Don't Bite the Botanist

By T. M. Kirk

Also by T. M. Kirk

The Don't Bite Me Series

Don't Bite the Director
Don't Bite the Botanist

The Onyx Palace Series

The Diamond Palace
The Golden Palace

The Magical Mishaps Series

A Fragile Spell

Author's Note

First off, I would like to thank you for picking up book two and welcoming these characters back into your life.

If you have not read book one, you can technically skip straight to this book, but there will be a few spoilers, a couple missed references, and enjoyment will greatly increase if you read Don't Bite the Director first.

I would also like to note that while this is a humorous romantic comedy meant to be lighthearted and fun, it is still intended for readers 18+ as it does contain multiple graphic sex scenes, adult language, PTSD, violence, death, blood, and a brief, non-graphic mention of assault that happened a very long time ago.

Reading should be a pleasant experience, and I hope you will take these themes into consideration.

Enjoy!
T. M. Kirk

For my own mom who helped shape me.

Thank you for putting up with all my thorns.

Chapter One

Tressa

A glistening drop of ruby red blood slid down the side of the woman's face, landed on her shoulder, and seeped into her white shirt.

Tressa suppressed the urge to lick it up.

It wasn't easy given how hungry she was, but at nearly three hundred years old, her restraint was borderline impeccable. Even when she was in a dire situation and had to resort to a natural feeding, she was always in control of the blood lust.

Today would be no different.

She just needed to block out the sounds of the hospital waiting room that were starting to grate on her and finish the job. The sooner she dealt with this hysterical woman, the sooner she could put the wailing ambulance sirens and rhythmic beeping of life support machinery in her rearview mirror.

Pasting a subdued smile on her face—one she had carefully curated over the years to portray sympathy and understanding—she reached a hand out to squeeze the woman's shoulder, careful to avoid the fresh blood stains blending into the rose pattern of the victim's blouse.

"Look at me," she told the late-twenties blonde who continued to weep softly. "What's your name?"

The woman sniffled a few more times, then swiped a hand over her eyes to brush away the bulk of her tears along with half of her eyeliner, the rest of which already coated her cheeks in thin black lines. "Re-Rebecca," she choked out. "But everyone calls me Becca."

Tressa nodded like she was hearing it for the first time, even though she'd already learned everything about the victims from the police. "You're going to be okay, Becca. You just need to breathe."

She'd long since lost track of how many times those exact same words came out of her mouth, but they never lacked sincerity. The woman *would* be okay. Or she would be once Tressa was done with her.

Fresh tears bubbled up in the woman's eyes. "But..."

"No buts," Tressa said firmly, drawing on her ability. "Just deep breaths. Can you do that for me?"

Becca dropped her face to her hands again and mumbled, "Yeah, I think so."

Of course she could. When Tressa allowed her soothing Gift to imbue her voice, it made dealing with the emotional victims much easier. She watched the woman take a few deep breaths, noting the tears drying up in the process.

That's it, Tressa thought. *Let the calm flow through you. Release yourself to it. Surrender your grief and just breathe.*

She didn't love using her Gift to manipulate people, but it was a necessary evil sometimes. And she wasn't messing with their brains too much. She just relaxed them a little. Like a walking, talking Xanax.

No, the manipulation would come in a few minutes when she had to use compulsion on the woman. That ability inherent to all vampires was the only way to convince Becca a rogue *hadn't* ripped out her husband's throat while their young daughter stood there and watched.

Tressa sighed. She didn't mind her job as the cadre's one-woman clean-up crew. She really didn't. She was giving these people peace after a highly traumatic incident. And if by doing so she also managed to keep the existence of vampires a secret, that was just a bonus.

Still... some days the years weighed on her, making her wonder if her life would ever be anything more than what it was.

"Who are you?" Becca asked, rubbing her bloodshot eyes.

Tressa took a second to analyze the woman's pulse and breathing. Becca's level of anxiety had dropped from a traumatic, life-altering event to something more like a minor car crash, and that would have to be close enough. She preferred them a bit more soothed, but the day was rolling into evening, and she was tired.

Not even vampires were immune to burn out.

"I'm a counselor," Tressa replied, offering up her tried and true lie. "And I just need a moment of your time."

The woman dropped her hands, meeting Tressa's gaze once more. "What do you want from me?"

Locking her eyes with Becca's, Tressa whispered, "Believe."

And here we go, she thought as the framing word took hold and the woman's eyes turned glassy and distant from the compulsion.

"Your husband was murdered this evening in a mugging gone wrong," Tressa said, maintaining the mental connection with Becca. "The mugger had a knife and stabbed him. It sprayed blood on your shirt. It was awful, but you don't want to think about it too much. You just want to focus on comforting your daughter and grieving for your loss. In the end, you'll both be okay."

"We'll be okay," the woman echoed in a monotonous tone, as if she were on autopilot.

With a deep exhale, Tressa let the connection slip away. She had no doubts the compulsion would hold. Even without the aid of supernatural abilities, people would always choose to believe the comforting lie. Nope, no murderous vampires hiding in the shadows. Just another example of human brutality. Tragic, but something that happened every day in the world.

Tressa gave the woman a pat on the shoulder and stood up. "You should go get cleaned off," she told Becca. "You don't want your daughter to see the blood."

The fogginess cleared from Becca's eyes as the woman shook the trance off. "You're right," she said, her voice steadier. "I should go do that."

Watching Becca hurry off down the hall toward the restroom, Tressa removed the clip that held her long black hair in a bun and let out a deep exhale of pleasure as the tension released from her scalp.

Another mission accomplished. Time to go home.

Well, almost. Tressa had already taken care of the daughter's memories, but things could be dicey with children's developing brains. Since the girl's trauma had warranted an overnight stay in the hospital for observation, Tressa might as well pop by her room one last time before returning to Fall River Mills and the cadre of vamps that was her family.

Strolling down the hospital corridor, Tressa chuckled as she thought back on everything her cousin, Saiden, had recently gone through to woo his new mate, Cora. The fiery horror film director had definitely disrupted their lives over the past couple weeks, in all the best ways possible.

Even though Cora hadn't wanted to become a vampire initially, she had taken to the undead life with ease. Not to mention her presence had turned Saiden from Sir Grumps-a-lot into Sir Grumps-a-little-less. He still sported his signature scowl most of the time, but whenever his eyes landed on his mate, it was like Tressa could see a weight being lifted off his shoulders.

And she loved nothing more than to tease him about it.

Cracking open the door to the girl's room, Tressa peered inside and found the young one fast asleep with a relaxed expression on her face, a crochet octopus clutched tightly in her arms. Tressa grinned at the familiar stuffed toy, then gently closed the door.

Pleased that everything was once again right in the world, Tressa took off at a brisk pace, heading toward the exit. She was already leaving later than she planned, but the police had detained the woman for longer than Tressa had anticipated, meaning the single blood bag she brought with her was long gone. The five-hour drive back to the compound in eastern California was going to seriously suck.

The hallway echoed with the satisfying tick tack of her lemon yellow pumps as she made her way out of the children's ward and back into the main corridor. Beyond that, the hospital was relatively quiet with daytime visiting hours nearing their end.

She turned a corner, and an intoxicating scent hit her like a punch to the face.

Creamy sweet vanilla.

Tressa froze mid stride and took a deep inhale. A groan nearly slipped from her lips as a shiver ran down her spine, and all thoughts of leaving vanished.

She didn't often eat food, but something about the smell made her mouth water, a hunger building inside her that was so foreign to the usual cravings for blood. Her feet carried her several yards down the hallway before she even registered that she was moving, her mind reeling from the scent and her body marching forward of its own volition.

She thought following her nose would take her toward the front of the hospital where visitors and overworked staff flocked to the café and gift shop, but nope. It took her down a hallway marked Long-Term Care.

Odd place for a bakery, Tressa mused as she drifted down the dimly lit corridor, drawn on by the hypnotizing aroma.

Seconds later, she found herself in front of room 113, the source of that creamy vanilla scent. Her shoulders slumped, her hopes crushed. It was probably just a 'get well' treat brought in for a patient.

Rising on her toes to spin back toward the exit, she glanced through the small window in the door, and her eyes landed on a body lying in the hospital bed. Something about the sleeping man caught her attention, and a slight tug in her chest prevented her from walking away.

He was cute, no doubt, even with all the wires hooked up to his body. Shaggy, dirty blond hair fell to his shoulders, and his chiseled jaw sported at least a couple months growth of facial hair. His expression was relaxed in sleep, but she couldn't help but notice the tension lines around his eyes, as if his dreams were filled with terrible images.

A strange sensation tickled the back of her mind, urging her to investigate, and Tressa's hand landed on the doorknob.

A gust of air wooshed out when she entered the room, and that siren scent smacked her in the face again. Even if she stuck her nose in a bag of fresh-baked cookies, the smell shouldn't be anywhere near that potent, heightened vampire senses aside.

She scanned the room, but there was no evidence of any tasty treats. In fact, the space was essentially empty aside from the medical equipment and an unused guest chair. No get well cards or photos. No flowers or balloons. No magazines or books to be read. Whoever this guy was, it didn't look like he'd had a single visitor.

Letting the door swing shut behind her, she took a few steps closer to the patient, intrigued by the mystery of the sleeping man. A chart hung at the foot of his bed, and curiosity had the file in her hand before she could even ask herself what the heck she was doing. She spent a lot of time at this hospital dealing with rogue vampire victims, and the last thing she needed was to get banned for sneaking into a patient's room and reading his private medical record. She could only compel one person at a time, so she'd be more than a little screwed if multiple security guards showed up to drag her out of the building.

And yet, not an ounce of that logic was able to silence the persistent voice in her head that whispered there was more to this guy than meets the eye.

Flipping open the chart, she read through the first page.

At first glance, it was all pretty basic. Name: Ethan Ambrose. Age: thirty-two. Occupation: botanist. She flipped over to the intake notes next, skimming through the documentation that said he was found unconscious outside his laboratory when authorities showed up to deal with a burning building. Under cause of injuries, it simply said, "animal attack."

Tressa scrolled through more pages, but nothing leapt out at her as to why she couldn't shake her curiosity about the man. Of course, there was a possibility the so-called "animal attack" was actually the result of a rogue vampire. It was a common enough rationalization they'd heard police officers use in the past. But why hadn't Baylin sent her to deal with his memories if that was the case? The question rolled around in her brain until she reached the very bottom of the page.

Status: Medical coma induced.

Medical coma? Tressa tossed a glance up at the sleeping man. Well, that explained all the wires, though she couldn't see any specific damage or injury from whatever had attacked him. Turning back to the file, she checked the date on the first note—three months ago.

Damn. That made the lack of cards and balloons even more depressing. Three months without a single visitor.

How was that even possible?

Making a mental note to call Baylin about a potentially missed vampire victim, she dropped the chart back on the hook and moved along the side of the bed to lean over him. His eyes twitched rapidly, which seemed strange for a coma patient, and the furrow etched into his brow only deepened as she brought her face closer to his.

She didn't know why, but for some reason, Tressa couldn't help but press her thumb to his forehead in an attempt to smooth out the tension lines.

The second her finger grazed his face, lightning shot down her skin, and steel gray eyes flew open, locking onto hers.

Then he started screaming.

Chapter Two

Ethan

A glistening drop of ruby red blood slid down the side of the woman's face, landed on her shoulder, and seeped into her white shirt.

Ethan suppressed the urge to vomit.

It wasn't easy given how much of his best friend's insides were now splattered across his lab, but dumping the remains of his ratatouille dinner on the floor wasn't going to save him from a similar fate.

He had to run. Had to get away. Had to tell... someone.

But who would listen to him? If he hadn't witnessed it with his own eyes, he wouldn't believe the truth either.

He'd known Jake for almost a decade and considered him a brother from another mother. Ethan was even the one who'd gotten him the job at VieTek Pharmaceuticals. A decision he deeply regretted when the dark-haired vampire dropped Jake's corpse to the floor and brushed the back of her hand across her mouth, smearing the blood on her lips into a hideous, crooked smile.

Vampire.

He still couldn't believe it, but there was no other explanation. Vampires were real, and one just viciously murdered his best friend.

The only thing that had saved Ethan was the fact he had been under a table cleaning up a spill when the door crashed open and the monster ripped Jake from his computer chair.

With a hand clamped over his mouth, Ethan watched the vampire's nostrils flare as she sniffed the air and started prowling around the lab.

Searching...

Hunting...

For him? Did he even stand a chance against that... that *thing*?

The slight ache in his thighs from crouching under the lab table turned into a burn, and Ethan could feel the imminent cramp digging its teeth in. He shifted slightly, and that tiny motion—that little squeak of his converse sneakers on the linoleum—was apparently enough to seal his fate.

Terror spread through his body when the vampire paused midstep, her head cocking slightly.

"I do believe," she said, spinning on her toes and stalking toward Ethan's hiding place, "that I've found my missing scientist."

Ethan huddled farther back under the table, tossing up a prayer to any deity that might be listening.

They weren't. They never were when it came to him. Although, the fact he didn't believe a higher power even existed likely wasn't helping.

A hauntingly beautiful face slid into his view as the vampire knelt down in front of him.

"Hello there."

Faster than Ethan could track, her hand flashed out and grabbed the collar of his lab coat, yanking him from under the table with inhuman strength.

She dragged Ethan up her body as she rose, holding his face inches from hers. He could smell the blood on her breath—Jake's blood—and the ratatouille roiled in his stomach.

The vampire closed her eyes, inhaling Ethan's scent. Then she pulled back and fixed an appraising stare on him. Her dark brown eyes took in every inch of his face, those nearly black irises expanding and contracting as they roamed over him.

"It's almost a shame," she said, her tongue swiping out to lick up a drop of blood from the corner of her mouth. "To have to kill someone so... intriguing. So intelligent. A pity, really."

Ethan swallowed roughly and struggled in her iron grip to no avail. The inevitability of his death lingered heavily in the air, his clock ticking down. If she thought he was going beg for mercy, though, she was going to be sorely disappointed. Ethan didn't beg for anything, and he certainly wasn't about to start in the final moments of his life.

"Do it," he bit out. "I'd rather die than spend another second looking at your hideous face."

Her lips twitched in a faint grin, like a snake amused that the mouse dared to fight back.

"In that case," she replied, the vacant depths of her soulless eyes offering him a glimpse of his fate, "your wish is granted."

A second set of teeth descended behind her normal ones, and when the fangs were fully exposed, she struck.

And Ethan let out a gut-wrenching scream.

Chapter Three

Tressa

Mate.

The word flashed through Tressa's brain like someone flipped the switch on a neon strobe light.

Mate. Mate. Mate.

The vanilla aroma suddenly made so much more sense. Of course the other half of her soul would smell like that.

He's my mate.

He's incredible.

He's... still screaming.

"Hey, calm down," she cried, grabbing the sides of his face with her hands. Those solid gray eyes locked on hers, but there was something empty in them, something that told her he wasn't actually *seeing* her.

Fuck! She couldn't compel him to relax because he was her mate, but maybe her Gift would still work on him?

"Ethan," she said firmly, gripping his face even tighter. "You're okay. Just breathe. Focus on me." She forced every ounce of calm she could summon into her words and waited for it to penetrate the haze of his panic.

The blood-curdling scream continued for another second before fading away. Ethan let out a small whimper, then collapsed back onto the bed.

"Are you—"

Tressa never got to hear the rest of his question because the door slammed open behind her, and a team of doctors and nurses raced in, shouting orders.

They elbowed her to the side, and she used the chaos of the moment to slip out of the room before someone started asking questions about who she was and why she was there.

Now more than ever she couldn't risk getting kicked out. Her mate was in that room, and nothing was going to keep her from returning to his side as soon as possible.

Two hours and four compelled medical professionals later, Tressa was able to get back into Ethan's room and take up a spot in the chair beside his bed. She couldn't tell if they'd sedated him again or he'd naturally fallen asleep, but regardless, he was snoring softly, and the tension lines around his eyes were back. Whatever knocked him out apparently hadn't sent him to a better place than before.

What exactly was he dreaming about that had him screaming bloody murder when he woke up?

Most likely whatever landed him in a coma, Tressa thought, scooting the guest chair a little closer to his bed. She was half-tempted to say fuck it and climb under the sheets with him, but she couldn't imagine that would be the best way to start their story. Just because women were considerably more forward in these modern times didn't mean Ethan wanted to wake up in a stranger's arms.

No, Tressa would just have to suck it up and settle for holding his hand, helpless to do anything to ease whatever torment was plaguing him. Now she had some inkling of what her cousin Saiden had gone through with Cora, and she felt a little bad about all the times she'd teased him.

But only a little. When you lived for centuries, you either became a cynic like Saiden, or you decided that forever was a long time to be unhappy, so you might as well shove all the unpleasantness somewhere deep inside and choose to have fun instead.

And the bit of fun she'd been clinging to for years was about to get exponentially more enjoyable now that she had Ethan to join her. It was like Lilith knew she'd been crawling the walls going crazy lately, so she dropped this incredible gift straight into Tressa's lap.

Surveying her mate lying in the bed, Tressa allowed her mind to run wild with thoughts about what kind of guy he was. Maybe he would be gentle and kind. He certainly didn't look like a jerk or the type of alpha male that would be possessive and domineering.

She noted a pair of wire-rimmed glasses sitting beside the bed and smiled. She'd always thought glasses looked sexy on a guy. Maybe her mate was a professor? Or a scholar? His chart said he was a botanist, but she had no idea what that meant other than something to do with plants. She turned his hand over and grazed her fingers across his skin. He had a few calluses lining his upper palm, but there were no scars or bumps on his knuckles. So he worked with his hands to some degree but was definitely not any kind of fighter.

A thousand possibilities spiraled through her brain, presenting her with scenario after scenario about what her mate was like. And all of it served one very important purpose—to distract her from that nagging thought in the back of her brain. The one that whispered...

What if?

What if he didn't want her? The mate bond drew you toward the other person, but it wasn't a guarantee they would actually be interested in pursuing anything romantic. And it definitely wasn't a guarantee he would want to become a vampire. What if she found her mate only to lose him in a few decades?

Nope, that possibility got buried deep inside with the rest of the things she chose to ignore.

Focus on the positive, she reminded herself. He was her mate, and they were destined to be together. You don't reject destiny.

When Ethan's hand twitched in hers and his eyes began to flutter, she released her hold on him and pushed the chair back slightly so she wasn't hovering. Brushing her skirt down over her thighs, she mentally prepared herself for the first conversation she would ever have with her mate.

She pasted on another of her patented smiles and took a few deep inhales to force her shaking hands to steady.

Calm, cool, collected. She could do this.

All she had to do was convince him that becoming a vampire was a gift unlike any other. Surely that would be easy enough after whatever injury he recently suffered. Who wouldn't want to be strong and healthy for centuries?

Chapter Four

Ethan

I need the pain back.

It was the first coherent thought that drifted through Ethan's brain as he struggled against the fog holding him under.

He'd been back there. Back with that... that *thing* again. Staring into the soulless depths of its eyes.

Then it sank its fangs into his neck once more and vanished. With the vampire gone, he was trapped between the real world and the dream world. The more he fought his way toward reality, straining to open his eyes, the more he realized there was no pain. Only a faint buzzy feeling throughout his body.

There should be pain. Pain meant reality. Pain meant he wasn't trapped in that never-ending nightmare. Pain was something he could latch onto as evidence that he was alive and awake. Pain was something he could remember.

And he could remember so many things. The agony of sharp teeth tearing into his neck. His bloody hands clutching at the wound and stumbling away on shaky legs as the creature laughed at him. Crashing into a table of beakers and microscopes, shards of glass stabbing into his hands and arms as they shattered under his weight. But the worst part was that he could remember sliding off the bloody table and landing on the floor next to Jake's body. For too long, he stared into his best friend's vacant eyes, savoring the pain that he was due.

Then everything went black, and he could remember nothing aside from the nightmare.

With a last effort of will, Ethan managed to pry his eyes open and drag a heavy hand up to block the bright lights above his head.

"You're awake."

The voice startled him, and most of his confusion dissipated between one blink and the next—high alert mode activated. His pulse raced, and a cold sweat broke out across his forehead as he snapped his head to the corner of the room, his gaze landing on an attractive woman watching him intently. There was something familiar about her, but he couldn't place where he'd seen her since his brain was still half lost in a bloody fog of screams and fangs. Glancing to the side, he found his glasses and settled them on his face.

Maybe I did die, Ethan thought as he took in the goddess perched on the edge of the chair. Her long black hair glistened like she stepped straight out of a cheesy shampoo commercial, and her smooth bronze skin had the kind of glow that normally only photoshop could achieve.

His eyes drifted lower as he took in her outfit. The pale yellow sweater popped against her darker skin, drawing him in like a beacon of light, and the matching short skirt slid up her enticing thighs when she crossed her legs. To his dismay, the image had something twitching under the thin hospital sheet that probably shouldn't be awake. Not when he was still trying to ascertain the where, what, and how that landed him in a hospital to begin with.

He should be dead.

"Are you a doctor?" he croaked out, his voice hoarse and scratchy as if he'd been screaming for hours.

A grin spread across her face at his words—a strange response to a legitimate question. Or maybe it wasn't legitimate given that women as gorgeous and glowing as her only worked in hospitals on TV shows. Every doctor he'd ever seen looked like they might slice him open and sell one of his kidneys for a cup of coffee or a twenty-minute nap. And he'd spent more than his fair share of time with them.

When the woman's smile faded and she hesitantly approached his bedside, flashbacks of his mother's illness pounded on the door of his mind. Nothing good ever happened when hospital staff addressed you with caution.

The woman must have tracked his apprehension, because she paused her approach and gave him that megawatt smile again. "Not quite," she said. "I'm actually..." Her words trailed off, and she chewed on her lip for a second.

The action was somewhat adorable, if oddly unprofessional. "Actually what?" he asked, pushing himself up in the bed. It was more difficult than it should have been, and his frustration leaked into his words. "Spit it out. Are you a nurse, then? I have more than a few questions, and I'd like to know if you're qualified to give me the answers I need."

The woman frowned, but Ethan could only bring himself to feel a little bad about his brusque tone. He'd been called blunt often enough to realize it wasn't ever a compliment, but this wasn't the time to worry about niceties. Because if he wasn't dead, then he had more important things to worry about.

It was still out there.

The monster.

Ethan didn't believe in flights of fancy or mythological creatures.

He believed in things that could be measured, studied, and explained. Every part of his scientific brain told him that thing couldn't be real. That he was suffering from some kind of trauma-induced hallucination.

But no matter how often he tried to get himself to accept that logic, it just wouldn't stick. He knew what he saw; it wasn't the kind of thing you just imagined.

And despite his rational brain's tendency to go full analytical mode, something about the being he'd encountered demanded he blow past researching its origins and skip straight to figuring out how to kill it. He'd looked into its eyes. There was no soul in that vampire. Nothing redeeming. Just a virus that consumed and destroyed. A virus, like so many others, that needed to be eradicated.

The woman studied him for a moment, and Ethan could practically see the wheels turning in her head. Deciding how much to tell him, probably. It seemed like hospital staff loved to make assumptions about how much truth he could handle. After a long, heavy moment, her expression shifted—a decision made.

"I'm a counselor," she said, her voice still unnecessarily perky but at least toned down a fraction.

Ethan groaned and slumped back, losing some of his vertical progress. "A counselor? Sorry, ma'am. I'm sure you're very good at your job, but I don't need a counselor. I need answers."

"I can help you with that," she replied, taking a step closer to the bed.

He eyed her warily. "Shouldn't I be discussing my situation with a doctor? Or at least the nurse who actually does all the work?"

The woman grabbed a clip from the seat behind her and focused on drawing her hair up into a bun, looking everywhere in the room but at him. "You're right," she said once she seemed satisfied that every strand was tucked away. "You should go over things with a doctor. It's just... the staff thought perhaps you might need someone to speak with when you woke up, given how things went last time."

He frowned. "Last time?"

Then it hit him. A split second of lucidity where he recalled images of people in white coats and purple scrubs shouting at him to lay down and breathe. But before that, before the noise and confusion, there had been... her. She had been the angel who pulled him from the dark, if only for a moment.

And he suddenly felt like a massive dick.

He scrubbed a hand down his face. "Oh, yeah, sorry about that."

"Don't be," the woman dismissed. "You've been through quite an ordeal."

"That's putting it mildly," he muttered, and his hand absently drifted up to his neck, settling on the patch of ridges that broke up his otherwise smooth skin. A not-so-small part of his brain wondered why it felt like a scar instead of a fresh wound, but he was preoccupied with the stunning woman in front of him. "So, what's your name, anyway? I don't want to call you Counselor."

She smiled again, and he couldn't help but be intrigued by the way the corners of her lips tugged up slowly, almost like she was deciding how big or wide to smile.

"Tressa," she replied pleasantly, holding out her hand. "And you're Ethan."

He shook her hand, flinching slightly when a zap of static electricity lit up his skin. She didn't seem bothered by his reaction, and he found himself reluctant to let go of her. "Thanks for the reminder," he said, eventually withdrawing his hand. "Good to know I'm not completely crazy."

Her grin dropped away. "Why would you say that?"

He settled back onto the pile of pillows. Maybe it was the drugs still coursing through his brain or maybe it was the fact that his 'give a damn' died with Jake, but he had no desire to lie to Tressa. Something about her made him think he could tell her anything. Maybe everything.

"Why do I think I'm crazy?" he asked.

She nodded.

"Because I was attacked by a vampire."

Chapter Five

Tressa

Well... crap.

A bead of sweat welled up on Tressa's forehead, and she started picking at her cuticles. Any damage she did would be healed in less than a minute, and the often subconscious action was like her version of snapping a rubber band on her wrist. It offered a distraction when unpleasant feelings wanted to pull her into a dark place. And learning her mate had indeed been attacked by a rogue—not an animal like she'd desperately been hoping—definitely qualified as a dark place.

Calm down. Just breathe, she ordered herself. *Maybe this is a good thing. Scratch that. It's one hundred percent a good thing.*

The internal pep talk was doing little to slow her racing heart, but she forced herself to focus on the positives. The biggest one being that he already believed in vampires.

Check that conversation off the to-do list.

Now all she had to do was convince him to become one. In all honesty, this was perfect. After only a handful of sentences with her mate, she was already halfway to her goal.

Apparently she'd been quietly hyping herself up in her head for too long, because Ethan huffed and crossed his arms, all the earlier levity she'd managed to pull from him gone.

"You don't believe me, do you?"

"No!" she blurted out before her brain could formulate a better response.

"Of course you don't," he muttered.

Wait, what?

"Shit, no, that's not…" she stammered. "I didn't mean that. The 'no' was for the not believing."

His brow furrowed, deepening the lines on his face. "So, no, you don't believe me?"

"No, I *do* believe you," she replied, using every bit of restraint to maintain a reasonable distance befitting a stranger when all she really wanted to do was pull him into her arms. "The 'no' was because I don't *not* believe you."

His eyes narrowed, but she caught the corner of his mouth curl up ever so slightly. "Granted I might have a head injury, but I don't think that response would make sense to anybody."

A tiny laugh slipped out, and her cheeks heated.

Wait, was she blushing? She didn't blush. She was a three-hundred-year-old vampire, not a twitterpated schoolgirl.

Be cool, Tressa, she reminded herself. *Be sexy and confident.*

"Oh, you're so funny," she gushed, tucking a non-existent stray hair behind her ear and giggling like the schoolgirl she absolutely was not. Guys liked giggles though, right? They liked being fawned over and told their jokes were hilarious?

Well, maybe every guy except the one looking at her like she should be getting fitted for a tight, white, self-hug jacket.

"Um, yeah, sure," he mumbled, casting his gaze toward the door like he hoped someone would come in and save him.

Okay, so maybe Tressa hadn't needed to impress a guy in, well, ever. Her life was pure survival mode right up until she became a vampire, and after that, she only cared about finding her mate. If a guy ended up between her thighs for some nighttime fun while she was waiting, cool. If not, no worries. She hadn't ever put much weight into caring what the male species thought of her.

There was a slight chance that everything she knew about men was wrong. That, or Ethan wasn't your average bear.

She groaned internally. Of course he wasn't average. Lilith would never give her an average mate. There was more to this guy than any of the one-dimensional scenarios her brain had offered up earlier, and the thought of unravelling his layers intrigued her. *He* intrigued her.

Not to mention the way her shirt became a little extra tight in through the chest when she got lost in his gray eyes, and she found herself with panties that needed to be changed sooner rather than later. She dragged the chair over to his bedside, sat back down, and resisted the urge to squeeze her thighs together.

"Sorry," she said, offering Ethan a sincere smile. "I was just trying to be reassuring after everything you've been through."

His lips flattened into a thin line. "Don't."

She cocked her head. "Don't what?"

"Reassure me," he answered, his voice taking on a detached tone that told Tressa he was not the type of person who desired anyone's approval or validation. "I'm not naïve, and I'm not crazy," he continued. "I know what happened. Or, I know what happened up until I should have died. What I want now is details about how I survived, any information on the attack, and most importantly, answers about how soon I can get out of here. So, thanks for the placating words and the offer of... counseling. But I'm good."

He glanced away in a firm indication he was done with the conversation, and Tressa's brain fully abandoned her on what to say next. Wasn't the mate bond supposed to create at least some level of attraction? She was definitely feeling a pull toward him, but either he had the restraint of a centuries old vampire or...

No. She wouldn't entertain the possibility that he had no interest in her at all. He was just dealing with the aftereffects of a traumatic experience. Something she could more than relate to.

But how to move forward and get him to let her in?

Should she admit she was a vampire and hope he didn't freak out?

Should she continue the counselor persona and save the v-bomb for after she endeared herself to him?

Or should she just abandon this whole mate idea and join a vampire nunnery?

Based on the freezing temperature of the cold shoulder she was getting from Ethan, her mind was leaning toward the last one. Thankfully, she was saved from planning her life of uncomfortable frocks and celibacy when the door popped open and an older woman strode into the room.

Tressa fought to keep the smile on her face when she recognized the nurse as the person she'd had the hardest time compelling earlier. The battleaxe had the least malleable brain Tressa had ever encountered and an attitude to match. She'd briefly entertained compelling a new personality into the woman after she handled Ethan far too roughly for Tressa's liking, but that was crossing a bit too far over the whole free will line.

"Oh, it's you," the nurse sneered at Tressa. "You need to clear out. Dr. Kim is going to want to do a full workup on Mr. Ambrose now that he's awake."

Tressa's cheeks were starting to hurt from maintaining the pleasant expression when all she really wanted to do was smack this rude woman upside the head. But she wasn't about to lend credence to the misguided theory that vampires were evil, violent creatures. Especially not when her mate who couldn't be compelled was sitting right there, and she had yet to fully suss out his feelings on the whole vamp thing.

Turning away from the nurse, Tressa's smile fell into something more natural when her attention landed on Ethan. "I'll see you later," she told him.

"I said I don't need counseling," he argued.

She gave him a quick wink. "Oh, you never know," she said. "You might change your mind."

With that last comment, she flitted out the door, trying her best to disregard Ethan's mumbled "highly fucking unlikely" comment.

Chapter Six

Ethan

An hour later, Ethan was seriously regretting his decision to send Tressa away. At least with her, he was getting a stunning face with his lack of answers. Even if she was unnervingly chipper.

Ethan rubbed at the scar on his neck. He needed to stop thinking of the charming counselor. She reminded him far too much of Jake. He also kept a permanent smile on his face regardless of how bad things got.

Except when he died. The last time Ethan would ever see his friend was the one time Jake didn't have his normal carefree expression in place. Those glassy vacant eyes, frozen in terror and pain, would haunt Ethan for the rest of his life.

And holding onto that was the least he deserved for surviving when Jake hadn't.

Yeah, probably for the best he told Tressa he didn't need counseling. He wasn't looking to get his body laid or his mind healed, so there was no reason to keep her around.

Now if his brain would stop throwing up images of that stunning smile, he could actually concentrate on the complete bullshit answers the doctor was giving him.

"Okay, Dr. Kim, let me see if I'm understanding you correctly," Ethan said, running a hand over the itchy beard growing wild from his normally clean-shaven chin. "I've been out for three damn months, and after all that time and investigating, no one has any idea what happened to me in the lab?"

The older Asian woman with short black hair grimaced, and it only accentuated the roughly thirty years' worth of hospital work that were etched into her face. "No, Ethan. As far as I'm aware, the police have no inkling of what occurred that night."

"Right." He pushed his sliding glasses back up on his nose. "And of course the building burnt down so there was no evidence."

The doctor grimaced again.

"And no witnesses that saw how I survived or managed to escape?"

The tired woman rubbed at her temples, then folded her hands in her lap. "I'm sorry I don't have more to tell you. The detective assigned to your case has been notified that you are lucid, and he will be here in the morning. Perhaps they have uncovered more information, but as far as my knowledge goes, you were brought in with severe trauma to the neck which was attributed to an animal attack, extreme blood loss resulting in hemorrhagic shock, and multiple contusions throughout your body. It was only by the grace of God that you survived long enough for us to induce a medical coma. In all honesty, you shouldn't even be alive right now."

Ethan tried not to bristle at her usage of 'God.' He'd stopped believing in an altruistic higher power the day his mom died. If he survived against all odds, it certainly wasn't because of some sky daddy watching over him. Which left the question of who, exactly, *was* watching over him? And why didn't that vampire finish him off?

"Yeah, well, thanks for nothing, I guess," Ethan told the doctor.

Then he tossed his glasses on the nightstand and rolled over onto his side, hoping she would take that as an obvious sign he was done listening.

He'd already endured an agonizing breakdown about his current health, and after the fourth time she mentioned additional lab tests and long-term monitoring, he had gotten the gist. His body was weak, and a lot of his muscles were atrophied, so life was going to be rough. Thankfully, he'd always kept himself in solid shape. Any time not spent in the lab was usually spent in the gym to combat the effects of his otherwise sedentary lifestyle. Even if he lost the definition of a six-pack, it wasn't like he didn't know how to get it back. Building up his strength to go after that creature was at the top of his priority list.

That demonic, soulless creature.

Anytime he closed his eyes, it was all he saw, so he didn't imagine sleep would be coming anytime soon. After the doctor quietly left his room, Ethan reached for his cell phone that had finally charged enough he could check his messages, of which there were many.

Not surprising after three months in a coma.

Fuck. When the doctor first mentioned how long he'd been out, he was still so fixated on the vampire aspect that it didn't fully register. But the enormity of his situation was starting to hit him.

He had no idea what his life even looked like now. Did he have a job? Would he be able to work at a different VieTek lab and continue his research? Hell, did he even have an apartment to go home to?

The answer to that last question came from listening to his handful of voice messages. And the rest came from his very full email inbox.

He groaned and slammed the infuriating device back on the nightstand. Between the messages from his now former landlord and the emails from his VieTek manager, Ethan had more or less no life waiting for him. No home. No job. No best friend.

No problem, he thought. *That all just means I can focus on what really matters.*

Hunting down the vampire he knew was still out there somewhere needed to be his sole priority anyway. He would never be able to relax until he could see for himself that it was dead-dead.

Closing his eyes, Ethan braced himself for the image of the monster to invade his mind once more so he could search his memories for any possible clues, but the black-haired female he found himself thinking about wasn't a vampire. She was a counselor. A sexy, friendly, *human* counselor.

Try as he might, he couldn't shake the image of her smiling at him. She was probably just doing her job—being nice and all that jazz—but for some reason, he didn't fully believe that. The way she'd looked at him was more than if he was any other patient on her roster. And even if she was just a distraction from what he needed to be concentrating on, maybe he could allow himself a brief reprieve from the darkness.

A little self-indulgence couldn't hurt, Ethan thought as his hand slid under the sheets to palm himself. Making a plan to hunt down the vampire could wait until tomorrow.

He just needed a quick confirmation that his cock still worked, and thoughts of Tressa would more than help in that endeavor.

Chapter Seven

Tressa

"You're fucked, Tress," Baylin said, having made no effort to conceal his raucous laughter after she finished recounting her meeting with Ethan.

Tressa glared at the phone in her hand even though her pseudo cousin couldn't see her face. "Thanks for that enlightening input, Bay. You maybe want to turn the volume down before you start in with your helpful observations?"

The grating sound of the screaming death metal her cousin was so fond of cut off, and she heard him take a swig of what was likely a disgustingly over-caffeinated energy drink before he responded.

"I gotta say, I thought Saiden's predicament was good, but damn. This is even more entertaining."

Tressa groaned and leaned back in the painfully uncomfortable chair in the hospital's waiting area. You'd think people worrying about their loved ones deserved some semblance of comfort, but apparently, the Good Samaritan Hospital didn't agree.

"While I appreciate that assessment," she told him without bothering to hide her sarcasm under her usual playful tone, "I'd like to know why you didn't tell any of us you were monitoring the victim of a vampire attack? I assumed you were just getting lax in your old age and missed this one."

"Eh," he replied dismissively. "Marquin knew, but I didn't think it was necessary to involve the rest of you until I had more information. I monitor the fallout after a lot of vampire attacks, Tress, but it's rare for anyone to survive unless Saiden is right there to intervene. And from what I've read about your Ethan in the hospital records, he shouldn't be alive either. Let alone awake. I wrote him off as a lost cause months ago."

Tressa noticed a young teary-eyed couple a few chairs away regarding her with curiosity, so she shifted a few seats over and lowered her voice. "It was the Spark. I think it woke him up. Fuck, Bay, what if I never touched him this morning? Would he have died before I even knew he existed? For Lilith's sake, I've been to this hospital four times in the past three months and never realized my mate was in a coma just down the hall. Why do you think fate is pushing us together now?"

"Beats me," Baylin replied, and she could hear him run a hand through his thick russet hair. "But Saiden's experience with his mate was less than smooth as well, so maybe that's just how it works. Maybe Lilith wants to prove your mate bond can overcome any obstacle."

She groaned again, then gave an apologetic look to the couple still staring at her from across the room. Dropping her voice to barely above a whisper since Baylin's supernatural hearing would pick it up fine, she said, "So Lilith decided to give me a mate who nearly died at the hands of a vampire? I still need to figure out exactly how much trouble I'm in fighting that potential prejudice, and I also need to know why he was attacked in the first place. Rogues don't break into pharmaceutical labs for a random evening snack, then burn down the building to hide the evidence."

"No, they don't," Baylin mused, and the sound of his fingers flying over a keyboard trickled through the phone. "I've been looking into what they were researching. They had to be targeted for a reason, but I can't crack the company's firewall."

"What?" she gasped, only partially mocking him. "Baylin, are you telling me you've encountered a website you *can't* hack into?"

Tressa hadn't known her easy-going cousin was even capable of the growl he let out.

"Bite me, Tress," he snapped. "I've been a little... distracted lately."

Tressa frowned and adjusted her position in the chair, making another futile attempt to get comfortable. "With what? You barely leave the compound, and I didn't think Saiden had an active case right now since we finished up this morning."

"Not important," he replied quickly. "Look, I'll get into the site. It's just a matter of time. If I can hack the Vampire Ruling Coalition's database, which by the way has a stronger firewall than the U.S. military, I think I can break into the cloud storage for a pharmaceutical company."

Tressa laughed, garnering her another look from the couple that now appeared more annoyed than grieving. Maybe they should thank her for the distraction.

"I don't know," she told Baylin as she climbed out of the chair and headed for an empty hallway. "The Ruling Coalition is only protecting knowledge that could mean life or death. Pharmaceutical companies are protecting their wallets. Pretty sure it won't be easy."

Baylin snorted. "Yeah, well, I welcome the challenge. But in the meantime, if you want to try seducing Ethan into revealing what he was working on, I fully support that."

"I'm not going to seduce him," she argued. Then a grin spread across her face. "Well, at least not for information. But no seduction of any kind will be happening until after I get something to drink. I'm not sure I could restrain myself right now, and I won't traumatize him even further."

Tressa ran her tongue along the spot in her gums where her fangs would descend. She was starting to develop an ache that told her it was well past time to feed, and if she didn't get blood soon, that couple in the lobby was going to be pissed at her for more than a minor disruption.

"Yeah, you have a big enough hill to climb," Baylin agreed. "Did you bring an extra bag with you?"

Tressa cursed her lack of preparedness. Saiden would be so ashamed of her, and of course Baylin would enjoy telling his brother all about her fuckup. "No, I didn't think I'd be here this long," she replied. "I'm just going to compel whoever is on security at the hospital's blood bank to let me inside for a minute. They won't miss one little bag, and I'm sure I can encourage a few people around here to make an extra donation. I just need you to clear the camera footage when I'm done."

"Now *that* I can do in my sleep."

"You sleep?" Tressa joked as she absently scanned a directory to locate the hospital's blood storage.

"I do," he replied dryly. "It's my second favorite thing to do in my bed."

Tressa fought the urge to shudder. While none of the cadre members that Marquin had brought together were actually related, they'd basically become a family over the past hundred years. "Gross, Bay. I don't need to hear about your sex life."

"You brought it up."

"No, I didn't." She sighed as she found the room number she was looking for and spun on her toes. "Whatever. Can you just update everyone on what I've told you? I'm going to attempt to get Ethan to come home with me, but it could take a while, so let Marquin know I might be unavailable for a bit."

"Will do, Tress," he replied.

"Thank you, Baylicious," she sang, her cheerful attitude returning when she used the silly nickname she'd coined for him. It was less fun than the hundred or so she'd come up with for Saiden, but it still always made her smile.

Choose happiness, she reminded herself. Those two words had become her mantra ever since she became a vampire, and she had a feeling she was going to need the reminder more than ever in the next few days.

Tressa hung up to the sound of Baylin laughing. He was the only one who took her love of teasing in stride. Not that anything bothered her cousin. He was nothing if not eternally entertained by the antics of their cadre. Still, it worried her sometimes. How he spent his entire life holed up in front of a computer. How was he ever going to find his mate if the only women he ever met were online?

Tressa shook off those potentially depressing thoughts and headed off toward the elevators that would take her down to the blood bank. She'd worry about Baylin's love life another time.

Right after she sorted out her own.

Despite sinking her fangs into a pilfered blood bag and sating the majority of her thirst, Tressa still had a shit evening.

She should have rented a nearby hotel room to get some sleep until she could talk to Ethan again, but the tug of the mating bond wouldn't let her stray too far from his side even if she wanted to. She couldn't stop thinking about him lying helpless in a hospital bed. The vampire who took a chunk out of his neck clearly wasn't your average chaotic maim and murder rogue, so what if they had targeted Ethan specifically? What if they were monitoring him just like Baylin was and needed to finish the job now that he'd woken up?

Ever since Saiden's encounter with the unhinged rogue, Bianca, the entire cadre had been a little on edge, wondering if there were more vampires out there with some larger nefarious plan.

A thousand horrific scenarios had raced through her mind, and in the end, the only way she could get even a few fitful hours of sleep was by crashing in that damned waiting area around the corner from his room. The hard hospital chair could give the rack a run for its money as the worst torture device ever, yet it was still less painful than being away from him. At least a dozen times, she considered compelling the nurse on duty to let her sleep in his room, but she was supposed to be a counselor, not a stalker, and she had no idea how she would explain her presence if he woke up in the night.

Which was why she needed an hour in the bathroom to make herself presentable before knocking on Ethan's door the next day. Her mate would inevitably get to experience her first thing in the morning messiness at some point, but they had an eternity for that. No need to rush into exposing him to her morning breath.

Tressa pushed open the door to his room, and a delightful shiver ran down her spine as Ethan's delicious scent washed over her.

"Good morning," she said, trying to keep her peppy persona dialed down to medium since most people tended to give her a nasty glare when she had the energy of a cracked-out squirrel before 9 a.m.

Ethan hit the remote control for his TV to silence the news report that had been airing and watched her enter with a mixture of curiosity and amusement on his face.

"Didn't I say no to the whole counseling thing?" he asked, leaning back against his propped-up pillows.

"You did," she replied, ignoring the sharp edge to his tone. "But I come bearing gifts in hopes of bribing you into reconsidering." She thrust out the overpriced latte she'd gotten from the hospital café.

He eyed the drink for a second before taking it from her. His fingers brushed against hers, and he jerked his hand back, spilling a bit of the coffee on his bed.

"Sorry," Tressa blurted out, glancing around for a napkin or towel.

Stupid Spark. It should be toning down by now. She knew she'd always feel a slight toe-curling tingle from touching Ethan, but it shouldn't be quite so shocking anymore.

"Don't worry about it," he grumbled, mopping up the worst of the spill with the corner of his blanket. "It was my fault. I think there's a lot of static electricity in here, combined with the fact that I'm still a little jumpy."

Tressa nodded and sank down into the chair beside his bed. "That's understandable after your ordeal," she replied, letting just a tiny hint of her soothing Gift slip into her words. She didn't want to abuse it too much when it came to her mate, but a small hit of calm wouldn't be too intrusive. "Would you like to talk about it?"

Ethan took a sip of the coffee and let out a moan. His eyes rolled back, a nearly orgasmic expression crossing his face, and Tressa was more than a little jealous that it was the coffee and not her causing that reaction in him.

"I see what you're doing here," he said, tapping the lid of the to-go cup as he settled back into his mound of pillows. "Trying to trick me into opening up. I'm seriously not interested in counseling, but I guess

I wouldn't mind chatting a bit. It's not like I have anything else to do." He gestured at the wires and IV keeping him tethered to the bed. "Plus, you did bring me the best latte I've had in three months."

When Ethan's lip quirked up, Tressa wished she could freeze time just to study all the nuances of his wry grin.

She held a hand to her chest in feigned shock. "Ethan Ambrose, did you just make a joke?"

His grin dropped away, and Tressa would have given up her eternal life to bring it back. It felt like every time she managed to put a crack in his wall, it immediately sealed itself up.

"Yeah, well, don't get used to it," Ethan said, picking at the heat sleeve on the to-go cup. "I've never exactly been the life of the party."

An ache settled into Tressa's heart at hearing the sadness behind his words. That wasn't an 'I dislike people, so I keep my distance' comment. It was a 'life hasn't been kind, so I've lost my sunshine' comment.

"And why is that?" she asked, hoping her coffee bribe elevated his mood enough for him to start talking. She might need to invest in pickaxes, but she was going to get his wall down one way or another.

Ethan shrugged and took another sip. Sadly, the orgasmic face didn't return.

"It doesn't really matter," he said. "Look, I understand why you think I could benefit from counseling. Fuck knows the TV shows don't accurately portray life after being in a coma. Because I have no family or friends to pay my bills, I woke up to my landlord telling me three months of unpaid rent meant my stuff got put into storage and he already leased my apartment out to someone new. Not to mention my position at work has been placed on an 'indefinite hiatus'"—he made air quotes with his fingers—"which probably would have oc-curred even without the coma since the laboratory I was working out of burned down. So I essentially have no job and nowhere to live. But that's not the kind of shit that's easily cured by a couple of hour-long sessions, no offense."

Tressa sat back in the chair, carefully evaluating Ethan's expression and body posture. His little speech had been more or less completely dispassionate given his situation, and it tugged at her heart—how he had so little left that he couldn't even summon rage or sorrow as he idly poked through the charred wreckage of his life. Did he really have no family or friends? And nowhere to live? She wanted to dive into the bed and crush him with a huge hug, but at the same time, all she could think about was how his tragic scenario might actually work to her advantage. Convincing him to come back to the compound with her would be a piece of cake if he had nothing tying him to San Jose.

Before she could say anything, he sat up straighter and fixed an intent stare on her. "But none of that even matters because we both know you're not a counselor, are you, Tressa?"

Wait, what?

She blinked at him, and her mouth opened and closed a couple times as she struggled to shift her thoughts back into gear.

"Don't waste your time coming up with a lie," Ethan said, leaning forward in the bed. "We both know the truth. So would you care to tell me who you actually are?"

"I... Um... What?" Her brain had been dancing in dopamine at the idea of how easy things were going with her mate compared to Saiden's situation, but the lake of happy chemicals was quickly drying up under the suspicious glare Ethan leveled at her.

He downed the last of his latte, dropped the cup in the trash, then crossed his arms. "I'm a scientist, Tressa. If nothing else, I'm extremely observant. I was willing to suspend disbelief yesterday since I had a few other things clouding my judgment, but there's no way I believe you're a counselor anymore."

"Uh... I mean... Why would you...?"

So articulate, Tressa. Way to look like an idiot in front of the genius.

"The signs are relatively obvious," he replied dryly, nudging his glasses back into place. "Your outfit is more cover girl than counselor. Not to mention you're wearing the same thing you had on yesterday, which wouldn't be the case if you'd gone home last night. Throw in the fact that you're far too gorgeous for a thankless job, you have no ID badge like everyone else, you didn't so much as blink when I mentioned vampires, and you somehow magically knew that I preferred vanilla lattes with almond milk over black coffee. No offense, but that all screams something is rotten in Denmark."

Well, fuck.

She'd brought him her own favorite coffee drink in hopes they had similar tastes, but that was just coincidence. And since when did guys notice a girl's clothing?

Wait, go back, did he say...

"You think I'm gorgeous?" she purred, unable and unwilling to hide the cheeky grin spreading across her face.

Ethan groaned and rubbed at his temples. "That's what you're focusing on?"

Tressa winked. "A girl's gotta have her priorities."

Okay, her appearance had never been anywhere near the top of her priority list, but she couldn't help the tingle in her abdomen at hearing her mate was attracted to her. It wasn't a declaration of undying love, but it was an improvement over his initial dismissal of her.

"Don't do that," Ethan said, his annoyed tone dampening her brief moment of joy.

"Do what?" she asked.

"Act like a ditz," he replied. "I'm not sure if you're trying to convince me or yourself with that shallow, happy-go-lucky crap, but it's clearly just an act. I can see it in your eyes."

Tressa went full on fish out of water for a moment. Who the hell was this guy that he saw through her carefully curated persona in less than twenty-four hours? Not even the cadre noticed how much pain she buried underneath her wide smile and forced optimism.

"There's nothing wrong with being happy," she told him, though her voice lacked a bit of the conviction that would have existed before Ethan called her out on the lie.

"Not if it's real," he replied. "But I don't see the benefit in putting on a show to please the people around me. So how about we try some truth instead? Drop the friendly neighborhood counselor act and be honest." He shifted forward, locking eyes with her. "Who are you, Tressa? Really?"

It was almost unsettling, the intense way he stared at her. Nobody had ever looked at her the way Ethan did. Like he really saw into the heart of her and wasn't put off by the darkness lurking inside. He gazed straight into her soul and didn't even blink at the suffering hiding under her sunny exterior.

"I'm…"

She trailed off. What should she even say? If she was being honest, it was the perfect opportunity to tell him the truth. To admit she was a vampire and deal with the fallout. They were mates, so even if he'd been attacked by a rogue, surely he could overlook that and accept all vampires weren't the same. Right?

"I'm…"

Shit. Tell him what she was and risk it? Or lie and buy herself some more time to convince him that her kind weren't inherently evil?

Truth or lie. Truth or lie.

Truth, she decided. Lying was the coward's way out, and she was a three-hundred-year-old badass vampire. She was no coward.

"I'm... a... vampire..."

Ethan's eyes widened.

"...hunter," she finished. "I'm a vampire *hunter*."

Okay, maybe even three-hundred-year-old badass vampires could still be cowards.

Chapter Eight

Ethan

"You're a what?"

There was no freaking way this skinny, adorable, perky woman was a Van Helsing in disguise. Not possible.

He'd been thinking maybe she worked for a rival pharmaceutical company and was going to offer him a new job. It would make sense to send a hottie to entice him, even though he was rarely swayed by a pretty face and was still bound by a strict NDA with VieTek. But he was a fairly well known entity in the pharmaceutical research world, being one of the few expert botanists who willingly worked in corporate America, so any smart company might see it as an opportunity to seize his vulnerable moment and lock him under a new contract.

Hell, he might have even believed she was a vampire herself showing up to finish the job. It would have made sense too, given how preternaturally beautiful she was. But a vampire wouldn't have the pain he'd seen in her eyes. And they wouldn't have Tressa's all-too-human nervous ticks—the way she picked at her cuticles or how she went all guppy-mouthed when she found herself in an unexpected situation.

No, there was no way she was a soulless demon. Still, it made more sense than the excuse she had gone with.

"I *am* a vampire hunter," she repeated with more confidence and a little defensiveness creeping into her voice. "You don't believe me?"

Ethan laughed and tucked his hands behind his head. "Sweetheart, it's not a matter of me believing you. Even if you are some kind of Buffy wannabe, it doesn't mean you could actually take down a real vampire."

She arched an eyebrow, but he just shook his head.

"I've seen one, remember? Up close and personal when it was tearing my throat out. And I was helpless. Completely unable to do anything but die a painful death. There's no way you're a hunter. Sorry, not to be a dick, but no."

"Well, fuck you too, Ethan," she shot back, all pretenses of little miss sunshine washed away by the venom soaking her voice. She stood up and stalked over to the side of his bed. "What kind of sexist, anti-quated, bullshit response is that?"

As much as he wanted to shout back that it was a logic-based response and there was no need to get pissy, the fire in her eyes was doing something to a certain part of his anatomy. She might be all 'look on the bright side' with everyone else, but there was fight in her. She was a woman who'd been through some shit and came out swinging.

Maybe...

"Okay, say I believe you," he offered, holding up his hands in a placating gesture. "I mean, you've certainly got the attitude for it, after all. But what are you doing here, then? If you're a hunter, why aren't you out there, you know, hunting?"

She huffed and took a step back, but only a small one. "I was sent to check on you," she replied stiffly, appearing only slightly mollified by his retraction. "My, um, organization that hunts vampires has been monitoring your progress after the attack. In case you woke up."

"Your organization?" He narrowed his eyes on her. "You belong to an organization that hunts vampires?"

She retrieved the chair she'd been sitting in and dragged it closer to Ethan's bed. "That's what I said. Did the attack damage your hearing?" She dropped into her seat and studied him carefully.

"My hearing is just fine," he snapped. "But what you're saying sounds like the plot of a bad movie. Next you'll tell me the government knows all about vampires, and it's a huge conspiracy to cover it up."

Tressa looked thoughtful for a second, tapping a slender finger on the arm of the chair. "No, I don't believe any of the world governments are aware of the existence of vamps. If they are, they're keeping it to themselves. We have a guy who monitors that kind of thing."

He blinked. "You have a guy?"

"Of course we do. How else would we keep track of everything?"

Ethan pinched the bridge of his nose, wishing he had another latte. Or seven. Three-month coma fatigue was not something cured by a single shot of espresso even when he wasn't struggling to wrap his brain around a substantial change to his world order.

"You're telling me you have a tech guy who spends his time in front of a large bank of computers and is somehow the best hacker ever?"

Tressa shrugged. "I won't tell him you said that, but yes. Baylin is pretty skilled with a keyboard."

"Okay, but you see how that's not helping with the whole bad movie plot, right?"

She rolled her eyes. "Oh, Cora would love you."

"Who's Cora?"

Tressa waved a hand. "Never mind. Cheesy film plot or not, it's true. There's a whole group of us who hunt vampires. They're... They're my family."

Something about the way Tressa said "family" hit Ethan like an elbow to the solar plexus.

"That sounds nice, I guess," he replied quietly. "Kind of like a whole Supernatural thing. The family business, yeah?"

Tressa cocked her head. "You make a lot of TV references for a scientist."

"Now who's being judgmental?"

"I... You're right."

And there was the fish mouth again.

"Sorry," she said sheepishly.

Ethan laughed. "It's fine. I tend to hit the gym late at night. Re-runs are the only thing playing to keep me entertained on the treadmill."

"Fair enough."

"Yup."

They stared awkwardly at each other for a moment.

"So, you're really a hunter?" he asked, trying to make his brain accept the notion. His mind was currently warring between disbelief that she was telling the truth and disbelief that he'd gotten so lucky. It had only started to dawn on him that he had no skills or connections to aid him with tracking down the monster. And then suddenly the answer to his dilemma walked into his hospital room wearing a tiny skirt and a heart-stopping smile? Maybe the universe was finally offering him a break.

For once.

She grinned. "I really am. We call them *rogues*, though. The ones that murder humans are rogues."

He scoffed. "Right, like there are good vampires running around not ripping out throats?"

"Actually," Tressa began.

"Save it," Ethan said, waving a hand through the air to cut her off. "I don't really care if your organization has some whole 'they're not all bad' ideology. I'm only interested in one. And it is definitely bad."

"It?"

"Yeah," he said, pushing his glasses back up on his nose. "The vampire. Or rogue, whatever you call them. The creature who killed my best friend. I'm going to find her, and I'm going to stake the bitch." He paused and pursed his lips for a second, running his eyes up and down her petite frame. "So, you in?"

Chapter Nine

Tressa

"So, you in?"

The words echoed in the small room, and Tressa was seriously regretting her little lie about being a hunter. When the word popped out, she hadn't fully considered how Ethan might respond. Now her mouth was writing checks her non-hunter ass couldn't cash.

Saiden was the hunter. Tressa was just the mind-altering clean-up crew. But she couldn't exactly tell Ethan that, now could she?

Fuck.

Hadn't she even lectured Saiden not that long ago about the importance of being honest with your mate?

Okay, this was fine. She could roll with this. If Ethan wanted to spend his time hunting down the rogue who attacked his lab, Tressa could work with that. If anything, it was an excuse to remain in his life. And if she managed to convince him that not all vamps were evil in the meantime, more the better.

Baylin was going to have a field day when she told him.

Deciding to commit to the ruse, she settled back in the chair and crossed her arms. "Am I in? Oh, Ethan. Sweet, misguided Ethan. It's me who should be asking *you* that question."

He frowned. "How do you figure?"

Tressa raised a slender hand and began ticking off her fingers. "Let's see. My organization has the means to locate this rogue. We have the knowledge to take them on. And we have the experience and weapons to be successful. What do you have? Piss and vinegar?"

"Hilarious."

"And accurate," she replied, barely suppressing her smirk. "Tell me, Ethan, what exactly was your plan if you're so hellbent on going after this rogue?"

"I..." He snapped his mouth shut and glared.

She didn't even try to hide her smirk anymore. "That's what I thought. So, allow me to ask you a question. Would *you* care to join *me* in hunting down this rogue?"

He bristled at her over-enunciation of the pronouns but nodded. "Yeah. I guess I could use your help," he replied in a tone that sounded like he just agreed to a four-hour root canal.

"Excellent!" Tressa chirped, her default optimism waking back up. "I have a feeling this is the start of a beautiful partnership."

"Baylin, I'm *fucked*," Tressa whispered into her cell phone.

After another fifteen minutes spent arguing with Ethan about the importance of him staying in the hospital for longer to heal, she'd ducked out to call her cousin.

"Like, literally?" he asked. "Because if so, damn girl. I'm impressed.

That was fast."

"Not literally," she hissed, slumping against the wall outside Ethan's room and sliding all the way to the floor. "But I may have just complicated things a little."

Tressa heard Baylin typing away on his computer for a moment before letting out a low chuckle.

"Bay, are you listening?" she demanded. "I'm having a bit of a panic attack here."

"Sorry," her cousin said. "I was just talking to... Doesn't matter. So if you're not fucking him, then what other problem do you have? You didn't do something crazy like confess you're a vampire right off the bat, did you?"

Tressa squeezed her eyes shut. "Um..."

"Lilith damn it, you did, didn't you?"

Tressa had to pull the phone away from her head, he was guffawing so loudly. Vampiric hearing was sensitive enough without her cousin braying like a donkey in her ear. "Baylin, would you stop for a second? No, I didn't tell him I was a vampire."

The laughing died down.

"I told him I was a vampire hunter."

And now she really did have to set her phone down or risk blowing out an eardrum. Curling her legs up under her, she let her head fall back against the wall, then banged it a couple times to dislodge whatever insanity gremlin had taken up residence in her brain. It was the only explanation for why she'd claimed to be a hunter. The cadre was never going to let her hear the end of this.

"Okay, but you see how that's worse, right?" Baylin wheezed several minutes later when he finally stopped laughing enough to resume their chat.

"No, I don't see how it's worse," she all but snarled into the cell-phone.

Choose happiness, she reminded herself, attempting to reign in her temper before she started cursing at her less than helpful cousin.

"Telling him you were a vampire was at least the truth," Baylin replied. "Even if he freaked out and fled the country to escape you, at least you were being open and honest. Telling him you're a hunter? No offense, Tress, but have you ever hunted anything in your life?"

Images of her bruised, emaciated frame stalking down a dark alley flashed in Tressa's brain, but she stuffed them down. "Yes, Baylin," she replied quietly. "I have hunted before."

"Aw, shit," he said. "I'm sorry. I didn't mean to dredge up the past."

"It's fine," she dismissed. Her family didn't know much about her pre-vamp life, but they knew enough to leave it be. "Listen, you can make it up to me by helping out with the cadre. I'm going to try to get Ethan to stay here while you work on locating the rogue, but he's so antsy, I doubt I can keep him in bed more than the rest of today. I need you to let everyone know about their new identities as members of an elite, secret vampire hunting organization."

He snorted. "Okay, you know most of that is ninety-nine percent true, right? Aside from the fact that Saiden does most of the actual hunting these days since Marquin has all but retired and Derrick only joins in when the mood suits him."

"In that case, easy peasy," she replied, her optimism returning as she realized she might be able to pull off her lie. "Just make sure most of the rooms are locked up so he doesn't stumble upon anyone's blood cooler, and we should be good."

"Yeah, I'll take care of it," Baylin assured her. "Shouldn't be a problem since the compound is kind of empty. Derrick's back from the mountains, but he's been moping in his room ever since he flew in. Not sure what's going on there, but he'll tell us eventually. Or not.

You know Derrick. Cora's pretty much holed up in her new studio day and night working remotely on her movie. And Raven... Well, she's Raven. She comes and goes, and currently she's gone. Liessa is also out of town still, but Saiden is heading your way. I'll give him a call before I update everyone else."

Tressa climbed to her feet when she noticed Ethan's doctor strolling down the hall in her direction. "Why is Saiden coming back this way?" she asked, darting around a corner. "He just left San Jose yesterday."

Baylin sighed. "There's been another rogue sighting. Saiden is hoping to catch this one before they kill anyone."

Tressa's stomach plummeted. "Another one?" Normally they went weeks between attacks, not days.

"Yup."

"Fuck."

"My thoughts exactly."

Tressa watched Dr. Kim disappear into Ethan's room, hopefully to talk some sense into her mate and convince him to stay in the hospital longer.

"What are we going to do, Bay?" she asked quietly. "Saiden's only one guy. And a newly mated one at that. He can't handle this increase in attacks."

"I know," Baylin replied, equally as somber. "Just keep a close eye on your own mate. With as brash as these rogues are getting, I'm not sure anywhere is safe. Right about now, I wish you really were a hunter."

"Me too," she replied, her mind drifting back to that night a few hundred years ago. The night she'd stood in the alley clutching a knife in her shaking hand, only to let it fall as she ran away, unable to kill even the one person who truly deserved it.

She might not be a hunter, but what happened after she'd ran away still reminded her that she was more than capable of taking a life if it came down to it. She wouldn't hesitate to protect Ethan from any rogue that tried to hurt him.

Maybe in the end, she would become a hunter after all.

Chapter Ten

Ethan

Holy shit.

He was really doing it. He was going to hunt down and kill a vampire.

Three months ago, his biggest concern was stabilizing the chemical compound for the new plant extract that might actually provide a lasting cure for heart disease. Not a small thing, and definitely not something he intended to forget about, but still...

Did this make him a vampire hunter now too? Did he need to stock up on garlic? Should he get one of those tattoos the Winchester brothers had?

He couldn't help but burst out laughing at that last thought. It was a rare occasion when logic took a back seat to fantastical notions in his life, but considering those fantastical notions were quickly becoming less fantasy and more reality, he needed to start thinking with his rational brain again. Which meant the first thing he needed to do was find out how much Tressa knew about vampires. He highly doubted the stuff he learned from TV was going to be accurate.

No, scratch that. The *first* thing he needed to do was get out of this damn hospital bed. His brief conversation with the detective on his case that morning told him he already knew more than they did, so nothing was going to happen until he got out there and started hunting the vampire down.

He glared at the stoic nurse who had just stabbed a needle into his vein with little warning and zero attempts at a gentle touch, but he doubted she noticed or cared about his reaction. Maybe she was a vampire for as much blood as she kept taking. It all felt so unnecessary. He was awake, and he felt... fine. More or less. He wouldn't be signing up for VieTek's annual half-marathon anytime soon, but he could mostly function. What more did they need to keep him there for?

He didn't want any more tests; he wanted to get out and hunt down that monster. Three months it had been roaming the streets, probably killing more innocent people. It could have gone anywhere in that time. It might not even be in the country anymore.

And these damn doctors didn't even want him getting out of bed? Fuck that shit.

Turning away from the pseudo-vampire-slash-nurse, he fixed his glare on Dr. Kim. "You want me to do what?"

She clicked a few buttons on the hospital computer before turning the monitor away to fix Ethan with the kind of no-nonsense stare that came from years of dealing with combative patients. "Ethan, we need to move you to a long-term rehab facility," she said plainly. "You've been in a coma for three months. It's going to require extensive physical and psychological rehab to get you back to one hundred percent functionality."

He scoffed and adjusted his glasses with the hand that wasn't still trapped by the blood-stealing nurse. "No offense, Doctor, but I feel fine. Yes, I'm a little weak, but that's nothing a few days in the gym can't fix."

The frown on Dr. Kim's face deepened as she folded her arms across her chest. "I don't think you fully understand the situation here, Ethan. You can't simply stroll out of this room and dive back into your old life and routine. Beyond the physical atrophy of your muscles, you may experience issues with breathing, swallowing, and walking. Not to mention the psychological impact. Many coma patients struggle with lifelong post-traumatic stress disorder after a near death experience like yours."

As if on cue, the image of the vampire's fangs descending on his neck popped into Ethan's head, prompting a bead of sweat to form on his brow. It was almost laughable to think any psychiatrist would be able to help him. He highly doubted many people had an experience like his and lived to get therapy for it. There was no diagnosis in the DSM-5 for vampire-related trauma.

Ignoring the queasy feeling in his gut that came from reliving his nightmare, he returned his attention to the haggard doctor, matching her unyielding expression. "I told you, I'm fine."

"And I'm telling you that you have no way of knowing that," she argued. "The body is a complex instrument, and many symptoms don't show up immediately. You might think you're fine, but all you've managed to accomplish so far is making it from the bed to the bathroom."

Ethan gripped the sheets, channeling his annoyance into his fingers so he didn't start shouting. "Yes," he said in a razor calm voice, "and I was able to."

"You fell twice."

"And I got back up."

"Ethan..."

He let out a small growl of frustration. It wasn't that he lacked respect for doctors or their medical knowledge, he just knew from firsthand experience they weren't always correct, and most of them rarely cared about the patient's opinion.

"Listen, Dr. Kim, I'm not trying to be an asshole, but I know my rights. You can't legally keep me here."

The woman grit her teeth. "Legally, no. But you leaving goes so far against my medical advice that—"

"I don't care," he interjected before she could get started on another lecture. "I'll sign as many releases or waivers as you want, but I *am* leaving."

She evaluated him for a long moment, then shook her head, clearly disappointed in his decision. "Will you at least stay overnight for observation?"

A muscle ticked in Ethan's jaw, but he nodded.

"Fine," the doctor said, rising from her chair. "I'll prepare the paperwork and send in a physical therapist to go over some exercises. Perhaps they can talk some sense into you and at least get you to commit to an outpatient program."

Not bloody likely.

The door swung open just as the doctor reached for the handle, and Tressa strolled through.

Doctor Kim barely acknowledged her, which seemed strange, but the pain in Ethan's arm kept him from thinking too much about it.

One down, one to go, he thought, flinching as the aggressive nurse all but yanked the needle from his vein.

Tressa stared daggers at the woman and muttered something under her breath he only partially caught, then sank down into the visitor's chair. He noted her intense focus as the nurse wiped up the small amount of blood oozing from the minor puncture wound.

"I'm fine," he told her. "They're just running some basic tests."

Tressa slowly pulled her eyes away from the assortment of blood tubes with different colored tops and met his gaze. "Of course. Standard procedure."

They sat there awkwardly in silence as the nurse labeled the samples before leaving without a single word. As soon as the door closed behind her, Tressa dragged her chair over to Ethan's side.

"Okay," she began, her face a contrast in emotions, as if she was equal parts excited and nervous. "So, I talked to my cadre, and we think—"

"Cadre?" Ethan interrupted. He rarely stumbled across a word he didn't recognize.

"Yeah," she said, shrugging. "That's just what we call ourselves. I'm not even sure who came up with the term, but we've all been using it for decades." Her eyes flashed wide for a heartbeat, and she coughed a few times before adding, "Sorry, I mean to say *they've* been using it for decades. I'm only twenty-seven, so obviously I haven't been hunting for that long. That would be insane."

He really shouldn't think it was so adorable when she got all flustered, but he couldn't help but grin. "Interesting," he said, adjusting his glasses on his nose. "A cadre of vampire hunters. I like it."

Tressa beamed. "I'm so glad you approve. Anyway, I spoke to them, and if you can just give us a few weeks to prepare while you heal—"

"No," Ethan snapped, then felt bad when he saw her flinch at his abrasive tone. Taking a deep breath to wash away the anger that lingered from his time with the doctor, he softened his voice before speaking again. "Sorry, that was a little harsh, but I just got finished telling Dr. Kim I'm leaving in the morning. Please don't make me fight you too."

Tressa pursed her lips. "You need rest."

"No, I need revenge."

"Getting out there before you're ready might cost you your life."

He stared blankly at her. "Okay. And?"

Tressa's mouth dropped open in horror. "Ethan, I won't let you go on a suicide mission."

He sighed, then tossed his glasses on the nightstand so he didn't have to see the judgment in her eyes. "I'm not planning on dying, all right? I still have work to do on a new medication that could help countless people, and I intend to finish it. But seeing as I currently have no lab to work in, I'm not just going to sit around and do nothing while that vampire keeps killing. My research might be on pause, but I can still save lives. I understand the danger involved, and I'm willing to take that risk."

When Tressa didn't respond right away, Ethan regretted removing his glasses. Even if there was a little judgment on her face, he really did want to see all the nuances of her expression. Ever since he called her out on the sunshine persona, he'd been noticing more of the real Tressa leaking through in their interactions, and he found himself craving those moments.

"Since you brought up your research," she began, shifting forward in her chair, "I have to ask, what were you working on? I'm just curious since it might explain why the rogue targeted you."

He waved a hand to cut off her train of thought. "It was just a new heart medication, and I can't imagine vampires would care about that. You'd think they would want their dinner in better shape. Like swapping a burger for a salad."

Tressa cringed and drew back. "I don't think that's how it works."

"Either way, it wouldn't make sense that my lab was targeted specifically. A lot of companies are working on heart medications. Maybe that thing was just prowling the streets for its next meal and saw the light in my lab was on."

She picked at her cuticles for a minute, and something about the small gesture made him smile. Another reminder that no matter how perfect and polished she initially came off as, she was only human, just like everyone else.

"I suppose you might be right," she conceded with a heavy amount of reluctance. "But if you would share your work with my organization, then..."

He shook his head. "Sorry. Can't."

"Can't or won't?"

"Take your pick," he replied. "I *can't* share it because I'm under the kind of strict NDA that popstars in fake marriages use. Also, I *won't* share it because it's not ready yet. I was almost there when that monster attacked, and I intend to go back and finish it as soon as she's dealt with."

"I understand that, but—"

"No buts," he insisted, crossing his arms. "I'm not sharing."

Tressa scrubbed her face and let out an agonized moan. "Let me get this straight. You won't take the time to heal so you can actually fight the rogue, and you won't share your research that might help us figure out a motive. What are you planning to contribute to this mission, Ethan?"

He grabbed his glasses off the table and pretended to clean them while he considered her question. When he felt confident there was only one realistic answer, he slid them back onto his face and stared at her for a long moment.

"Passion," he declared.

Tressa met his gaze, and her eyes widened, a flash of heat in their depths. "Passion?" Her voice came out barely more than a squeak.

"Yeah," he said. "I'm passionate about killing this vampire."

Tressa blinked, then sat back in the chair, her shoulders drooping slightly. "Oh, right. Of course. Vampire killing."

"What else did you think I meant?"

"N-nothing," she stammered, her deep bronze skin turning a pretty shade of copper from what could only be a blush. "I just... It doesn't matter. If I can't change your mind, I guess I'll see you in the morning, then. It'll take about five hours to get to the compound in eastern California."

He settled back onto his bed and studied the captivating woman in front of him. The way her eyes glowed when he'd said "passion" intrigued him. And that blush...

Keep it in your pants, Ambrose, he scolded himself. *You need to kill the vampire first. Then you can think about planting your zucchini in her secret garden.*

If she was even interested. For all he knew, this strange connection he felt might only be one-sided and her uneasiness simply came from him seeing through her facade.

He kept his mouth shut, and Tressa must have seen the resolve on his face because she gave him a small nod and stood up.

"Get some rest, Ethan," she said, pushing the door open. "I'll see you in the morning."

And then she was gone in a swirl of shiny black hair and a curious bubble gum scent.

Inhaling deeply to catch the last lingering traces of her perfume, he felt his dick hardening. Groaning slightly, he slid back down in the bed and pressed a hand firmly to his groin, as if he could will his soldier to stand down.

Mission first, he reminded himself. *Keep your focus on what matters.*

Chapter Eleven

Tressa

Strolling down the hall outside Ethan's room, Tressa's thoughts swirled with her latest encounter. She hadn't wanted to leave him, but it was clearly written on his face that pushing him would get her nowhere. And if she stayed, she wouldn't be able to help it. He was her mate, and he was injured. Every instinct she had inside her screamed to keep him wrapped up in a healing cocoon of safety.

No part of her was surprised that Ethan refused to stay in the hospital, but she had to give it her best effort. She would just need to keep a really close eye on him to watch for any post-coma issues. The last thing she wanted was for her mate to die before she could convince him to turn.

Tressa had seen what that did to Raven—losing a mate—and now that she found Ethan, she was committed to keeping him alive. Even if he was a little stubborn and pigheaded. It drove her insane how someone who based his life on science and logic could even consider something as crazy as taking on a vampire after months in a coma. He might not know it, but he needed her in his life, if for nothing other than to give him something else to focus on. It wouldn't do him any good to lose himself to revenge. Maybe if she opened up to him about her own experience with that...

Tressa was so far down the rabbit hole of envisioning her future conversations with Ethan that she missed the nurse walking in her direction and bumped into the familiar middle-aged woman.

"Oh, I'm sorry," she said, placing out a hand to steady her.

"It's fine," the older woman said politely, her voice sounding a bit different than before. "It was completely my fault for not paying attention. I apologize."

Odd, Tressa thought, surprised at not only the hint of an accent she'd missed previously, but also the formerly-harsh nurse's extreme shift in attitude from their earlier interactions.

Maybe all the bitterness was just exhaustion leaking through. It had to take a toll, being so overworked all the time for crappy pay and no respect. Tressa didn't like to use her vampire powers for frivolous reasons, but if the woman had somehow found a little extra kindness and cheer, she deserved to keep it. Especially if she had a long shift ahead. Tressa's Gift was essentially limited to calming and relaxing, but compulsion could work. She could make sure the nurse held onto to her happiness throughout the evening.

"Hey," she said, gently grabbing the woman's arm before she could walk away. Tressa locked eyes with the nurse and waited for the mind link to settle into place.

And waited.

And waited.

"I do really need to be going," the nurse said with a forced politeness as she tugged her arm easily from Tressa's grip.

What the...?

Tressa's jaw all but hit the sterile hospital floor. How was that possible? The only person a vampire couldn't compel should be their mate. And hers was lying in a bed six doors down.

"Sorry," Tressa mumbled.

The nurse gave her a small smile, then rushed off.

Tressa watched her scurry down the hall and was about to head toward the waiting room to call Baylin about the bizarre encounter when she noticed the nurse enter Ethan's room.

Wasn't she literally just in there five minutes ago taking his blood?

There were probably a hundred reasons the nurse would need to return to Ethan, but Tressa couldn't shake the weirdness of not being able to compel the woman.

Trusting her instincts, she walked back toward Ethan's room to take a look. Once she saw he was fine, she would get Baylin on the phone to figure out why there might be a human other than her mate who couldn't be compelled.

When she peeked through the window into Ethan's room, though, all thoughts of her cousin vanished, and pure, undiluted terror raced down Tressa's spine. For a single second, every muscle in her vampiric body went into full on lockdown as she processed what she was seeing.

Then she was bursting through the door with enough force that the door partially ripped off its hinges.

"Stop!" she screamed, rushing toward Ethan's bed and the nurse who had a pillow pressed onto her mate's face.

The nurse popped her head up, but only mild annoyance rippled over her slightly wrinkled features as Tressa flung her away from the bed, sending her into the wall with a crunch of broken plaster.

Tressa took a second to evaluate Ethan, her pulse pounding wildly at how close she came to losing him. His eyes were closed, and his face was slack, but his heart still beat, though not as strong as she would like.

"You really couldn't leave well enough alone, could you?" the nurse said, sounding strangely unconcerned about being caught trying to smother a patient. "Do us both a favor and walk away before you get hurt. I have no grievance with you, but I'm not going to allow you to disrupt my plans either."

Tressa whipped around. "Walk away?" she growled. "You tried to murder him!"

Despite the pure rage building inside, she kept her voice low enough that she wouldn't alert any hospital staff. Whoever this nurse was or wasn't, Tressa wanted to deal with it herself. She hadn't killed a person in nearly three hundred years, but all that went out the window the moment she saw her mate in danger. Saiden hadn't been kidding when he said the protection instincts were no joke.

The "nurse" pulled herself from the divot in the wall and rose to her feet, brushing gypsum dust from her scrubs. "Yes, and once I've dealt with you, I'll finish the job. His death is inevitable, but yours needn't be."

"Like hell you're going to touch him again," Tressa snarled.

She blurred around the bed to snatch the woman's neck but stumbled into the broken wall when her fingers grasped only empty air.

"What the fuck?" She whirled around to see her target leaning against the door frame without a care in the world. "How did..."

The woman sighed as if the whole situation was little more than a minor inconvenience. "I would think you of all people would know the answer to that." She cocked her head, then added, "Although, I suppose 'people' isn't the right word, is it?"

Vampire.

Tressa analyzed the woman, scanning her face for any of the tells that were so common to her kind—preternaturally flawless skin, lush and healthy hair, eyes that almost glowed. "But you look human," she said when she found nothing but paper-thin skin with numerous wrinkles, frizzy gray hair, and dark circles under the eyes.

The woman laughed. "Not quite."

She waved a hand in front of her, and Tressa gasped when the woman's appearance rippled like the surface of a placid pond disturbed by a dropped stone. The ripples grew and twisted until a stocky middle-aged nurse no longer stood before her, replaced by a statuesque beauty with wavy dark hair and tan skin—a woman whose appearance matched that smooth voice tinged with a Mediterranean accent. She'd look like a goddess if it wasn't for her ominous eyes, the irises so dark they were nearly indistinguishable from her pupils.

"You're a shape shifter?" Tressa whispered, confusion and fear warring for dominance in her brain.

"Nothing so exotic," the woman replied. "Just a little perception filter. My Gift from Lilith. I can appear however I choose."

With the confirmation that she wasn't facing an unknown entity—just another vampire gone off the deep end—Tressa's unease dissipated under a wave of anger. "What did you do to the real nurse?" she demanded.

"Her blood is in my veins, and I'm sure her body will turn up sooner or later," the rogue replied, her tone void of any emotion. "I don't actually enjoy killing, but I had to keep her hidden, and..." She shrugged. "Waste not, want not."

"We don't attack humans," Tressa hissed, even though she doubted there was any point in reasoning with this vampire. Once they hopped on the murder train, it was essentially a one-way ticket. They almost never came back.

"I do what is necessary," the rogue replied, her eyes drifting over to Ethan. "Though you shouldn't be worried about that. You should be more concerned about your mate and how you will console yourself once he's gone."

Tressa's eyes widened, and the rogue let out a small, almost sad, laugh. "Yes, it's quite obvious you're mates. Congratulations by the way. Though you may not believe it, I truly am sorry that I need to kill him."

"You can try," Tressa taunted, pointedly shifting her body between Ethan and the rogue.

The vampire gave her a pitying smile. "Truly, I have no desire to eliminate you, but I will if I have to. In fact..." She waved her hand again, and the ripples appeared once more, shifting and reshaping until Tressa found herself staring at Ethan.

Her head swung toward the bed, needing the visual confirmation that yes, her mate was still unconscious.

"That's better," fake Ethan said, and Tressa gawked at the feminine voice coming out of his mouth.

"You can't win against me," the rogue said, stalking closer to Tressa. "But even if you did stand a chance, could you really strike your own mate?"

"You think I care about your parlor trick?" Tressa replied, though she couldn't deny her tone lacked the confidence she would have preferred. The vampire wasn't wrong; every instinct inside of her wanted to protect this person who resembled her mate. Not harm them.

She took a deep inhale and latched onto the rogue's decaying flower scent.

This is not my Ethan.

Her fangs descended, itching to tear out the throat of this rogue who dared impersonate her mate. "You have no idea what I'm capable of." Tressa rolled onto the balls of her feet, preparing to strike.

She never got the chance.

Moving faster than even Tressa's vampiric eyes could track, the woman blurred forward and clamped her hand around Tressa's neck, cutting off her air supply. "Oh, my sweet summer child. I know more about you than you could ever imagine. You're the one with the calming Gift. The perfect beauty who never lacks for a smile. The Eternal Optimist." She paused. "Or so you've managed to convince everyone. But I know the truth. I know what lurks in your past, haunting you."

Tressa struggled in the vampire's grasp, but the rogue was clearly older. Much, much older.

"You're wasting your energy," she said, lifting Tressa off her feet, slender fingers digging into her windpipe and cracking something that was probably important. "You can't stop me. You're not a killer."

"She might not be, but I am," a deep male voice said from the doorway, and the rogue swung around.

Stars burst in Tressa's vision as she was wrenched about like a helpless rag doll.

The woman tightened her grip, holding Tressa in front of her like a shield as her body rippled and flowed back into the tall female form.

"Saiden," Tressa gurgled, but she couldn't get anything else out because the lack of oxygen was starting to take its toll. She imagined she only had two or three minutes left before she passed out. Vampires might be champions at holding their breath, but their bodies still needed oxygen to power the brain.

She'd just found her mate and was already failing him. Tressa shot a glance over at the bed, at Ethan's sprawled form, and she took in his too pale skin with a slight tinge of blue to his lips. Fire burned in her gut, and something extra sparked to life inside her. She refused to go down without a fight, redoubling her efforts to kick and squirm her way free.

Her struggle seemed to matter little to the vampire who was now focused on her cousin. "Ah, yes," the rogue said, sneering. "Saiden. The Enforcer. Murderer of his own kind."

Ever the tall, dark, and intimidating figure, Saiden took a step into the room, his hands settling on the daggers at his belt as he kicked the door shut. "Glad you've heard of me. That means you know exactly how easily I'm going to kill you if you don't release my cousin."

"Oh, this cousin?" the woman asked innocently. "She's all yours."

One second, Tressa was struggling to maintain consciousness, and the next, she was flying across the room. She slammed into Saiden with enough force to send them crashing into the wall, adding a second sizable dent to the room's decor.

Before they could untangle themselves, the rogue blurred over and held Saiden down with one foot on his chest. "Since you're so adamant about fighting, let's do this another time away from humans. But just so you know, this is not a gift. Ethan *is* going to die, and the more time you spend with him, the more it's going to hurt." She darted out into the hall but tossed a glance back at them. "And when that day comes, do remember that I tried to make it quick."

Then she was gone.

Tressa groaned and rolled off Saiden. "You didn't see that coming with your Gift?" she muttered, her throat still hoarse despite her accelerated healing working to repair the damage.

Saiden pushed up off the floor, then held out a hand for Tressa.

"You know my Gift only triggers in potentially lethal scenarios," he replied, pulling her up. "Besides, you're lucky I decided to stop by the hospital before heading out to hunt. If I hadn't heard your little scuffle in here from the waiting room, I might be having a rather uncomfortable talk with Marquin right about now."

"Awww," Tressa cooed before kissing Saiden on the cheek. "If I didn't know any better, I'd think you were fond of me, Sadie Cakes."

Rolling his eyes, he swiped a hand through the long strands of dark hair that only hung down on the left side of his head, smoothing them back into place. "So," he said, walking over to the side of the bed. "I take it this is your mate Baylin was telling me about?"

"Yeah," Tressa said, coming up to his side. "Saiden, meet Ethan Ambrose."

Saiden huffed. "He looks decent enough, I guess. You like him?"

Tressa smiled and brushed her hand over Ethan's cheek. "I do. He's a bit like you, actually. Kind of a grump sometimes. But he's got a heart of gold. And he's smart. Some type of plant medicine scientist. I think I could fall in love with him quite easily."

Saiden grunted, and Tressa took that to be about as much sappy emotional stuff as he could handle. "You get anything out of him about why he was targeted?" her cousin asked.

She let her hand drop back to her side. "Not yet. He's keeping the details of whatever he was working on pretty close to the chest. But whatever it was can't be good if the rogue came back to finish the job."

"I don't like it," Saiden grumbled as he righted a fallen chair and sank into it, stretching his long legs out in front of him. "Mindless rogues killing people to feed I can handle, but this?" He waved a hand at Ethan. "And showing up so soon after the vamp that killed Cora? There's something going on, and I don't appreciate stumbling around in the dark."

"And see here I thought you had perfect night vision."

"Cute."

"I know."

He sighed. "I take it you're going to continue this vampire hunter charade you told Bay about?"

Nodding, Tressa dropped down on the side of the bed. She slid Ethan's hand onto her lap and wound her fingers through his, needing to remain as close to him as possible after the attack. Every inch of her skin buzzed with the ocean of adrenaline coursing through her, and his touch anchored her amidst the maelstrom of worry, fear, and anxiety thrashing in her head. "What else am I supposed to do?"

"Tell him the truth."

Tressa's right eyebrow quirked up. "Oh, like how you told Cora she was your mate?"

Saiden fixed his most intimidating glare on her—the one that sent both humans and vampires running—but it only amused her. "At least I didn't hide that I was a vampire," he shot back.

"Oh, bite me, Saiden," Tressa teased, falling into their usual habit of goading each other. "You want to give me shit about this? I could tell the rest of the cadre what I found in the trunk of your McLaren. I always thought it was strange most of the kids I've had to compel were clutching little crochet animals."

He froze. "You wouldn't."

A slow grin spread across Tressa's face. "Oh, I very much would."

Saiden narrowed his steely eyes on her. "Fine. He's your mate. Do whatever you want, and I'll stay out of it. But when this all blows up in your face, and trust me, it will, I get to say I told you so."

"Deal." Tressa grinned wider. "I have to ask though, why pick crochet as a hobby? Why not origami?"

Saiden pushed out of his chair and stalked toward the door. "Bye, Tressa."

"Or maybe baking?" she called after him. "You'd look adorable in a frilly pink apron!"

He flipped her the middle finger and disappeared into the hall.

Turning to Ethan, Tressa evaluated his now steady breathing and rhythmic pulse. At least there were no new injuries she could see beyond a slight pallor to his complexion.

Moving at top speed before anyone was alerted, she unhooked the wires from his body, flicked off the monitor that started beeping frantically from the disconnections, then slipped her hands under his back to pull him up into her arms. He might be pushing two hundred pounds, but that was nothing for her vampire strength.

Nudging the door open with her foot, Tressa quickly carried Ethan toward the back exit.

Baylin wasn't going to be thrilled when he got another phone call from her about wiping more security feeds, but her cousin would just have to deal. There was no way in hell she was leaving her mate in the hospital, exposed and vulnerable to another attack.

The long five-hour drive back to the safety of the compound still held a distinct lack of appeal, but with any luck, Ethan would remain asleep the entire way.

She glanced down at his face. His features were hard, yet so innocent at the same time.

"It's okay, Ethan," she whispered. "I'll protect you."

That rogue bitch would be toast before she laid another finger on her mate.

Chapter Twelve

Ethan

"It's almost a shame," the vampire said, her tongue swiping out to lick up a drop of blood from the corner of her mouth. "To have to kill someone so... intriguing. So intelligent. A pity, really."

Ethan swallowed roughly, putting all his strength into wrenching free from her tight hold that refused to yield. "Do it," he bit out. "I'd rather die than spend another second looking at your hideous face."

Her lips twitched, almost as if she was suppressing a grin. "In that case," she replied, her hollow eyes drawing him into eternal darkness, "your wish is granted."

A second set of teeth descended behind her normal ones, and when the fangs were fully exposed, she struck.

And luscious lips caressed his neck.

Jerking away, his body no longer locked in place, he stared at Tressa as she smiled at him. "It's okay, Ethan," she whispered. "I'll protect you."

He sank into the depths of her bewitching gaze, a sense of warmth and security pulling him in. She would protect him. He didn't know where the sense of absolute certainty came from, but he trusted her.

"Tressa," he murmured, holding her tight against his body. He dropped his mouth to her neck, smelling only that delicious bubblegum aroma. The cloying coppery scent of blood faded away until there was simply her and him. No monsters. No murdered best friends. No laboratory coated in streaks of red.

He peppered kisses up the long line of her neck, pausing for some reason when he felt the steady drumming of her pulse beneath his lips. Moving without thought, he gave a tiny nip. He'd never been into biting before, but with Tressa, it felt right. To sink his teeth into her sweet skin and relish in the moans that followed.

The soft whimper that came from her was a stark contrast to the hard length growing in his slacks. "You taste so good," he mumbled between kisses as he made his way to her lips. "And you feel even better."

"Ethan," Tressa sighed, running her hands along his taut chest.

"Fuck..." He let out a deep, desperate groan. "I need you. Why do I need you so bad?"

Tressa wrapped her arms around him tighter, the iron grip triggering something at the back of his mind, but he mentally brushed the distraction away.

Then all thoughts disappeared entirely when her pebbled nipples brushed against his chest. "Take whatever you need, Ethan," she purred. "I'm yours."

He captured her mouth with his own, his hands gliding along the smooth skin of her bare shoulders. Every part of her was silky and sensuous, and it awoke something inside him when she surrendered so completely to him.

As his tongue delved into her mouth, she pressed her hips into him, rubbing herself along the length of his very ready and willing cock.

He met her teasing with his own, grinding against her just as hard as she worked him. Then he slid his hand lower and cupped the treasure between her legs that was already so wet he could feel it through her thin, *silky pants.*

"Ethan," she moaned, gently rolling her hips against his strong palm.

"Tressa."

"Ethan."

"Tressa."

"Ethan?"

Her voice changed, the sensuality giving way to confusion. "Ethan, are you with me?"

He wanted to say yes, of course he was. But her voice grew distant, as if drifting through a cloud.

"Tressa?" he called. She was still in his arms, but she sounded miles away.

"Ethan, you need to wake up."

The words jolted him out of sleep, his eyes flying open. He blinked furiously at the sunshine streaming in through an open window as he drowned in a haze of blinding light and bubblegum scent.

Then reality smacked into him, and he realized just where that scent was coming from.

Tressa. In his arms. Wearing only a thin pair of teal satin pajamas.

And his hand was still between her legs.

"Fucking hell!" he shouted, scrambling away from her.

What was going on? And what had he been about to do?

A quick glance down told him the only clothing on his body was an unfamiliar pair of black athletic shorts that were currently being tented by his raging hard-on. His hands dropped to his crotch in a useless attempt to hide his obvious arousal.

Promptly abandoning that pointless mission, he leapt from the bed and grabbed a pillow. Holding it in front of his erection with one hand, he grabbed his glasses off the nightstand and backed up a few steps. Fumbling awkwardly, he shoved his glasses on his face, then forced himself to look at Tressa, prepared to see the worst.

She rolled over and studied him but remained lying in bed, her face showing nowhere near as much outrage as he would have expected.

"You know," she said, "you can feel free to relax. I'm already intimately aware of what's going on behind that pillow."

Ethan gawked at her. Why wasn't she screeching and cursing his name? He had essentially assaulted her in his sleep!

"But... but... why?" It felt like his brain was bouncing around in his skull on tumble dry and he couldn't find the off switch.

Tressa cocked her head. "Why am I aware of what you're packing downstairs? Well, you see, when a man presses himself against a woman, that woman can feel every bit of—"

"Stop!" Ethan yelled, backing up even farther until he slammed into a solid oak dresser, knocking over whatever picture frames had been decorating it. "I'm very well aware of what was happening in that regard. But *why* were we in bed together? And why is that bed not a hospital bed? And why aren't you pissed as hell at me for touching you like... like that! Why aren't you trying to kick my ass?"

Tressa ran a hand through her messy hair and collapsed against the pillow, the movement pulling her satin camisole up enough to expose a wide expanse of smooth, toned skin.

Ethan clutched the pillow even tighter as his cock tried to burst through the thing like a damned alien facehugger.

"Wellll," Tressa drawled, oblivious to his internal struggle. "That's a lot of questions for so early in the morning, but I'll see what I can do. Long story short, you were attacked in the hospital. I fended off the vamp but decided you weren't safe there, which is why I brought you back to the compound last night. It was late, and everyone was asleep when we arrived, so I figured we could share a bed for the night. I didn't want you to wake up alone and confused in a strange place."

She paused, and her eyes crawled over his body, landing on the pillow he held with a white-knuckled death grip. "When I made the call, I didn't realize you were such a nocturnal cuddler."

There was no mirror in the room, but Ethan was pretty sure his pale face turned bright red. He couldn't say he was surprised he woke up wrapped around Tressa if they'd been sharing a bed. He hadn't been with a woman in, well, long enough he would need to check a calendar. Not to mention she was sexy as hell. Of course he would gravitate toward her in his sleep. And clearly something about her presence chased away the nightmare that had continued to plague his unconscious mind. A fact he didn't want to think too closely about right then.

But none of that explained...

"Okay, but why are you so cool about this?" he demanded, then decided aggression was the absolute wrong emotion for the scenario. Taking a deep breath, he let it out on a slow exhale.

The problem with releasing his anger, though, was it left behind only complete and utter embarrassment with an epic side helping of shame.

He dropped his eyes to the floor as he mumbled, "I was... you know, I was..."

"Very close to getting me off?"

His eyes shot up to meet hers, and for a solid minute, he could do nothing but gape at the relaxed woman reclining on the bed with a wide, mischievous smirk on her face.

"You know what I meant," he protested. "I was touching you inappropriately, and we only just met a few days ago."

"Why, Ethan," Tressa gushed, rolling onto her side in a way that gave him a tempting view down her tank top. "Who knew you were such a gentleman?"

Eyes on her face, Ambrose, he ordered himself. *Eyes on her god-damned face.*

"Although," she continued, "maybe you aren't all gentleman. That tattoo on your low back tells me there might be a wild side to you."

Her eyes gleamed with amusement, and he would have emptied his entire bank account for a hole to open up and swallow him. Of course she'd seen *that* tattoo. "I died," he muttered quietly to himself. "I died in that coma, and this is hell—embarrassing myself in front of a hot woman."

Tressa's smirk grew into a full-blown grin when he said the word "hot," but she must have registered the distress overtaking him because her amused expression faded as she sat up, thankfully making it easier for him to look at her face. "I appreciate the chivalry and distress on my behalf," she said, "but have you looked at you? Regardless of the circumstances that led us here, I'm not going to complain if you want to get some horizontal exercise in. Although, I clearly made the right call by waking you up since you seem so horrified by the thought."

The shame overwhelmed him to the point that his cock finally decided to stand down, and something about the blood no longer rushing south reminded his body that it was still weak. His knees shook, and he let his full weight fall back against the dresser, forgoing the no longer needed pillow in lieu of gripping the wood with both hands.

"No, I'm not..." He frowned, fully aware he was traipsing through a mine field, and one wrong step could mean disaster. "I'm definitely not... because you're..."

Fuck, he couldn't even speak.

"Look," he said, pushing up to standing when he felt certain his legs would hold him. "You are... I mean, you're incredibly beautiful, Tressa. You know that. I know that. A blind preacher would know that. Any man would kill to be with you."

She arched an eyebrow.

"And I'm including myself in that 'any man' statement, obviously," he added before she could get the wrong idea. "But my mom raised me right and taught me that consent matters, so—"

"Ethan," she interjected, swinging her legs around to sit on the side of the bed. "You more than had my consent."

Her words eased a bit of the tension in his body, and he pushed off the dresser to take a step forward. Without something to occupy his hands, though, they quickly made their way into his standard crossed arms position.

Which apparently sent the wrong message. Again.

Tressa pursed her lips, assessing him with shrewd eyes. "It seems I should be more concerned about your consent since you were the one still asleep and clearly disturbed by what happened."

"No!" Ethan shouted. Fueled by fear that he'd royally fucked up, he darted over to sit beside her on the bed and grabbed her hand. "Tressa, I would very, *very*, much like the opportunity to be with you. But right now..." He glanced around frantically for something to focus on besides those wide brown eyes that were now flooded with uncertainty.

Seeing no obvious way to change the subject, he pulled off his glasses and began wiping the lenses on his shorts while he gathered his thoughts. How exactly was he supposed to explain to the most beautiful woman he'd ever seen that despite being more than attracted to her, he couldn't handle any distractions from his mission. And the stiff nipples pressing against her thin satin camisole were one—make that two—very big distractions.

"Breathe, Ethan," Tressa said, running her hand down his back and sending tiny shocks straight to his groin. "I get it. You just got out of a coma, discovered vampires are real, and have plans to hunt one down. You got a lot on your plate. And while I would love for you to add me to that plate, I'm going to guess you're not really hungry for more?"

Anxiety drained from his shoulders as her soft fingers traced soothing, nearly hypnotic patterns across his bare skin, and before his brain could contribute to the conversation, he responded, "Tressa, I would love to dine on you, but..."

Her lips ticked up into a grin, and he groaned when he realized what he'd said.

"Dine *with* you!" he blurted out. "Or, no, that's not what I meant either. Fuck, can we use a different metaphor here?"

Ethan didn't think he could blush harder. He'd never been nervous around women before, but for some reason, he couldn't view Tressa the same as just any woman. She wasn't a fellow scientist he met in the hotel bar at a pharma convention looking for a one-night stand. And she wasn't a gym bunny who saw his muscles flexing on the weight bench and thought he would make an excellent additional workout. No, there was something different about her. Something special. Something he might very much want to pursue after the vampire was dealt with.

So long as he didn't screw up his chances beforehand.

"Look," he said, putting his glasses on and shifting to face her. "My blundering responses aside, you were right when you said I have a lot going on. This whole vampire thing kind of turned my world upside down, and I need to get a handle on that before I..."

"Get a handle on me?" she finished in a teasing tone.

He let out a small laugh. "Yeah. Pretty much."

"Well, in that case, no harm no foul," she said, her voice resuming that chipper tone he knew wasn't entirely authentic. "I'm guessing by the way you flew out of this bed, though, your strength and mobility are coming back?"

Ethan glanced down at his legs. He couldn't deny the muscle fibers were twitching overtime at the level of exertion he'd just used, but he hadn't collapsed during their conversation which he was eternally grateful for. That extra layer of awkwardness would have made things beyond unbearable.

"Yeah, I think I'm doing okay," he told her. "I doubt I'll be bench-pressing my own body weight in the next day or two, but I think I can walk on my own at least."

"Great," Tressa said, and Ethan could have sworn her smile was more forced than usual. "In that case, why don't you take a shower while I go update the cadre about the latest attack. I'll be back with breakfast shortly, and then I can show you around."

She hopped off the bed, grabbed a robe from her closet, and wrapped it around her.

Ethan eyed the tightness in her face. Her bubbly facade was normally much more intact than this. Was she really that upset he didn't want to pursue something with her right away? Fuck. He'd never been suave, never needed or cared to be, but for some reason, he didn't want her shying away from him.

"Tressa..."

"Shower, Ethan," she said quietly. "I'll be back in a bit."

Then she was out the door, leaving only a cloud of intoxicating bubblegum scent and the unsettling feeling that she was more hurt by his dismissal than she had let on.

Chapter Thirteen

Tressa

Lilith take me now and put me out of my misery.

Tressa slumped against the wall just outside her bedroom. When she'd woken up to Ethan cuddled against her, part of her hoped he was fully awake and initiating something. Something she was more than interested in. But the moment she realized he was dreaming, she had no choice. She couldn't take advantage of him like that. Even if he didn't know what it was, he would feel the pull of the mating bond.

And judging by his reaction, she'd made the right call. If things had progressed much further, she wouldn't have been able to stop herself—wouldn't have wanted to—and she had a feeling he would have been halfway back to San Jose when he realized what they'd done.

She thumped her head against the wall a few times, then climbed to her feet. Wallowing in what could have happened wasn't getting her anywhere. That rogue was still out there, and her mate was still in danger. While the compound might be the most secure place they could hole up, the incident with Bianca a few months back had shown them it wasn't entirely impenetrable.

Which meant she needed intel, and she needed it fast.

Tressa knocked once on Baylin's door, then pushed it open before he could say anything. Entering the sterile room that contained little more than a wall of computers, a blood cooler, and a door that led into Baylin's actual bedroom, she paused briefly when she saw Derrick slouched in a chair off to the side, his face drawn with melancholy.

"Morning, Derrick," she chirped, but he only grunted in response. She waited for his typical smirk and a snarky quip—two things you *always* got from Derrick—but he just folded his arms and scuffed a shiny loafer on the marble tiling. Since he wouldn't meet her eyes, she turned to the other male in the room.

"Hey, Baylicious," she said, dropping into the computer chair beside her cousin, careful not to knock over the open can of Red Bull that sat a little too close to the edge. She picked it up and read the label, cringing when she saw the amount of caffeine. Her cousin was the only vampire in the world who seemed to crave more energy than they were naturally blessed with.

"Hey, person who doesn't wait for permission to enter," Baylin replied without pulling his eyes from the monitor. A chat box was open on one of the screens, but he closed it before Tressa could see who he was talking to.

"Oh, come on," she teased, kicking up her bare feet to set them on the arm of Baylin's chair. "At least I knocked. Saiden doesn't even do that much."

"And he's fully aware how I feel about that."

"So why not lock your door?" she asked, poking his ribs with her big toe.

Baylin grabbed her feet and dropped them to the floor before snatching the energy drink from her hands. "No reason. I just keep forgetting."

Tressa studied her cousin and the complete lack of annoyance on his face. That, combined with the fact Baylin never forgot anything, made her wonder if some part of him actually enjoyed how they entered his space so casually.

Like a family would.

They all knew how Baylin had been turned and abandoned, left in a back alley of Galway to either die or become a rogue. It was only by the grace of Lilith that Marquin found him and taught him how to function as a real vampire. Baylin's life before that, though, he never talked about. Not even with Saiden, who was more or less his brother since they were turned around the same time and grew into their fangs together with Marquin watching over them.

It was almost like an unspoken rule in their cadre. If someone wanted to volunteer their history, great. But you didn't ask.

You *never* asked.

And she had every intention of hiding behind that rule.

"So what's he moping about?" Tressa thumbed a finger at Derrick who only scowled at her in response.

Baylin shook his head, then turned his attention back to the monitors. "That is... not my story. Just leave it alone, Tress. He'll tell you when he's ready."

Ignoring Baylin's advice, Tressa scanned her sulking cousin—the tension in his body, the almost greasy appearance of his normally coiffed hair, and the wrinkled Armani dress shirt that looked like it had been slept in. Twice. Whatever had her cousin tangled up must be major for him to be anything but runway ready. "Derrick?" she asked, hoping he might offer her a brief distraction from her own issues.

He ran a hand through his messy blond hair and shook his head. "Not now, Tressa. I'll... I'll tell you later. Why don't you update us on your own mate? Bay says you took him to bed last night?" Derrick's voice held a hint of teasing, but there was no levity behind it. None of the normal joy he would take in tormenting one of his family members.

Deciding it would be best to let it go, Tressa sagged back in the chair. "What update would you like? The one where he woke up in my arms completely freaked out because he thought he was taking advantage of me and I can't tell him he's my mate so it was a perfectly normal reaction? Or the one where I can't stop panicking about how he almost died in that hospital so now he lives here and I have to make sure absolutely nobody exposes our vamp-ness before I'm ready to tell him the truth?"

"Ooof," Baylin said, only half paying attention to her while the other half of his brain was clearly occupied with whatever the lines of numbers on his computer represented. She couldn't even be mad about his lack of concern for her problems since that was pretty standard for Baylin. If you ever had his full attention, something was seriously wrong.

"Yeah, oof indeed," she replied. "We need to find this rogue and take her out so I can focus on convincing Ethan that not all vamps are evil."

Baylin laughed. "So, what I'm hearing is that operation VAJ is making a return?"

Tressa blinked. "Operation what? Scratch that, I don't want to know. What I do want to hear is what you've found out about her. I'm going to assume you haven't been doing anything but researching ever since I told you."

Baylin slid an eye in her direction before taking a sip of his energy drink. "I do have a life, you know. It's not cadre business a hundred percent of the time."

"Good one, Bay," she said, grinning. "We all know you only leave this room to go into town like once a month."

He drained the last of his Red Bull, wadded it up like a paper ball, and tossed the crumpled can over his shoulder, where it sailed perfectly into the trash bin on the other side of the room.

"Whatever," he huffed out. "I talked to Saiden about the attack when he got home this morning and then pulled some footage from the hospital cameras. I found your vamp in the Ruling Coalition's database, but I didn't alert you right away because it honestly doesn't make any sense." He tapped a few keys, and a new screen popped up. "Her name is Renata Da Silva, and she was born in Portugal in 1502. According to her file, she has been a model vamp. Five hundred years without a single mark against her. Not even a natural feeding gone wrong before the invention of blood banks. She's as clean as they come."

Tressa frowned at the photo on the screen. "Any chance it's not actually her?"

Baylin spun in his chair and raised an eyebrow. "What do you mean?"

"Her ability," Tressa said, leaning forward to scan the file more closely. "She has some kind of perception filter Gift. She can look like whatever she wants. Maybe she's just pretending to be this person?"

"Doubtful," Bay said, pointing to the bottom of the screen. "Her ability is noted right there. Not to mention I caught her on a traffic cam minutes after the attack on the lab. A perception filter doesn't work on cameras. No, it's her all right. And if she's started killing humans, not only is it a recent change, but she's managed to stay off the Coalition's radar somehow."

Tressa continued to study the photo as if something might pop up and scream, 'This is why I went rogue.' When nothing solidified, she sighed and turned to her other cousin who had remained suspiciously quiet. "Derricula, grab me a bag, would you?"

Ignoring his pained groan, she held out her hand and wiggled her fingers insistently. He snagged a blood pouch from the small cooler beside the sofa and tossed it over to her.

Piercing the bag with her fangs, she sipped on the blood and read through the details of the file again. Baylin was right. Not a single red flag to be seen. "What's her motivation, then?" Tressa mused aloud. "How do you go from five hundred years of squeaky clean to murdering humans and destroying labs?"

Baylin just shrugged, but Derrick scoffed. "Maybe she got dumped and went on a rampage."

At his bitter tone, Tressa whirled around. "Okay, what is your deal, Derrick? Did some girl reject your advances or something? I know it doesn't happen to you often because of your Gift, but not every woman is going to fall for your so-called charm."

Derrick clenched his jaw for a moment, then sprang to his feet. "I'm going to see if Saiden is up for training. I'll catch you two later."

He stormed out of the room, and Tressa turned back to her less angry cousin. "What in Lilith's name crawled up his ass and died?"

Baylin waved a hand. "Not my story," he reminded her.

A strong part of her wanted to go after Derrick and make him spill the beans about whatever had him pissier than a teenage girl on her period, but that would have to wait. There was a bigger mystery staring at her from Baylin's computer screen.

"So, any theories?" she asked.

He shook his head. "I'll keep looking, but I got nothing. It might help if we had some idea what Ethan was working on because I doubt it was just a simple heart medication. With Renata going rogue out of the blue, I have to imagine it's related. If we can uncover that connection, we might be able to figure out her motive and what her end game is."

Tressa drained the last of her blood bag, then tossed it in the trash. "A great plan in theory, except for the part where Ethan's staying mum on his research."

Baylin waggled his eyebrows. "Does that mean we're back to the idea of you seducing it out of him? Use that mate bond attraction to suss out the dirty deets?"

Tressa smacked his arm hard enough to bruise a human, but her cousin didn't so much as flinch. "First off, no," she told him. "Ethan and I are not getting busy any time soon. For multiple reasons. And secondly, don't say 'dirty deets.' I know your Gift is absorbing in-formation at a crazy rate, but can you maybe not adopt *every* bit of modern slang you find?"

He rolled his eyes. "Sorry, didn't mean to offend your delicate ancient sensibilities."

"Aren't you older than me by a decade or two?"

"Maybe. But I'm not delicate."

Tressa scoffed and rose from the chair. "Whatever. I need to get back to Ethan with breakfast. Everything is in place with the staff?"

Baylin nodded. "Yup. All the rooms with blood storage have been locked up tight, and the human employees have all been compelled to keep the vamp thing under wraps. Anyone he runs into will support your bullshit spiel about this being a group of vampire hunters."

"I wouldn't call it bullshit," she argued. "You even admitted that's basically what we are. Just... a very specific kind of rogue vampire hunter."

He laughed and turned back to his monitors. "If that's what you need to tell yourself to feel better about lying to your mate, then by all means. Keep repeating it."

"Bite me, Bay."

"No thanks. I already ate."

"Cute."

"So the ladies tell me."

Tressa reached down to the black mini-cooler that Baylin kept hidden under his desk and pulled a can out. "Have another energy drink, why don't you?"

He held a hand out without shifting his attention from the computer, and she slapped the can into his palm before striding toward the door.

"So what's your plan?" he called after her.

Tressa stopped and glanced back at her cousin who was still mostly absorbed in whatever chat screen he'd pulled up. "Well, first I need to get my mate some food," she answered. "After that... I might have an idea. Heck, it worked on Cora, maybe it'll work on Ethan."

"Cora knew about us, though," he replied absently.

"Details," Tressa tossed over her shoulder as she raced off down the hall toward the kitchen.

Step one was grabbing a plate full of their chef's buttery croissants to bribe his stomach.

And if that worked, she'd move on to step two—showing him the compound's massive garden in hopes she could bribe his heart as well.

Chapter Fourteen

Ethan

Ethan stepped out from under the warm spray of water and reached for his fogged over glasses. Normally he showered so fast they didn't have time for condensation to build up, but after his... encounter with Tressa, he'd needed a few extra minutes under the water. No matter how ashamed he'd been about his unconscious advances, he couldn't deny his body wanted her.

And his heart was starting to catch up. Thankfully, his brain had always been the one in charge of decision making, and any romantic entanglements were on pause until after the vamp was pushing up daisies. Then he would be more than willing to spend all night fucking Tressa's brains out. Provided she still wanted him, of course. It wasn't like he had anything to offer a goddess like her, what with currently being homeless and jobless.

He stared into the mirror for a minute and evaluated his new physique. His hair was in serious need of a trim. The strands he could usually control with a swipe of gel now hung down like a curtain over his face. It had gotten to the point that he had to either tuck them behind his ears or walk around half blind. Not to mention his normal chin scruff had grown to full on beard status. But facial hair aside, his biggest concern was the new sharp angle to his cheeks and taper to his waist. He'd worked his ass off to fill out his frame with enough muscle to ensure his lab job wouldn't turn him into a scrawny nerd, but alas, his lot in life seemed to find him anyway.

Well, maybe scrawny wasn't the right word. He shifted side to side, running his hands down his broad shoulders and the chest muscles that were now more lean than bulky. Maybe it wasn't so bad. When he hit thirty a couple years back, he'd started to question just why he spent so many nights at the gym to maintain the sculpted look. He hadn't been on a date in over a year, so really, who cared if he was ripped or not as long as he was healthy. And Tressa hadn't exactly seemed like she was repulsed by his physical appearance, so maybe...

Shaking his head, he grabbed the only towel hanging on the rack—a fluffy pink one—and wrapped it around his waist. He was starting to feel like a kid who just went through puberty and now wanted to do nothing but stare at his new body.

Stepping back into the bedroom, he paused his adolescent musings.

Well, shit.

He'd likely been sporting nothing but the highest hospital gown fashion when Tressa brought him to this place which meant... Yup. He had exactly nothing to wear. A quick glance around showed him the starchy garment was nowhere to be found, and even the black shorts he'd left on the floor had been whisked off to who knows where.

Great. He upgraded from a hospital gown to a pink towel. A surprisingly large towel that hung well past his knees, but a towel nonetheless. Not exactly conducive to tracking down a vampire.

Although, if this really was a compound filled with hunters, one of them had to be a guy who was roughly Ethan's size. He was a little taller than the average male at just over six feet, but he'd wear cut off jean shorts if it meant he could burn that disgusting hospital gown.

Seeing as he had no desire to wander the compound half naked looking for Tressa, he strolled around the room, taking in the unique art pieces that adorned the walls. The space had a whole cozy vibe going on with mahogany furniture and a pair of plush beige recliners, but it was the explosions of color everywhere that turned the room from boring to exciting. The paintings varied in style from expressionism to watercolor, and they were all landscapes from around the world, most of which Ethan didn't immediately recognize. One in particular, though, drew him in, and he stepped closer to analyze it.

"I painted that," Tressa said, and Ethan leapt back so fast his towel slipped off his hips in the process.

"Fuck!" he screamed, and not a manly scream either. It was a 'seven-year-old girl who just saw a spider' type of high-pitched scream he would give anything to take back.

Snatching the towel off the floor with lightning reflexes he didn't know he was capable of, he whipped around to take in Tressa's smirking face. The multiple sudden movements left him more than a little woozy, but he wasn't about to dump fertilizer on the invasive weeds of his embarrassment by leaning against the wall for support. Instead, he carefully secured the pink towel around his waist again, his toes gripping the plush carpet tightly.

"Oh, no need to get dressed on my account," she said with eyes that sparkled in the light. "The others might prefer you in pants, but I'm more... flexible."

Ethan's face heated, but he wasn't sure how to respond. He'd had his fair share of women hit on him before, though none had the ability to tie his tongue like the one standing before him.

The one holding a tray of croissants and orange juice.

Ethan let out a much more manly shout of joy that hopefully drowned out the loud grumbling from his stomach and dove for a pastry. In his haste to snatch up a flaky croissant, he nearly lost the damn towel a second time.

"Fuck me," he moaned after sinking his teeth into the soft buttery treat. The garbage the hospital staff had the audacity to call food had done nothing to welcome him back to the land of the living.

Tressa raised an eyebrow, and his blush returned in full force.

"Uh, sorry," he muttered. "I just meant this is really delicious."

"Well, good to know the standard for pleasing you starts somewhere around tasty pastry. I look forward to seeing where we can go from there." She gave him a wicked grin.

Holy shit, this woman was testing his resolve.

She must have seen the torment on his face because she just laughed and set the tray on the dresser before plopping onto the freshly made bed. The level of bounce from the cushy mattress drew his eyes to the way her breasts jiggled in the tight lavender tank top she'd thrown on. It was a step above her silk PJs in terms of temptation, but she'd paired it with a short, white tennis skirt that exposed far too much bronze skin for him to focus, so the outfit was more or less a lateral move.

"Relax, Science Boy," she said, tucking her legs up underneath her. "I'm just teasing."

"Science Boy?" he grumbled after swallowing another bite. "Not to be *that* guy, but you do know I have a Doctorate in Botany and a Masters in both Microbiology and Bioorganic Chemistry, right?"

Tressa tapped her chin for a second. "Hmm... Should I call you Doctor Science, then?"

Ethan groaned. "How about not?"

"I have to call you something," she protested. Then her eyes positively lit up with mischief, and Ethan braced himself.

"I got it!" she shouted. "Your last name is Ambrose. Amb. Rose. You have a rose tattoo on your ass, and you're literally a rose doctor! Dr. Rose is the perfect nickname for you!"

Despite how proud of herself Tressa seemed, Ethan couldn't help but cringe at the reduction of his life's work down to a silly moniker. "Or you could just call me Ethan, like the rest of the world does. Please don't tell me you're one of those people who thinks everyone needs a nickname?"

She shrugged. "Why not? I think they're cute. And who doesn't want a little fun to lighten up their day?"

He shoved the rest of the croissant in his mouth to buy time to formulate a response. He didn't want her to think he was a complete stick in the mud, but he couldn't deny the truth. "To be honest, that's not a big part of my life."

"Fun? You don't do fun? Come on, Ethan," she said, giving him a dubious look. "Life is too precious to be so miserable all the time."

The last bit of pastry soured in his mouth, but he choked it down. "I guess I've just been through a lot in my life, and my ability to be so carefree vanished somewhere along the way."

Tressa's smile flickered, then reappeared with less sincerity. "We've all been through a lot, Ethan," she replied calmly, regarding him with rich brown eyes that were filled with the remnants of an old pain hidden but not forgotten. "I've been through more than you could possibly know, and while I can't change the past, I can choose how it affects my present. I can crumble under the suckiness and let it define me, or I can give it the middle finger and choose happiness instead."

There was a strange hesitancy to her words, as if she'd said them many times but didn't necessarily believe them herself.

"You do know it's not that easy, right?" he said, trying and failing to keep the bite out of his tone. Just because she wanted to bury her trauma in a field of dandelions didn't mean he had to indulge her. "Some of us can't just choose to be happy."

She studied him for a long moment. "Not right away, no," she admitted, her perky persona fading away into something more honest and genuine. "But eventually the wounds start to heal, and you decide how you want to move forward. You can let whatever you went through shape you into something dark and tormented, or you can step into the light and declare in a loud voice that you are more than the awful things that have happened to you."

Her words drew him closer to the bed, and his hands gripped the towel tighter so he wouldn't reach out and drag her into his arms. "I take it awful things have happened to you?"

"You have no idea, Ethan," she said quietly, her gaze dropping to her lap where she absently picked at her cuticles.

"Was it also a vampire?"

Tressa flinched, then let out a sigh that carried far too much weight for someone as young as her. "Yes and no," she replied. "I do have a vampire to thank for my place here at the compound, but my life was... difficult even before that."

Ethan nodded, realizing he might have bitten off more than he could chew with his desire to see what Tressa hid from the world. For as much as he'd been through, he still had no idea how to console another human being.

"So, you said you painted that?" he asked, stepping away from her and gesturing toward the art piece.

"I did," she replied, and he could have sworn he saw a flash of relief on her face before her standard smile snapped back into place, the heaviness of their conversation set aside for another day.

"It's Fiji, right?" He ran his fingers over the vibrant blues and greens. "Was that home for you?"

Tressa blinked at him, and her jaw dropped open slightly. "Uh, yeah. How did you know that?"

"Deductive logic. Your physical features are a key indicator, plus I thought I heard you say *'magaitinamu'* to the nurse in the hospital. And I'm fairly certain I recognize this image as the Sawa-I-Lau Caves."

When the shock on Tressa's face turned to mortification, he couldn't help but grin.

"Wait, wait, what?" she stammered, sitting up straighter. "You knew what I said in the hospital?"

He appreciated how red her face turned beneath her golden-brown skin. It wasn't fair he'd been the only one blushing up a storm that morning. Smirking, he said, "I did. And Tressa, who knew you had such a dirty mouth?"

"But... I..." she sputtered. "How?"

Abandoning the safety of the space between them, Ethan sat next to her on the bed, still clutching the towel at his waist with both hands so they didn't go wandering. "I spent six months in Fiji as part of my master's program studying the indigenous plant life," he explained. "I became friends with a few locals, and you know the first thing they always teach you are the swear words."

Tressa threw her head back and laughed. "Yeah, I'm not surprised."

"So have you visited recently?" he asked.

Her expression darkened, and she pushed up off the bed. "Not in a very long time," she answered with her back to him, her voice somber. When she whirled around, though, a smile was firmly plastered on her face once more. It was like a light switch, the way she could instantly turn it back on. "Are you done eating? I have something to show you that I think you might enjoy."

Ethan eyed the remaining croissants on the plate, their smell taunting and teasing him almost as badly as Tressa did. "Yeah, I guess so," he told her sadly. "They mentioned in the hospital that I shouldn't indulge too much right away since my stomach is still adapting to solid food again."

"In that case," she said, snatching him by the wrist and pulling him off the bed, "I'll give you a minute to get dressed, and then we can go on a brief tour of the compound. After that, I have a surprise."

"Umm..." Ethan glanced at the towel, then gestured around at the room that lacked a closet full of men's clothing.

Tressa grabbed a black duffel from the hall. "Courtesy of my cousin, Saiden," she said, handing it over. "I think you guys have pretty similar builds. Just warning you, though, his wardrobe is pretty monochromatic."

"As long as my dick is covered, I'm happy," he muttered, reaching for the bag.

"Well, that makes one of us." She winked at him, then pulled the door shut behind her as she slipped out.

Ethan stared dumbfounded at the space where she'd been standing. He could typically analyze a person for a day or so and have a firm grasp on who they were. Tressa, on the other hand, continued to keep him guessing at what might come out of her mouth next.

And he didn't think it would take much to fall for a girl like that.

"I'm in love," Ethan breathed out, his eyes widening as he took in the beauty that greeted him. The garden sprawled out for what had to be acres, and before he even stepped past the first hedgerow, he could already see at least three plant species that should not be growing in the United States.

He couldn't believe she'd dragged him through the entire house for almost an hour and even showed him an indoor swimming pool while saving this gem for last.

Although, he couldn't deny he'd enjoyed listening to her share all the lore the hunters had learned about over the years. Hearing vampires had supposedly been created by Lilith as a revenge against Adam and his human kin had been fascinating, if a bit hard to swallow.

Okay, make that *very* hard to swallow. He might believe vampires were real because it was a little hard to deny the existence of something that had chewed on your neck, but the scientist in him still assumed it was some kind of viral mutation, not the result of a biblical break up.

Despite his protests, Tressa asserted it was the truth. When Adam rejected Lilith and cast her out of the Garden of Eden, she turned to Samael and asked him to help her create a being that would eternally crave the blood of Adam's descendants. Of course, the hardest part of her story—and the thing that kept him from accepting it—was the fact that it implied beings other than just vampires were real. Beings like angels, demons, and... God?

Ethan had fought to suppress his laugh when she was telling him about it, barely managing to keep his reservations to himself. Tressa was so committed to the myth he didn't want to break her heart and reveal that his only true religion was science. Instead, he'd distracted her from continuing the story by asking about all the other vampire traits he'd heard about.

Thankfully, she told him most of it was false, and they didn't turn into bats or mist. The dismissal of those Bram Stoker qualities was only more fuel for his viral theory, though. She'd been starting to go into detail about what they did know to be true about vampires when they'd arrived at the garden and Ethan nearly fell to his knees.

"I'll add this to the list," Tressa said jokingly, apparently having heard his earlier confession. "Flowers," she explained when he gave her a curious look. "So far I have croissants and flowers as things that make you happy."

"Oh. Yeah, I guess so." He brushed his hair out of his face. "That's pretty much my life in a nutshell. I eat delicious food and spend most of my day with plants."

"Well then," Tressa said, stepping closer and tucking a stray hair he'd missed behind his ear. "I'm glad I was able to *please* you, this morning."

Her wicked grin combined with the way she said "please" sent a burning need coursing through him. His borrowed track pants were suddenly much tighter through the crotch, and he was grateful this Saiden guy was at least a size bigger than him so his cock didn't immediately make its presence known.

In an attempt to escape the seductive smile that was becoming harder to resist, he stepped around her and headed into the garden.

"Wait," she shouted, and he whipped back around.

"You have to take your shoes off," she told him, making it sound as if he'd been about to commit a grave sin. "The grass is so luscious, it's like you're one with nature when you walk through the hedges barefoot." Tressa bent over, placing her delectable ass front and center as she removed her shoes.

Swallowing, Ethan used the full extent of his willpower to pull his gaze away and reach down to untie his own sneakers.

Wriggling his bare toes in the grass, he had to agree with her. Whoever maintained their zoysia was doing an impeccable job.

Tressa linked her arm through his and directed him into the garden. They veered off to the right in a slow meander as his gaze swept over the place. The entire thing was laid out like a maze, except the various hedges only came about chest high and were periodically broken up by bushes exploding with exotic flowers he itched to examine. Any direction he turned, he was greeted by new wondrous plants he hadn't seen since his college days.

"Holy shit," Ethan breathed out. His feet locked in place, and Tressa nearly pulled him off balance before realizing he'd stopped moving. "Is that..."

Unhooking his arm from hers, he took a tentative step forward, then pulled his glasses off to wipe the lenses. He was hallucinating. Had to be. A side effect from the coma most likely. Because there was simply no way his eyes weren't playing tricks on him.

A few cautious steps closer, though, confirmed that, no, he was not actually hallucinating. Whirling around, he fixed a hard, almost accusatory stare on Tressa.

"This is a Middlemist Red Camellia," he snapped, waving a hand at the plant sitting innocuously amongst a row of other flowering bushes.

She frowned and glanced between him and the Camellia. "But it's pink."

His jaw dropped. "That's what you're focused on?"

Her eyes darted around the garden, and she rubbed at the back of her neck. "Sorry, I don't know much about flowers. Um, it's really pretty?"

There was so much genuine confusion on her face that Ethan knew she had to be completely oblivious, but how could she not know what they had planted on their property?

"The name Middlemist Red Camellia really doesn't mean anything to you?" he asked cautiously, his eyes searching her face for any hint of deception.

"Nooo," she drawled, her brows furrowing. "Should it?"

After another glance at the flower to confirm one final time that he wasn't losing it, he turned back to her. "Yes, it should." He let out a long exhale and shook his head. "Tressa... this is widely considered to be the most rare flower in the world. There are only two known shrubs, one in New Zealand and one in the UK. And they are both less than half the size of this one."

"Oh," Tressa said, grinning. "That's cool."

"*Cool*?" Ethan sputtered. "It's not... It doesn't even come close to..." He fought back the urge to grab her by the shoulders and shake her. "Imagine if I found out vampires were real and just said 'cool.' No matter what you're feeling, 'cool' is so far from an adequate response."

Tressa bit her lip. "Um... I'm not sure what you're looking for here, Ethan. While I find your enthusiasm to be absolutely adorable, it's just a flower."

"Just a...?" Ethan couldn't even bring himself to look at Tressa until he calmed down, so he spun around and stared at the plant that shouldn't exist on this side of the Atlantic. His fingers itched to reach out and touch it, to caress the petals, yet at the same time, he was terrified of the oils from his skin damaging the delicate cell structure.

"Hey," Tressa said softly, gently tugging his chin around to face her. "I didn't mean to sound like I don't care. I do care. If it has you this flabbergasted, I want to know more. Teach me, Ethan. Tell me about this plant."

Ethan gazed into her brown almond-shaped eyes that shone with not only an internal glow and warmth, but also genuine interest. She really wasn't placating him. She had no idea what the plant was, but for some reason, she legitimately wanted to learn.

He couldn't help but lose his heart to her just a tiny bit more. He might have taken a job in pharmaceutics because it was the shortest path to what he wanted to achieve, but a not-so-small part of him had considered academia for a while since he loved to teach.

"Okay," he said, his annoyance fading into the excitement that always built inside him whenever he got to share the wonders of the botanical world. Grabbing her hands, he tugged her closer to the plant but stopped a few feet away so she wasn't tempted to reach out and touch it. "I wasn't exaggerating when I said it was the most rare flower in the world. I've been trying to get a cutting for years so I could propagate it here in the States, but neither of the owners are parting with them. They probably like the prestige of the rarity. Which is damned selfish because the pharmaceutical possibilities for this flower are endless. It has immense antioxidant properties which could lead to serious breakthroughs in treating cardiovascular disease and even some kinds of cancer."

He turned away from her and analyzed the bush in front of him. So many blooms with vibrant petals and healthy stamen, the plump anther ready to release its pollen. His brain swirled with all the possibilities this flower could offer to his research. If they had it growing successfully, he could probably transplant some cuttings to breed even more. And with such a large supply, he could conduct an endless number of tests. Fuck, he could potentially find a cure for heart disease altogether with this flower.

He started mentally compiling all the various steps he would need to take to get a lab up and running. VieTek would fund the whole thing in a heartbeat when he explained the situation. Or maybe he could cut them out entirely and get his own private lab going so he could control what happened with the medication. He would need a loan to do that which would be hard without a job, but...

His hopes came screeching to a halt when his brain landed on the most important thing any pharmaceutical botanist needed—a competent organic chemist.

He rubbed at his chest as the ache deep inside blossomed anew. Jake had been his chemist. For years, they'd worked together, researching side by side with the goal of developing a medication that could truly change the world. They'd become brothers in all but blood. He should be here. He should be at Ethan's side, embarking on this incredible new journey with him.

Only he wasn't.

Because of the vampire.

Jake's dead eyes, staring for eternity, pleading, accusing.

His ideas swirled down the drain in his head as he remembered his true priority. The vampire needed to die first. Then, and only then, could he allow himself to think about developing a new medication.

"Hey, Earth to Ethan," Tressa said, waving a hand in front of his face. "Where did you go just now?"

Ethan removed his glasses and wiped them on the hem of his borrowed Linkin Park T-shirt while he composed himself enough to answer. "This plant..." he began, placing the glasses back on the bridge of his nose. "The potential it could offer the world is incredible, but Jake should be here for this. He was my partner. He was the chemist to my botanist. He kept me tethered to the world." Ethan paused, and a small grin tugged at his lips. "Jake is the reason I have that rose tattooed on my ass."

Tressa's eyebrow quirked up. "Go on..."

"Let's just say I lost a bet over how many hydrogen atoms are in the chemical formula for caffeine. In my defense, it was two in the morning and we'd been drinking."

"Why Ethan, who knew you had such a wild side?" Tressa teased, bumping his hip with hers.

Ethan stumbled slightly but caught himself before he accidentally fell into the Middlemist Red Camellia. Straightening up, he said, "Yeah, but that was years ago. Lately it's been all work. The medication we were developing together had the real potential to significantly decrease fatalities from cardiovascular disease. But this"—he gestured to the Camellia—"this plant could let me develop a treatment that might eliminate them altogether." His voice choked up. "And Jake will never be around to see it happen."

"I'm so sorry," Tressa whispered, leaning her head on his shoulder. "I know what it's like to lose people. Why don't you tell me more about him? Or tell me about that medication you were working on."

Ethan sighed. "There's really nothing more to mention beyond what I've said, and the mechanism of action would probably just bore you." He gave her a small smile. "Unless maybe you're a doctor on top of being a vampire hunter?"

He was only partially teasing, but honestly, she seemed intelligent enough that he wouldn't be surprised.

"Not quite," Tressa said, but she didn't seem as interested in playing as she had before. "Why don't we continue on? There's a lot of the garden left to see."

Ethan drug his eyes away from her face to stare at the pink flower for another second, reminding himself that it was real and in good shape.

She laughed and tugged on his shoulder. "It's not going anywhere, Ethan. I promise."

Reluctantly, he let Tressa lead him deeper into the garden. An assortment of other rare plants greeted him, but he'd pretty much shot his load with the Middlemist Red Camellia. Nothing else could even come close.

His mind drifted once more to the possibilities of the exotic flower, and he vowed he would return for it.

Just as soon as he got revenge for his partner.

Chapter Fifteen

Tressa

"I have to ask," Ethan said, breaking the silence that had lingered since Tressa pulled him away from the rare plant. "How do you have all of these? *Why* do you have all these? You must keep an army of gardeners to maintain them since some are very finicky. This chocolate cosmos is especially difficult to keep alive. So why go to the trouble? What do vampire hunters need with plants?"

Tressa bent down to sniff the deep burgundy flower Ethan had gestured to, allowing her vampire senses to absorb all the nuances of the smell. Lovely, but not as appealing as her mate. "I think our boss just wanted us to have something peaceful and relaxing since this is home for us," she replied, standing up. "A happy place to escape the less pleasant aspects of our lives. 'Flowers are the smiles of nature,' right?"

Ethan blinked at her. "You've read Ralph Waldo Emerson?"

Tressa grinned, pleased he recognized the quote. "I have a lot of free time on my hands. You'd be surprised at how many books I've read."

His eyes locked on hers, searching her face in a way that made her both thrilled at the intensity but also a little nervous at what he might find. Clearing her throat, she forced herself to turn away and continued down the row of vibrant flowers, running her fingers over a few of the silky leaves.

"As I was saying, we all live here at the compound. That's why we have things like this garden and the pool. Marquin, the one in charge of the cadre, is sort of a father figure, you might say. I think that's why he likes to spoil us. He also has more than enough money, so I doubt maintaining this garden makes even a dent in his finances."

Tressa glanced over her shoulder in time to see Ethan arch an eyebrow. "So, your boss is rich, generous, and a vampire hunter?" he asked. "Sounds like a paranormal Batman."

Tressa burst out laughing. "Please, I'm begging you, when you meet him, I need you to call him that."

Marquin would have a field day with the comparison, and it would give Tressa an unending source of fuel for teasing. She couldn't get him to so much as blink whenever she tried out a new nickname for him, but this might be her in. She was one of the few people who knew about the comic books in Marquin's office—the ones he hid in a secret panel behind his bottles of expensive scotch. Tressa knew everyone's secrets, in fact, even if none of them knew hers.

Dismissing the all too familiar melancholy that tugged at her heart, she turned back to Ethan and caught him staring at her.

"Beautiful," he murmured.

"What? The flower?" she asked, glancing back at the chocolate cosmopolitan or whatever Ethan had called it.

"No," he said quietly. "Your laugh. It's incredible."

Her lips curved up into a small, genuine smile. "I got it from my mom," she told him. "People used to always say we had identical laughs."

"Yeah, I used to get that with my mom too." His words were hesitant, but not as sad as she might have expected from him.

"What was she like?" Tressa asked, wanting to know more about the woman who had clearly shaped Ethan's life. She just hoped it would bring up some happy memories. Despite all her own trauma, thoughts of her mother could still bring her joy most of the time.

Ethan chuckled and continued through the hedges, thankfully in the direction of the exit. Tressa would need more than one bag of blood after spending the morning in the sun, but she'd gladly empty out an entire blood bank if it meant getting to see Ethan in his element.

"Well," he said with a new lightness in his tone, "if you believe her word, she was a witch."

Tressa's eyebrows shot up, and she looped her arm through his once more. "Okay, you have my full attention. Tell me more."

"Calm down, it's not quite so exciting as all that," he said, a hint of teasing to his voice. "I grew up in Seacliff, Oregon, though I doubt you've ever heard of it. There was a large community of women there who called themselves witches, but I think they were just really into nature. That's how I became fascinated with all this." He waved his hand around at the bushes. "My mom used to teach me about plants and their different properties. I didn't quite take to the metaphysical side like she did, but I was always curious about the medicinal aspects. I was never given pills or anything as a kid. If my stomach hurt, I didn't get antacids, my mom just gave me a bit of ginger to chew on. When the summer mosquitos got to me, she would rub the inside of banana peels on the bites instead of using anti-itch creams. It always worked, too, and the older I got, the more intrigued I became by plants."

"Sounds like she had a huge impact on you."

Ethan shrugged, his face closing off once more. "Yeah, well, I never knew my dad. My mom said he was a passing fancy who left her with the best gift ever, and that was all she wanted from him. Don't ask me why she gave me his last name when I was born, considering she refused to talk about him."

Tressa bit back the urge to say anything. She already knew his dad wasn't in the picture since Baylin had relayed that little tidbit after his initial investigation into her mate. She could tell Ethan it would be easy for her cousin to find the man if he wanted, but since it didn't sound like his father was a happy subject, she opted to leave it be.

"Sounds like your mom did an amazing job raising you all by herself."

"She did," Ethan replied somberly. "She was the most important person in my life. Then she died when I was nineteen. It was..." A flash of pain rolled over his face, the deep-seated kind Tressa often saw in the mirror. "It was awful. She suffered for a long time until the cardiomyopathy killed her." At Tressa's blank look, he added, "It's a type of heart disease. Genetic, I guess, since I'd never met a healthier person. It's why I went into pharmaceuticals. I wanted to make damn sure nobody else lost a loved one for no fucking reason other than their DNA."

"I think she would be really proud of what you've achieved," Tressa offered, rubbing his arm. The mate sparks had died down to the point that they weren't distracting, and she couldn't help but seize any excuse to touch him.

"Yeah, I think so too," Ethan said, placing his hand over hers. "She was always proud of me."

Tressa briefly debated whether now would be a good time to press him. She didn't want to ruin the way he was currently looking at her, or stop the gentle circles he was now massaging into the back of her hand with his thumb, and yet... "Do you think she would be proud of what you're doing now?" Tressa asked softly. "Hunting down this vampire? Obsessing over revenge?"

Ethan stiffened, and Tressa almost whined when he pulled away from her. "Of course she would," he said firmly. "She would want that vile creature eliminated, same as me."

Tressa winced. She wasn't shocked at his response, but it still hurt. "The one that attacked you, yeah. But you don't think they're all evil, right? Because we've found evidence that—"

Ethan scoffed, the harsh noise cutting her off. "Please tell me you're not about to spout some good vampire nonsense again. I already told you, I'm not buying it. I saw that thing. I saw the emptiness in its eyes. There aren't good ones or bad ones because that would imply they have souls. It's a monster, Tressa. An abomination. Nothing more."

Abomination.

The word rang in her ears. Not that she hadn't heard it before. Over the centuries, she'd dealt with more than her fair share of humans who believed they were all soulless, bloodsucking fiends. She just didn't think Ethan, a man who was so logical, would have that same closed-minded mentality. Why couldn't she have met him before Renata attacked?

Tressa hadn't ever put much thought into what her mate would be like, but the last thing she saw coming was a grumpy pharmaceutical botanist with a vendetta against vampires and a rose tattoo on his ass.

Allowing her frustration to be replaced by the amusing memory of seeing that bright pop of color on his perfect pale butt, she followed after Ethan as he raced toward another plant with deep purple blooms. Obstacles or no, she would do whatever it took to convince Ethan that he was wrong about vampires. There was more to him than logic and hatred, and she would uncover every layer that made up her unique mate. Even it meant spending the morning in the blazing sun being jealous of a damn flower.

Chapter Sixteen

Ethan

"That was incredible," Ethan breathed out, emerging from the garden back onto the expansive lawn. "And we didn't even get to see all the flowers because several of those breeds are night blooming. Honestly, I could set up a tent and live in there."

"You're welcome to visit anytime," Tressa said, picking up her shoes. "But I think sleeping in a bedroom would be a better idea."

Ethan reached down for his own sneakers he'd left outside the garden. "Yeah, about that. You have a room for me, right? I feel a little weird crashing in yours."

Tressa froze with her foot half into her shoe, then let out what he could only describe as the most pitiful laugh in the history of time. "Oh, uh, yeah, of course we have a room for you. You don't want to share a bed with me..."

The way she trailed off while studiously avoiding meeting his eyes felt a little like a trap to Ethan. Like she wanted him to protest.

Did she want him to protest? He knew she was interested in things being more physical between them, but they didn't need to share a room for that to happen. So why did it feel like he suddenly found himself standing in a patch of poison sumac, and one wrong move could leave him blistered and rashy for weeks?

"Right," he said.

Tressa's face shot up to meet his, and the heartbreak that flashed across her face was worse than any plant poison he'd ever experienced.

Okay, so that was the wrong thing to say, he thought. But what kind of woman wanted a guy to move into their room days after meeting them? Everything about Tressa screamed independent, vampire-hunting badass who didn't need a man for anything. Was there a chance she was feeling the same intense pull that he was? That reluctance to be apart?

Part of him wanted to retract his statement and say that he'd love to share her room, but he knew exactly where that would lead. If he had to endure another night within arms distance of her, inhaling her intoxicating scent, he was going to lose the ability to be a gentleman that his mom worked so hard to instill in him.

Sighing, because he could tell from her body language alone that he'd fucked something up, he trudged back toward the house with her lagging behind.

His legs grew weary with every step he took. He'd probably pushed himself too hard with the tour that morning and the time spent wandering around the garden. Just as he was about to pause for a brief thigh massage, his legs made the decision for him. His right quad seized up, and he pitched forward, throwing his hands up to prevent eating a face full of grass.

But his palms never reached the ground. A tight band around his midsection held him aloft for a long moment before hauling him back upright.

He gave Tressa a bewildered look. "Uh, thanks. Nice reflexes you got there."

She released her hold on him and turned away. "Comes with the training. You know, gotta be able to keep up with the vamps and their superpowers."

Ethan nodded, studying the woman in front of him who was suddenly preoccupied with the row of tall sunflowers planted alongside the patio steps.

They were fitting for her, he mused. *Cheerfully bright and bold.*

"Well, the training paid off. You're a lot stronger than I would have guessed."

She chewed on her lip, still running her long slender fingers over the delicate yellow petals. "Like I said, training."

"Of course." He cast furtive glances back at her as he slowly made his way up the steps.

When he got to the top, he leaned on the railing and took in the expansive patio. Elegant French doors were flanked by Grecian statues, and the entire space was surrounded by tall oak trees that cast a dappled shade over them.

"So, um... what now?" he asked.

Tressa's eyes dragged up and down his body in a way that was more clinical than seductive, and he doubted she missed the beads of sweat on his forehead or the shakiness in his legs he was unable to hide.

"You should probably rest," she said gently. "You're still recovering, and obviously your body needs a break."

Ethan shook his head. She might be right that he overextended himself, but he wouldn't get stronger by taking a nap every time he got a little unsteady. He would rest when either he or that creature was dead.

"I don't think I could manage that right now even if I tried," he told her. "What's going on with finding the vampire? What can I do to help?" He wasn't exactly a computer whiz with tech skills, but he was nothing if not a quick study.

Tressa waved a hand dismissively. "Baylin is on it. Anyone else would only get in his way. He'll find her soon, Ethan. I promise."

"Yeah, okay," he replied, wiping his brow and gripping onto the railing for a little more support. "I just feel weird not doing anything. What about research? Finding weaknesses or things like that?"

Tressa hopped up on a patio table with ease and perched on the edge, crossing her legs in a way that dragged the hem of her skirt enticingly high. If he shifted to the side just a bit, he was certain he would catch more than a glimpse of a luscious bronze ass cheek.

"Ethan?"

He snapped his attention back up to Tressa who was smirking at him.

Busted.

"I'm sorry," he said, hoping she wouldn't call him out on the blatant ogling. Just because he hadn't been laid in forever was no excuse to be eye-fucking the poor woman. "What were you saying?"

She watched him with amusement twinkling in her gaze for another moment before thankfully letting it drop.

"I was saying, we already know everything there is to know about vampires. So there's not really any research to be done."

"Oh," he replied, dissapointed. "Well, in that case, tell me about their weaknesses. How do you take one down?"

"Oh, the usual ways you would kill a human. You just have to make it count since we are able—" She choked on her words, coughing violently.

He rushed to her side and slapped her on the back. "Hey, you okay?"

"Yeah," she said, clearing her throat. "Just, um, a bug or something."

He gave her a curious look but returned to the railing. A safe distance where she was out of touching range, because otherwise he would have kept rubbing her back. Which would have led to rubbing... other things.

"Anyway," she said, brushing her hair out of her eyes. "I was going to say that vampires are able to heal really fast. So if you want to kill one, it needs to be swift, accurate, and permanent. Lop off the head, sharp implement to the heart, bullet to the brainpan."

"Squish," he added with a grin, but the strange look she gave him said the obscure Firefly reference was lost on her. Pity. Maybe he could introduce her to some of his favorite classic sci-fi shows. His mind conjured an image of them curled up on a couch, munching on popcorn, his hand sliding up her thigh...

Focus, Ambrose, he chided himself yet again.

"Well, that's all good to know, but what else do you have? Is there some way to lay a trap once we find her? I might be grasping at straws here, but is there anything vampires care about more than blood and murder?"

Tressa flinched ever so faintly, but he caught the movement and wondered what he had said wrong.

"Vampires care about a lot of things," she said quietly as she picked at her cuticles again. "But they care about their mate more than anything else."

"Mate?" he asked, wrinkling his brow. "Isn't that like a wolf thing?"

Tressa laughed. "Yeah, kind of, but also not at all. Basically, a vampire has one person that is their destined love. Their mate. Someone the universe pushes them toward because they belong together. The one individual they can easily spend forever with and never grow bored." She paused for a second, eyeing him carefully. "Most vampires would do anything for their mate, Ethan. To keep them safe, keep them happy. The bond between mates is more than just love. It's... destiny."

He couldn't deny the little tingle in his chest when she said "destiny." Even if the whole thing sounded like another vampire myth they got a kick out of humans believing in, right up there with garlic and holy water. But if it was real...

The hairs on the back of Ethan's neck stood on end, and his hand drifted unconsciously towards his scar as the nauseating slurping sound of the creature feeding filled his mind once more. He noticed Tressa's eyes tracking his hand, so at the last minute, he diverted it over his shoulder to knead at the ropey knots in his upper back.

As beautiful as this mate concept was, he couldn't reconcile it with what he knew of vampires. "Okay, I'm not sure which is more ridiculous," he said. "The whole 'fated by some mystical higher power to be together forever' thing, or the fact that the monster who killed my friend could even be capable of love, let alone the kind you're describing. It's a beautiful fairytale, but I'm not buying it."

Tressa shrugged. "I could say I don't believe in the moon's gravitational pull, but the ocean tides would still rise and fall. Not believing in something doesn't make it any less real. Losing a mate is actually how a lot of vampires go rogue. To be sentenced to an eternity alone is..." She sighed. "It can make people act crazy."

"Except she's not a person, Tressa," he reminded her, annoyed that she was still on about some vampires being good. It didn't even matter if the mate thing was true or not. He didn't care how the rogue lost her gourd; he just wanted to smash it before she hurt anyone else.

Tressa didn't argue, but she also didn't agree with him either. She just regarded him thoughtfully for a second, then hopped off the table. "Right, well, I'm sorry we don't have any way for you to help right now. Just know that when we do find her, we're fully prepared to handle it."

Ethan nodded. "Gotcha. In that case, how about we try some of that superior training you mentioned? I think I could use a few workouts to get back into shape before we go after her anyway. And I'm feeling much better." He pushed off the railing and took a steady step toward her as proof that he wasn't the weak fawn she seemed to view him as. "So what do you say? You down to get a little sweaty?"

When Tressa's eyes bulged, he quickly added, "In the gym, of course. You know, training."

"Of course," she replied with a subtle grin. "I have some things I need to take care of, but I'll see if Saiden or Derrick can meet you in the gym. Just... take it easy, Ethan. I know you want to get your revenge, but you're still healing. The effects of a three-month coma don't just disappear overnight."

A flash of blood-soaked fangs appeared in Ethan's mind again, and he shook his head, trying to dislodge the image. He massaged his neck as if working out a kink, but really, he was trying to rub away the pain of phantom fangs sinking into his skin. "I know, but I can't just sit around. I have to do something."

Tressa peered at him for a moment. "Can I ask you a question?"

"Always."

"Why is this so important to you? I know what she did to your friend and the fallout with your job, but it feels... *more*, somehow."

Ethan contemplated her words. He knew the answer he wanted to give her—that the rogue made him feel powerless. Pathetic. That she'd forced him to watch as yet another person he cared about died in front of him while he stood by, helpless to do anything but whimper like a child. He was always left behind to pick up the pieces after far better people were taken from the world. Jake should have been the one to survive. Just like his mom should have been. But the world was cruel and unfair, and monsters like the rogue only proved his point.

He knew Tressa would understand his suffering and might even have a similar story, but for some reason, the words wouldn't come. He couldn't admit the painful truth quite yet. He wasn't ready to rip open his bleeding heart and show her all his wounds. So he took the coward's way out.

"No, there's nothing more. She's a blood-sucking monster who killed my best friend and countless others. Of course I'm going to make removing her from this world a priority."

Tressa studied his face for a long moment, then sighed. "Okay. In that case, let me show you to the gym."

Chapter Seventeen

Tressa

Tressa lingered in the doorway, watching as Ethan joined Saiden and Derrick who were stretching on the floor of the gym. More than anything, she wanted to go over there and join them. Maybe offer to massage Ethan's healing muscles. *All* of Ethan's healing muscles.

Instead of giving into her desires, though, she closed the door. She'd already messed up once when she caught his fall. If she spent time training with him, there was no way she would be able to hide her vamp strength. As her mate would say, science was science, and her body with a notable lack of visible muscle mass could only realistically achieve so much. If she wasn't careful, Ethan was going to start asking questions she couldn't answer.

Saiden and Derrick could handle it. They were both fairly ripped, so any inhuman slips might be more easily dismissed.

She debated simply sitting on the sidelines and observing as Ethan trained with her cousins. She imagined watching his muscles bunch and strain, his shirt darkening with sweat as he exerted himself. Possibly removing said shirt when he got hotter. She could envision him dropping into a deep lunge, the waistband of his sweatpants riding low to reveal that tattoo on his ass that begged to be nipped...

Fuck. And now she needed a cold shower. Stat.

But more than that, she needed advice. Tressa would normally go to the most level-headed member of their little cadre, but Raven had been struggling ever since Saiden found his mate, so she was off on a 'soul-searching journey' as she put it. Raven would never admit the real reason for her vacation, but Tressa knew it was all the old emotions that had come rushing back in.

Raven losing her mate to a back alley mugging before she had a chance to turn him was not something she could just get over. A hundred years later, and there was still a deep sorrow that lived in her eyes. It scared Tressa, that sadness. She had fought tooth and nail to overcome her tragic past, but if she lost Ethan?

She understood it now. How when Raven's mate died she became suicidal, picking a fight with every rogue she could find in the hopes one of them would end her lonely eternal existence. Even after Saiden saved her and brought her into the fold, Tressa suspected Raven still lived with the kind of pain that no amount of family could cure.

If Ethan died, Tressa couldn't imagine going on. It was like living your entire life in a dark cave and then finally emerging into the sunlight. Once you know what you'd been missing, how could you ever live without it?

Sighing, she considered her other options for advice. Marquin and Eliana were like parents to them all, even though technically Marquin had only sired Saiden. Tressa couldn't really see herself doing boy talk with her father figure, though. Eliana, Marquin's mate, would probably be open to offering her input, but Eliana wasn't just a vampire. She had been a seer before she was turned, and it made her a little... unique. Nobody had any idea how old she was, but given she'd sired Marquin, she had to be borderline ancient. That, combined with her visions, usually meant interactions could take a weird turn fairly quickly.

Tressa had been talking to her a few weeks back about having the gardeners plant some pear trees, and Eliana grabbed her wrists tightly and screamed, "No!"

Tressa had no idea why a few trees would elicit such a reaction, but then again, Eliana never shared the reasoning behind what she said or saw. Regardless, no pear trees had yet to join the orange and lemon grove toward the back of their property.

So Eliana and Raven were out. And Liessa, her other cousin, was still freediving in the Bahamas. That left...

She smacked her forehead. Of course. Who better to discuss her mate issues with than someone who was human herself only a few months ago?

Striding down the hall, she just hoped Cora wasn't too busy.

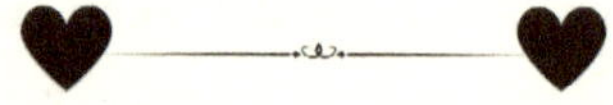

"I will sink my fangs into you and drain every last drop of blood from your body until you are nothing but a shriveled husk," Cora growled at her computer when Tressa nudged the door open.

Blinking at the newest addition to their cadre, Tressa tried to make sense of Cora's words. More than anyone, Cora knew the importance of hiding the existence of vampires. So who was she threatening so blatantly?

"Uh, Cora?" she called out tentatively.

The new baby vamp spun around and grinned when her eyes landed on Tressa. "Hey, Tress. Just give me a second."

She turned back to the set of monitors and adjusted the microphone on her headset. "Okay guys, take five. Jinx, please work with Nick, and make sure the next time he delivers that line he says it with the kind of violence I'm looking for."

Cora tapped a few buttons on her keyboard, then hopped off the chair and plopped down onto the gray microsuede couch next to her desk, her long auburn braid whipping about her shoulders. She patted the spot next to her, and Tressa took a seat, curling her legs up under her.

"Sorry," Cora said. "With Saiden's financial contribution, we were able to hire a much better actor to play the villain in my film, but he's still lacking the kind of deep, menacing vibe I need. I guess I was spoiled with my own real-life vampire. No one else comes close to matching Saiden."

Tressa grinned and sank back into the plush cushions. "Fair enough. Saiden does have the kind of resting murder face that makes you think he'd slit your throat then go home to a cup of tea."

Cora laughed and shook her head. "He doesn't drink tea, but I could totally see him doing that. What does it say about me that I fell in love with him?"

"It means you have good taste."

They both giggled at that for a second. "While I always love our girl time, Tress," Cora said, glancing at her watch, "I can't leave the crew in LA waiting too long. What's going on? I know you didn't come in here just to catch up."

"No, I have a reason," Tressa mumbled, picking at one of her cuticles. "A six-foot two reason with glasses and a brain the likes I've never encountered in the male gender before."

Cora shifted forward and crossed her legs in a way that reminded Tressa of a therapist preparing to dispense some profound insight.

"Ah, yes. Saiden mentioned your mate. I've been meaning to find some time to slip away and come find you, but..." She waved a hand toward the monitors. "We're in the last few days of principal photography, and things have been chaotic to say the least."

"No worries," Tressa replied. "I figured as much. I could use a quick piece of advice, though. Seeing as you were basically in Ethan's shoes a few months ago."

"How could I ever forget?" Cora said with dry amusement. "But I'm more than happy to help. What's your question?"

"How do I convince him that vampires aren't evil so I can confess my true identity to him and live happily ever after?"

Cora burst out laughing. "Tress, no part of this conversation is going to be quick if that's your situation."

"Yeah, I was worried that might be the case." Tressa dropped her head against the back of the couch.

"Look," Cora said, placing her hand on Tressa's knee. "As much as I wish I had the magic answer, my scenario was completely different because A, Saiden told me he was a vampire pretty early on, and B, I've never lost someone I cared about to a rogue. I can tell you this much, though. If I had witnessed a vampire tear out Jinx's throat, I'm not sure anything would change my mind about them being evil."

Tressa grimaced. "I was afraid of that."

"I wish I could brainstorm this with you, but I have to get back," Cora said as she struggled to extricate herself from the deep cushions. "Here's the best I got for you. Things between Saiden and I almost fizzled before they sparked because he lied about the mate bond and turned me without my permission. So just be honest with Ethan, and whatever you do, don't make him a vampire until he's willing."

Cora gave Tressa a sympathetic look, then sat back down at her computer and slid a headset over her ears. "Okay, I'm back. Jinx, let's go from the top."

Tressa watched Cora give instructions for a moment, then headed out of the room to allow their resident director to work her magic in peace.

"Be honest and don't turn him?" she huffed out as she strolled down the hall. "Pretty sure the moment I'm honest I'll never see him again."

Sighing, she made her way toward the kitchen to look into getting some food prepared for Ethan. Maybe if she was lucky, the chef would teach her how to cook, and she could make something for him. Her mate did mention he loved yummy pastry, and she'd always heard the way to a man's heart was through his stomach.

Chapter Eighteen

Ethan

"Get out of my kitchen and never come back!" an older male voice bellowed as Ethan rounded the corner and saw Tressa scurrying away from a white-tiled room filled with stainless steel furnishings.

"Oof," he grunted when she barreled straight into him, knocking them both to the floor. Her flour-covered form landed on top of him with a thud, but he couldn't summon any annoyance at being plowed into. Not when he saw her face covered in chunks of lemon.

"You okay?" he asked, reaching up to pluck a bit of fruit from her hair.

"More or less," she said sheepishly, tossing a look over her shoulder at the irritated man who just glared at her before slamming the double doors shut.

"Pastry mishap?" he asked, barely suppressing his grin.

"Yeah, I was trying to learn how to make lemon tarts. Turns out I'm not meant for the kitchen."

She dropped her head to his chest, and the movement molded their bodies together even deeper. She hadn't made an attempt to get up yet, but for some reason, he was okay with that despite the squishy wet chunks dampening his shirt.

Ethan glanced at the trail of flour leading from the closed doors to Tressa. "I'd say that's a safe assumption. Though I don't think that's a bad thing. A badass vampire hunter like you shouldn't be hidden away in a stuffy kitchen baking for other people."

"I just thought it might be nice to make a treat for you," she mumbled into his chest. "To help with settling in here."

He cupped her face with his hands and lifted her head so he could see her properly. "While I appreciate the gesture," he said, brushing a smudge of flour off her cheek with his thumb, "you don't need to bake for me, Tressa. Ever. Though you do have good taste. Lemon tarts are one of my favorites."

Her face lit up. "Oh, well, I'll have someone who is much more qualified make you some. Any other favorites I should let the chef know about?"

He shook his head. "I'm pretty easy. As long as you don't put pears or apricots in anything, I'm happy."

She jerked backward, and the motion shifted her body along a part of him that was growing more awake the longer she remained on top of him.

"Pear?" she asked. "What do you have against pears?"

"I'm deathly allergic, and I'm pretty sure you guys don't have a spare EpiPen laying around."

She narrowed her eyes, almost as if the information carried more weight than something so simple should. "You're allergic? To pears?"

Ethan shrugged. "And apricots. Could be worse, though. I could be allergic to something I love, like apples."

He didn't think his answer was anything surprising, but Tressa's eyes grew comically wide. He would have to ask her what the big deal with fruit was.

She climbed off him, and it wasn't until her weight disappeared that he realized how much he'd enjoyed having her in his arms. She held out a hand, and he took it, blinking at how easily she pulled him up. Someone as strong as her would definitely be wasted in a kitchen. In fact, he was more than a little disappointed she didn't join him and the others for training. He'd love to see what kind of fighting skills his little Sunflower was hiding.

Wait, since when did he use nicknames? And when the fuck did he start thinking of her as 'his?'

Shaking his head, he brushed off the bits of powder and lemon that had transferred to his clothing.

"So, I take it you're done training?" she asked, eyeing his pants and shirt that had been clean moments ago.

"Yeah," he said, running a hand through his still damp hair. Three months without a trim had been annoying at first, but he was getting used to the longer strands and how they curled slightly at his shoulders. "I wanted to go until dinner, but Saiden is a bigger hardass than you when it comes to not pushing myself. He gave me some stretches to do for ten minutes every other hour to keep things loose, but otherwise I've been banished from the gym for today."

Tressa laughed. "Well, since I've been banished from the kitchen, how about we go check out your new room? I had some of the staff make up a bed for you."

"Sounds good," he said, taking her offered hand. His skin tingled when her fingers laced through his.

More static electricity? It had been happening to him a lot the past couple days.

She guided him through a series of long halls, making a few familiar-looking turns. When she pushed open the door to the room beside hers, he arched an eyebrow. "You trying to keep an eye on me, Tress?"

He could have sworn he saw an embarrassed grin before she hurried inside. "It was just the easiest room to prepare. The rest are all pretty dusty and need a lot of cleaning."

"In that case, I guess we're neighbors." He stepped through the door and paused for a second to take in the gothic room. The four-poster bed with gossamer crimson curtains, rich mahogany furniture, and wine-colored velvet drapes made his beige spartan apartment seem downright depressing in comparison. Well, former apartment, that is. This new space that looked like it belonged in a medieval castle was apparently his home for the time being.

Oddly enough, the unique decor wasn't even the most bizarre aspect. The strangest thing was how the bed was pushed up against the east wall. It felt... out of place. Like the room had been designed for the bed to be smack in the center but the housekeeping crew had forgotten to move it back after cleaning the rug beneath. He could even see four slight depressions in the thick weave.

"Can't say I would have chosen the creature of the night vibe," he said, turning to Tressa. "But I guess it makes sense. Get inside the mind of the vampires you're hunting and all."

"Uh, right," she stammered. "That's exactly it. Anyway, I'll let you get settled in. Our staff went into town and got you some clothing, so you can change if you like." She pointed to an assortment of bags tucked off to the side. "Everything should fit, so you won't have to borrow from Saiden anymore. There are also some toiletries in the bathroom just through that door." She gestured to the back of the room. "If you're missing anything, let me know and I can send someone to pick it up."

"Thanks," he murmured. He pulled a plain blue T-shirt out of the bag closest to him and held it up to his chest. She was right, her staff got the correct size. He set it on the bed along with a pair of gray sweats, then turned back to Tressa. "I just realized I haven't properly thanked you. And I don't mean for the clothes, I mean for all of this. You could have left me in that hospital and taken care of the rogue on your own. I know I'm a liability to your well-honed operation, so the fact that you're letting me help is... well, I appreciate it. More than you know."

He stepped closer and dislodged another piece of lemon, his fingers lingering in her silky black hair for a second longer than was necessary.

"You're welcome," she said softly, her attention focused on the chunk of fruit in his hand. "And I know what it's like to want revenge but not be able to make it happen. How could I deny you yours?"

He frowned, wondering just what revenge Tressa had been denied.

She plucked the lemon from his hand and backed out of his room. "I should go get cleaned up. Dinner's in a couple hours, so I'll come knock on your door then."

He shoved his hands in his pockets so he wouldn't prevent her from leaving. "Sounds good. And thank you again, Tress. I mean it."

She gave him a small half-smile, then pulled the door shut.

And maybe he was imagining things, but he could have sworn he heard her mutter, "Don't thank me yet."

Chapter Nineteen

Tressa

"Sleep well," Tressa told Ethan, then closed the door behind her, fighting the urge to barge back into the room and tackle him onto the bed.

Dinner, at least, had been a wild culinary success with the chef preparing a meal big enough to feed an army. Most vamps only indulged in human food occasionally out of nostalgia, so the poor man typically spent his time making standard American faire for their human staff despite his Michelin star status. That was probably why he'd been more than happy to jump on her request for corned beef palusami, even though he was still a little bitter that she'd coated his kitchen in lemon and flour—who knew mixers needed a lid?

While most of the cadre joined them for dinner, talking and laughing enough to hide how they weren't really eating much, Tressa had gotten to hang out alone with Ethan on the patio afterward. They'd spent hours just chatting about his life growing up in Seacliff and his time in Fiji while she ducked every question about her own life like a champion dodgeball player. If Ethan caught on to the fact she hadn't revealed anything more than her favorite hike—which was a gamble since she had no idea if the trail still existed after three hundred years—he hadn't let on. Every time the conversation drifted toward her past, she expertly steered it back to his life.

But as much as she loved learning about his college years and hearing him talk in general—she could listen to his rich voice read the damn phonebook—not once did he reveal any information that helped her figure out why his research had been targeted.

Slumping against the door to his bedroom where she'd deposited him after it became too late to justify continuing their patio chat, Tressa grit her teeth to suppress the frustrated groan that roiled deep inside her.

A groan that had nothing to do with the lack of progress on their hunt for Renata and everything to do with the fact that her mate was sliding under the covers a few feet away while she had no right to join him. She briefly debated knocking on the door and asking if she could cuddle up beside him, but she didn't get so far as to raise her hand before reminding herself that idea was more than absurd. He'd made it clear he was keeping things between them PG until the rogue was dealt with, and she wasn't going to push him.

That didn't mean she was going to be happy about sleeping without her mate, though.

Kicking the door to her own room shut behind her, Tressa flopped face down on the bed she had pushed up against the wall. Part of her worried Ethan might comment on the fact that his own bed had been moved to the side when it clearly belonged in the center, but if she was going to sleep alone, she was going to do it as close to him as possible. So yeah, she'd shifted the feng shui of his room a tad. And maybe she'd laid in the bed for a couple minutes so she could perfectly visualize him in the same spot later that night. So what? It wasn't anything worse than Saiden had done when he was obsessing over Cora.

Rolling over to the side, she rested her hand on the wall and let the image of him fill her head.

Ten inches, she guessed. Ten inches of wood and plaster between her and Ethan. It might as well have been ten miles for as lonely as she felt, but it would have to suffice. The longer she left her hand in place, the more she could sense him, and she couldn't help but wonder...

Was he leaning up against the wall on his side?

Was Ethan fighting his own urges?

Was he feeling that tug to dash from his room into hers and wrap Tressa up in his arms?

Heat spread through her body as her mind ran wild with thoughts of her mate. An ache developed between her legs, but she couldn't stop the images if she wanted to. She closed her eyes, and Ethan was there, kissing her. She opened her eyes, and she could still visualize him, like a slow motion fantasy playing out—him bursting through her door, shirtless, sweeping her up in his tight embrace. No matter how much she tried to think of anything else, she couldn't escape him.

She didn't *want* to escape him. She just wanted the reality more than she wanted the fantasy.

But since reality wasn't on the menu, she would have to make do.

Sliding her hands down her stomach toward the pulsing need that called her name, she sent out a brief thank you to Baylin for ensuring their rooms were all soundproof. She would have a hard time explaining the noises to Ethan if he overheard.

Unless... those same sounds were coming from his room. Tressa had no way of knowing for sure, but the thought of Ethan on the other side of the wall, touching himself and thinking about her, had a gush of wetness soaking her panties.

"Fuck," she moaned, rubbing herself through the thin fabric of her underwear. As her speed increased, her mind drifted to the drawer of toys beside her bed. After a few decades, sex had a tendency to become boring with most humans since she had to hold so much of herself back or risk breaking them. Most of the time, she relied on something battery-powered to scratch the random itches that arose, but just the concept of anything other than Ethan between her legs had her lip curling with disdain.

She wanted her mate, not some shitty silicone approximation.

So her hand continued to work herself as she pictured all the things she would do to Ethan if he became a vampire.

When, she corrected herself.

When he became a vampire.

When they lived happily ever after.

When she finally got to fuck him until his body begged for mercy. Or until hers did. Something about the way her mate trained in the gym suggested he would be more than able to match her pace in the bedroom.

"Ethan..." Her hand dipped inside her panties, no longer satisfied with a simple bit of friction. She slipped a finger inside, and then a second one, pumping them in and out as she imagined it wasn't her hand, but Ethan's. They were his long strong fingers, the same ones that had caressed the plants so delicately. So tenderly. Only now they were being put to a better use—caressing her own rose bud.

The warmth that had bloomed inside her grew more intense as she pumped her fingers into her wet heat while rubbing her palm against her clit.

She needed Ethan. Needed him to make her come. Needed his body pressed against hers.

She slapped her other hand against the wall, half crazed and wanting to put her fist through the damn plaster to get to her mate. The wall shook a bit from the impact, but she couldn't be bothered to care.

Wanton moans escaped her as she ground her hips into her own hand. Squeezing her eyes shut, she imagined Ethan on the other side, touching himself, until finally, the visual was enough to send her over the edge.

She drenched her own fingers to thoughts of Ethan in his bed, stroking his cock and thinking of her.

Chapter Twenty

Ethan

He stroked his cock, thoughts of Tressa filling his mind. When she'd first left him alone in his room, he almost ran back out and asked her to stay. She'd made it clear she was more than interested in seeing where things might go between them sexually, and he couldn't deny that the feeling of her in his arms earlier had felt so right it was scary.

He wanted her. He wanted her delicious body that called to him, and he wanted her fierce attitude that challenged him. It hadn't escaped his notice that she refused to talk about her past, and he could only imagine what she'd gone through to remain that tight-lipped. But she didn't let it define her. She fought through the trauma and became this powerful, confident, sexy woman.

She was everything he ever wanted in a partner, but he still couldn't have her. At least not yet. He wasn't an idiot. He knew she was the kind of woman who was end game. The kind you would never let go if you ever found yourself blessed enough to call her yours.

If Ethan allowed himself a taste of Tressa, it would be the death of him. He would fall so hard, the impact would shatter any other motivations he had. And Jake deserved better than that. He deserved better than a best friend who forgot about his revenge because he couldn't stop touching the goddess in the next room.

And he wouldn't be able to stop.

So he had settled for the next best thing.

He'd locked the door to his bedroom and slid under the covers before shucking his pants and boxers. Just the thought of being with Tressa had him painfully hard, so he'd gone straight to work, gripping his cock and imagining it was Tressa's hand working him up and down.

Fuck, the bed even smelled like her, all sweet and fruity. She'd said their staff changed the sheets, but she must have rolled around in them afterward, because damn. The scent only increased the pace at which he jerked himself off.

She was so fucking far away in the next room, but it felt like she was right there beside him. Like she was with him, bound by the same strong connection he felt.

It drove his arousal to new heights, and he threw his head back, stifling the moans that threatened to escape. He wouldn't be able to look Tressa in the face if she heard him masturbating like a teenager on the other side of the wall.

But that was what she made him feel like. A horny teenager who wanted nothing more than to get his dick wet. Only he didn't want just any pussy. He wanted *hers*. He wanted to feel how tightly she clenched around his cock when he finally claimed her.

He'd never been a particularly rough lover before, what with his fear of accidentally hurting a partner, but something about Tressa told him she could take it. She could take everything he wanted to give and then some.

Despite her petite appearance, she wasn't delicate like his flowers, she was strong. And fuck did he want that strength wrapped around him, choking his cock until he erupted inside her.

His hand worked his length harder and faster as he imagined her there on top of him, bouncing up and down with those perfect tits right in his face.

It was that final visual that finished him, and he couldn't fight back the loud moan that escaped as his release exploded all over his hand.

Fuck, he'd never come so hard in his life. He simply couldn't deny the power Tressa had over him. At one point, it even seemed like the walls shook from the force of his orgasm, but that couldn't be real.

He snatched a couple tissues from the box on the nightstand, cleaned himself up, then collapsed back into the bed, sending a fresh cloud of bubblegum scent wafting into the air around him. His hand drifted over to the wall, and it was like he could sense her presence on the other side. He didn't love the idea of sleep, fully aware the nightmares would inevitably visit him once more, but knowing Tressa was next door helped ease his anxiety a bit.

Ethan shifted over so he was pressed against the wall. Closer to his salvation. Because that's what she was. He knew it in his bones. She was the one who could make the nightmares go away. If only he was strong enough to be with her.

But he wasn't. He was weak, both in body and mind. The vampire had done that to him, reduced him to a pathetic version of himself, but no matter what it took, he was going to kill it and get his strength back.

His goddess deserved better than a broken man.

Chapter Twenty-One

Tressa

"You need to tell Ethan the truth."

Tressa wiped the water from her eyes and looked up to see Saiden and Derrick looming over her. Groaning, she let go of the edge and sank back under.

Unfortunately, she couldn't hide at the bottom of their swimming pool forever. And even if she could, it wouldn't matter. Her vamp hearing could pick up their voices just fine underwater. It was how she knew it was her cousins and not Ethan who'd entered a few moments earlier. She'd been keeping one ear open just in case Ethan wondered in and she needed to reduce her level of vamp speed that made Olympic swimmers look like kids with floaties.

"You know we're having this talk whether you come out or not, right?" Saiden asked.

Tressa glanced up to see the distorted face of her cousin leaning over the edge, glowering at her. Well, maybe not glowering so much as looking at her with his normal menacing expression.

Accepting that her peace and quiet were gone, she pressed hard against the bottom of the pool to launch herself up and out of the water to land next to her cousins. Snatching the offered towel from Saiden's grip, she wrapped it around her body.

"Okay, fine," she said, collapsing onto a lounge chair and staring up at the night sky visible through the open ceiling. Marquin had the retractable roof installed at her request since she was pretty much the only one who used the pool regularly. There was something about swimming under the stars that reminded her of the few peaceful moments from her childhood.

An outdoor pool would have been ridiculous, given they had to severely limit their time in the sun unless they drastically increased their intake of blood. So she accepted the cloying smell of chlorine in the enclosed room as long as she could open the roof when she swam at night.

Tressa cracked her neck side to side, then glared at her cousins. "Let's get this over with. You do know I already got a lecture from Marquin a couple days ago?"

"Clearly it didn't take," a smooth, cultured voice came from behind Saiden and Derrick.

Tressa glanced around them to see Marquin and Eliana strolling through the doors to the pool. They practically looked like twins with their long blond hair and icy blue eyes, though Eliana was likely hundreds of years older than him. They were all curious about her age, but nobody wanted to risk their undead life enough to pry the actual number out of her.

Tressa groaned and dropped her head into her hands as her pseudo parents joined Saiden and Derrick. "So this is what?" she asked. "An intervention? Shouldn't Baylin be here?"

"Baylin is... occupied," Eliana said as she gracefully lowered herself onto the chair beside Tressa.

"Not with finding Renata," Tressa muttered. She knew Baylin was likely doing his best to locate the rogue, but it still itched at her. The way he immediately closed a window on his computer whenever she went to see him for an update. Whatever he was working on was keeping him from the search for Ethan's attacker. Even though she knew his facial recognition programs ran in the background, she still felt like he was... distracted.

"The rogue will be located when the time is right," Eliana said, her tone leaving no room for argument. Not that anyone ever argued with Eliana. Her delicate beauty might give her an angelic appearance at first glance, but there was death in her eyes.

No, you didn't argue with Eliana. You bowed your head slightly and accepted whatever she said. Which is exactly what Tressa did.

"Okay, then," she replied, switching her attention to Marquin. "Are we going to do a repeat of Monday's discussion? Because I told you, I'm waiting for the right moment to tell Ethan about us. He's still not budging on the whole vamps are evil thing."

"Well of course he isn't," Derrick huffed out. "Until you tell him the truth, all he has is the one experience."

"But if I tell him the truth, he'll leave."

Derrick shrugged. "Then he leaves. Maybe it wasn't meant to be."

"Derrick!" Eliana scolded. "You will not bring your own issues into Tressa's predicament."

Everyone's head rotated toward Derrick. "What issue is she talking about, Derricula?" Tressa asked, amused that she was no longer the one in the hotseat.

Derrick glared at her, then stormed out of the pool, tossing a "Fuck you guys," over his shoulder.

They all glanced back to Eliana who just waved a hand. "Do not ask. Derrick's story is his own to tell."

Okaaay, Tressa thought, wondering what, or who, had her arrogant cousin on edge. It couldn't be that he found his mate because he wouldn't be hanging around the compound if that was the case, but something clearly had his Armani boxers in a twist.

Saiden shoved Tressa's legs to the side and sat on the edge of her lounge chair. "We're worried about you, Tress. Ethan has been here over a week now, and it's getting increasingly difficult to keep our identities secret. I slipped up the other day when we were working out and mentioned something that happened forty years ago. How was I supposed to remember that? Time sort of loses all meaning shortly after you turn two hundred."

Tressa sighed. "I know. I've had my own fair share of near fuckups. But I swear, I've been trying to open his eyes to our kind. Anytime he's not in the gym, I'm talking to him about how our research has shown that rogues are not the same as other vampires."

"And how is that going?" Marquin asked as he took a spot against the wall, crossing his arms and legs in a pose that exuded relaxed and casual. Or it would if you didn't know Marquin. Relaxed and casual on the outside meant you could be seconds away from either getting a lecture or getting murdered.

Tressa thought back to the conversation earlier that day when Ethan had asked her if she'd been brainwashed for her continued assertions that some vamps might be good.

"Not amazing," Tressa answered. "He's just been so focused on getting his strength back for his revenge mission. He's not really open to hearing anything that isn't that."

"Tell me about it," Saiden grumbled. "He's got me in the gym training him to fight multiple times a day, and he won't shut up about how he's going to murder that vamp. It takes everything in me not to laugh and reveal this whole training bullshit is just a ruse. I'm kind of starting to like him, and I feel bad about the lies. He genuinely has no concept of how much stronger we are than him."

"So perhaps we educate him," Marquin mused.

Tressa's head snapped up. "Say what now?"

"I'm merely suggesting that if he's fixating on his revenge because he thinks he has a shot at eliminating Renata, then maybe you should let him encounter another real vampire. He might realize just how outclassed he is. I could ask one of the members of the East Coast cadre to come visit for a few days."

Tressa leapt out of the chair, nearly kicking Saiden in the balls as she did. "Are you insane?" she barked. "You think having him get attacked by another vampire is going to help? Every night I sit outside his room for a few hours with the door cracked, listening to him whimper in his sleep from the nightmares he's still dealing with. It kills me not to hold him in my arms and tell him it's going to be okay. And you want to put him through that again? Have you lost your marbles in your old age?"

"Careful," Elianna said quietly from her seat. "I might take offense at that considering I'm older than everyone in this compound combined."

They all stared at her for a moment, each of them likely doing the math in their heads. It was the closest Eliana had come to revealing anything about her age. If she was older than all of them, that would put her at well over a thousand years.

Okay, so Tressa would definitely not be arguing with Eliana anytime soon.

"If you would let me finish," Marquin said, his voice dangerously calm. "We could have him encounter another of our kind in a non-hostile scenario. Perhaps we tell him that we've been working with them to hunt down the rogues. It would give him exposure to a friendly vampire and let him see that even a young one would overpower him in seconds."

Tressa pondered his plan for a moment, then shook her head. If anything, the fact she actually considered his insane idea for even a minute made her realize just how far she was going with her deception. Cora's words flitted through her brain multiple times a day, and she couldn't deny it had all gone on too long. She'd been banking everything on Baylin finding Renata right away so she could tell Ethan the vamp was dead at the same time she revealed the truth about herself. Sort of like softening the blow with a head on a platter. Not literally of course, she wasn't that gross, but if Ethan knew she killed the rogue for him, surely he could see that she was one of the good ones?

But days had passed, and they were no closer to finding Renata. It was time she accepted the truth of the situation. The sooner she ripped off the bandage and told him what she was, the sooner she could start repairing the wound.

"No," she told Marquin. "I can't keep piling on more lies and deception. I already have to deal with his inevitable feelings of betrayal when he hears about us. I don't want to tangle up the web anymore. It's time I told him what's really going on."

"Are you being serious?" Saiden asked, narrowing his eyes at her. "You're going to confess everything to him?"

Tressa nodded. "I am. He deserves the truth." She paused, then added. "Tomorrow. He deserves the truth tomorrow."

Saiden quirked an eyebrow at her.

"Come on," she said, backing toward the exit. "It's after midnight. I'm not waking him up to shred his world."

"I doubt he's asleep," Saiden replied.

Tressa continued to head for the door. "Best not to risk it. Tomorrow, I promise."

"You better," Marquin called. "Or we will, and I don't think we'll be as gentle as you might be."

Tressa waved a hand over her shoulder as she left the pool.

Her hopes that she could put off telling Ethan the truth until after the rogue was dealt with had been delusional thinking born out of fear. There was no way Ethan would actually believe Renata was dead unless he saw it happen with his own eyes, and they would have to reveal their true nature to accomplish that. Which meant it was time to come clean and beg him to let her turn him.

She just needed to butter him up first.

Chapter Twenty-Two

Ethan

"Croissant?"

Ethan whipped his head around and nearly stumbled on the tread-mill. He slammed his hand down on the emergency stop and grabbed a towel to wipe the sweat off his face. He ignored the blinking numbers reminding him how out of shape he still was and instead focused on the gorgeous creature holding out a plate of those delicious breakfast pastries.

"Um, I'm good," he forced out. More than anything he wanted to hop off the damn treadmill and enjoy a buttery croissant with Tressa, but every time they started chatting, he lost hours of his life. Over the past week, they'd spent more and more time just lounging on the back patio at night or reading books together in the library. It felt right, being near her. Like that was where he belonged.

And maybe someday he could give in, but he couldn't ignore the painstakingly slow progress of his recovery. Sure, Saiden had said the very fact that he was in the gym pushing himself daily was more than most coma patients could hope to achieve in such a short time, but it still didn't feel like enough. Any day, Tressa's cousin might locate that vamp, and he needed to be ready.

"Come on," Tressa said, waving the plate under his nose. "They're freshly baked. And you can't deny that you need fuel. What is it people say, flowers can't grow without fertilizer?"

"Pretty sure that's not a common saying."

Tressa rolled her eyes. "Whatever. Doesn't make it any less true. Seriously, Ethan, you know you want to take a break."

He grit his teeth and shook his head. "I need to get more run time in."

Tressa sighed and set the plate off to the side. "Ethan, you're pushing yourself too hard. Can you even say you enjoy this?" She tapped a finger on the treadmill.

"Not really," he admitted reluctantly, swiping his towel over the back of his neck. "Even before the attack, I hated running in a stuffy gym. But I need to get my strength back up, Tressa. I *need* to."

She eyed him carefully, and he could practically see the gears turning in her brain. "Was there anything you used to do that you did actually enjoy? To work out, I mean."

"I do usually love running," he said, taking a swig from his water bottle. "Just not indoors. I used to hit my favorite trails whenever I had the time to get out of the city, but my latest project had me stuck in the lab pretty late most nights. I've had to make do with the equipment at my 24-hour gym. Still, there's something incredibly peaceful about running in nature. Connecting with the plants and trees. No matter what I was struggling with in the lab, a good jog through the forest always put me in a better mood."

Tressa's eyes lit up like someone flipped a switch on the side of her head. "That's perfect!" she exclaimed.

He cocked his head. "Perfect how? I know your compound is big, Tressa, but I don't think you have a ten-mile trail out back."

He paused, considering the extravagance of the garden and the sheer amount of money this operation clearly had. "Unless you do. Does this property really go back that far?"

Tressa chuckled softly. "No, that's not what I meant. I mean, yeah it goes on for miles, but that's just the privacy buffer for the outside world. Though, we could put in a trail if you want..."

Ethan blinked. Tressa was talking like he was going to be around for a while, but he'd just assumed once the vamp was dead, he would be on his way. Hopefully with some clippings of the Middlemist Red Camellia, but on his way nonetheless. He needed to get another job and continue his research. Or look into opening up a new lab. He couldn't play vampire hunter forever.

Fuck.

He'd been so fixated on revenge, he hadn't thought about the details of after. He couldn't ask Tressa to leave this life behind and return with him to San Jose. Hell, would he even still be working in San Jose? If he stuck with VieTek, they would have to send him to a different lab, one that hadn't been reduced to rubble. Her life was here, and his was... not.

Something about that thought made it feel like the protein bar he had for breakfast was attempting a coup in his stomach.

"Ethan?"

Returning his attention to Tressa, he realized he missed whatever she'd just said.

"I'm sorry. What was that?"

"I said I know the perfect place to take you running. I've been there many times myself, and I think you'll enjoy it. What do you say? Want to jailbreak this compound?"

Ethan frowned for a second, then relaxed. There was no reason he couldn't leave. If Baylin found the rogue while he was out with Tressa, that was what cell phones were for.

"Sure," he said with a grin. "I'm in."

Maybe it was time for him to stop and smell the roses. If he was being honest, he could use a little fresh air and a break from the monotony of work out, eat, repeat. Besides, he was technically still training if they went out for a run. It wasn't like they were going on a date or anything.

Chapter Twenty-Three

Tressa

Yes, Tressa cheered internally. She was finally getting Ethan out on a date.

Okay, so they were only going for a run, but if she had her way, they wouldn't be stopping there. Hitting the trail was just the perfect start to her plan. She had built an entire day for them together, all designed to put him in the best mood possible before she broke the news about her V-card.

Giving him an "I'll be right back," she blurred down the hall to her room and threw on a pink sports bra and black spandex shorts. Was it shameless? Maybe. But she didn't need shame. She needed to show her mate what he was missing out on by trying to be honorable. And if a little light seduction put him in the mood to ignore the teensie weensie lies she'd told him, all the better.

"That was fast," Ethan remarked when she ran back into the gym a few minutes later. "You know you can..."

His words died with a choking sound when he turned around, and his eyes went damn near cartoon levels of wide.

She suppressed the massive grin that tugged at the corners of her lips, aiming instead for a casual saunter over to the bench where he was sitting. "What was that, Ethan?" she asked as she crouched down right in front of him to secure the laces on her shoes that were more than tight enough already. Holding the position that left her head inches from his groin, she glanced up at him through her eyelashes. "You were saying I can do something?"

She couldn't resist. She licked her lips and blinked innocently before sparing a brief glance at his crotch.

"Um, you can, uh…" he sputtered.

She grinned when the bulge in his pants grew before her very eyes. "Finish that thought, Ethan," she purred. "Tell me what I can do."

Okay, at this point she was just tormenting him, but that didn't mean she was going to stop. Unless she started making him uncomfortable. She would never cross that line with anyone, let alone her own mate. But until he said or indicated otherwise, she couldn't help but play with him just a bit. Watching his jaw clench as he stared down at her with a look that could only be described as "molten" was simply too much fun.

It was at least another sixty seconds before she saw the switch in his brain flick back on, and he scooted off the side of the bench to stand up, not so subtly adjusting himself in the process.

"Uh, sorry. I was just noticing your running outfit. Looks like quality fabric."

That was what he was going with?

Poor boy, Tressa thought. She probably should stop messing with him. It really wasn't fair given he didn't know the truth about her. She had no plans to go all the way with him until after he knew what she was, so she was basically just being a tease. Yeah, she should definitely stop messing with him.

Later.

She would stop messing with him later. Just because she wasn't going to go all the way with him didn't mean she couldn't go *some* of the way. There were a lot of very fun rest stops on the road to Pleasure Town.

"Oh, it's definitely quality fabric," she said as she climbed to her feet. "So velvety," she added, running a hand over her breasts.

She glanced at Ethan and saw him swallow roughly, his eyes locked on her chest.

This is almost too easy.

"Do you want to touch it?" she asked him, dropping her voice an octave.

Ethan took a step forward, his hands twitching at his sides.

Just give in.

"What do you think, Ethan?" she asked seductively. "Do you want to feel how soft I am right now?"

Human ears might not have heard the tiny whimper that escaped her mate, but Tressa definitely caught it.

Oh yeah, I've got him now.

Ethan lifted his hands and...

...shoved them in his pockets. "I'll take your word for it," he choked out.

Damn.

Why did her mate have to be the only male in existence with willpower?

Ethan cleared his throat and strolled across the room to grab his water bottle. "Um, anyway, I was just going to say earlier that you can save the running for the trail. You know, don't tire yourself out too soon."

Oh, he had no idea.

"I guess I'm just excited to get out," she said. "I don't usually hang around the compound for long periods of time. I tend to be on the road a lot. You know, life of a vampire hunter and all. Gotta go where the action is."

A flash of something like disappointment flickered over Ethan's face, but it vanished quickly as he said, "In that case, let's head out."

"Sounds good," she chirped, then made for the door. Pausing at the threshold, she tossed him a wicked grin over her shoulder. "Oh, and just so you know, I don't tire easily. You might even say I can go all night." When he made that painful choking noise again, she laughed. "Running, I meant." She winked at him. "Get your mind out of the gutter."

She left him standing there flustered in the gym and headed for the garage, confident he would follow once he regained his senses. If he thought that teasing was bad, he had no idea how far she was willing to go.

Game on, Ethan.

Chapter Twenty-Four

Ethan

"Holy shit," Ethan breathed out, staring at the massive trees looming above his head. There were some decent arbors in the San Jose area, but they were nothing compared to these ancient giants. "Sequoiadendron giganteum," he whispered, running his hand reverently along the bark.

"What?" Tressa asked, coming up beside him.

"Oh, sorry. It's the scientific name for these. Giant redwoods. I didn't know they had any in this part of California."

Tressa shrugged. "I think most people only know about the famous one that you can drive a car through. Very few tourists make it all the way out here."

"You're not kidding," Ethan muttered, glancing around. They'd driven past Burney Falls a while ago, and ever since then, he'd seen nothing but trees that kept getting bigger and bigger as Tressa drove farther into the forest. By the time she pulled off onto a dirt road that ended at a small trailhead, he hadn't seen another living being for miles.

"So you approve?" she asked, and he thought he detected a hint of worry in her tone.

How could she be nervous that he wouldn't like this? His eyes traced up the colossal sentinels that bordered the parking area and then down the murky pathway they flanked. Craning his neck, he could barely see where it twisted off into the heart of the forest. There was just enough light to make out the trail, and that was perfection for him.

"I love it," he told her. "I had no idea it was so secluded. You're not secretly a vampire, are you? Because this would be the perfect place to dump my body if you were." He chuckled, feeling proud that he actually could joke about it after what he'd been through. He wasn't a therapist, but that felt like progress.

Unfortunately, Tressa failed to see the humor.

The pleased expression that lit up her face when he said he loved it dropped faster than his erection near a woodchipper. And he would know because he'd been using that image to keep from being hard as a rock anytime Tressa was near him.

"I was just kidding," he said, stepping closer and taking her chin in his hand. "I know you're not one of those mindless killing machines."

Her eyes dropped, and he felt like a total dick for whatever he'd done to upset her. It killed him to know he was in some way responsible for the downshift in her mood when he only ever wanted to make her smile.

"Ethan, I..." She picked at her cuticles, refusing to look up at him.

"What is it?" he asked, rubbing his thumb along her cheek and trying to ignore the small jolt that always seemed to echo through him when he touched her skin. "What's wrong?"

He racked his brain in an attempt to figure out what he'd said that made her look like the sky just opened up and started pouring rain. Was it the vampire joke? Did she actually think he believed her to be like one of those creatures for even a second?

She didn't answer him, but her warm brown eyes searched his, looking for... something.

"Hey," he said. "You can tell me anything. I hope you trust me when I say that even though we haven't known each other for very long, I still care about you." He huffed out a laugh. "Probably more than I should."

She raised an eyebrow at that, and while it wasn't a smile, it was progress.

"Seriously, Tressa," he said, brushing his thumb over the corner of her mouth as if he was physically trying to coax a smile. "If I said something dumb, please let me know. Otherwise, I'll probably say it again. And knowing me I'll do it often and in public."

Her lip twitched.

Come on, he thought. *Let me see that smile.*

"It's nothing," she replied. "I'm just being weird. Ignore me."

His hand slid around to the back of her neck in a gesture that felt far too comfortable for his liking, and his voice dropped lower. "Tressa, I don't think that's ever going to be possible."

She finally smiled up at him then, a full proper smile, and the shady forest no longer seemed so gray. It was like a damned ray of sunshine, that smile, and if he wasn't careful, it just might be the thing that broke him.

He took a deep inhale of the clean, woodsy air and let out a small shudder of pleasure, his shoulders fully relaxing for the first time since the attack. "Come on," he said, prying his hands away from her soft skin. "Let's go running. Maybe I'll even go slow so you can keep up."

Her laughter echoed through the forest, and he couldn't decide which was more intoxicating, that or her smile. Either was likely to bring him to his knees.

"Whatever you say, Dr. Rose." She dashed off down the trail, and despite the ridiculous nickname, he couldn't help but chuckle when she shouted back, "How about we see if *you* can keep up with *me*."

Oh, he could keep up. He might have lost some muscle mass, but working out constantly over the past week combined with a lifetime of running meant he was still damn fast. And when he caught her, he'd make sure he put an end to that nickname.

Grinning, he took off down the path after Tressa.

Damn, he thought, watching her race away from him, her tight ass on full display. *Maybe I shouldn't run too fast after all.*

Chapter Twenty-Five

Tressa

"Come on, slowpoke," Tressa called behind her as she emerged from the tree line an hour later. She shouldn't tease him about being slow when it really wasn't his fault. Not even the fastest human sprinter could keep pace with her, and Ethan was still recovering. She just couldn't help it, though. He always looked so flabbergasted when she messed with him. Like he wasn't sure if he was allowed to laugh and be silly for once.

Huffing and puffing, Ethan came up beside Tressa and laid a hand on the hood of her car. Well, technically it was Saiden's car since she "borrowed" his McLaren, but she thought Ethan might enjoy the sweet ride. Sadly, he'd shown more interest in that fancy flower than the two-hundred-thousand-dollar vehicle most guys would fawn over. Just another reminder that her mate wasn't like most men.

After a few minutes of Ethan wheezing like the post-coma patient that he was, his eyes finally rolled up to meet hers. "How…"

"Yes, Ethan?" she asked, waiting for him to catch his breath a little more.

"How the…"

"Finish your sentence."

"How the fuck do you run so fast?"

I'm a vampire.

The words were on the tip of her tongue. She'd planned to wait until the end of the day, but maybe this was the perfect time to tell him. It was becoming more difficult to endure his anti-vampire comments without feeling like they were a smack in the face.

She should just confess to him what she was so they could start the healing process. And the trailhead was as good a place as any. They were secluded, so he couldn't exactly escape. He said runs always put him in an upbeat mood, and exhaustion aside, he'd been all smiles on the trail. Plus, she wasn't entirely sure how long she could last when the urge to throw him up against one of those giant tree and fuck his brains out kept getting stronger the more time she spent around him.

I'm a vampire.

She just needed to open her mouth and say those three words. Those three life-altering words. Once she spoke them, everything would change, but maybe, just maybe, it would be for the best. Three words to tell him the truth, and then she could deal with the fallout, however bad it was.

Just three little words.

"I'm a vampire," Tressa said.

Ethan laughed and pushed off the car. "Good one. That would explain a lot. But there's only one problem with that..."

Tressa bit her lip. "Um, what's that?"

Ethan stared at her for a second, then stepped closer, his breathing heavy but no longer uncontrolled. He brushed a lock of hair off her forehead and grinned. "You're way too sweet to be a monster."

He leaned in, and Tressa went still.

Was he finally going to kiss her?

Wait, should she let him? And if she did, could she bring herself to stop before things went too far? She wanted to say yes, but at the same time, a resounding *no* echoed in her brain.

On the other hand, she *had* told him the truth, so technically she was no longer deceiving him. Was it really her fault if he didn't believe her?

His lips brushed against hers, and sparks of lightning exploded under her skin, making her entire body tingle in the best way. She wanted to sink into his embrace and never leave. If he was willing, then who was she to push him away? Everything she wanted was right there in her arms.

Only he didn't *really* know the truth, and she couldn't deny that he'd been very clear about how important consent was for him when it came to sex. So, as much as she yearned to say 'fuck it' and take what she wanted, she couldn't bring herself to do it. Not to her mate.

Breaking the kiss, she took a step back.

Dang, she thought. *Apparently he isn't the only one with willpower.* Though she wasn't entirely sure that was a good thing considering the nearly painful throbbing between her legs.

"I'm sorry," Ethan said, running a hand through his sweaty hair. "I shouldn't have done that. I just... I forgot for a second. About everything."

"No," Tressa said, placing a hand on his arm. "I wanted you to. I still want you to. You have no idea how *much* I want you to. But when you kiss me, I want all of you to be with all of me. I want you to see me completely."

Ethan fiddled with the drawstring on his running shorts, refusing to meet her eyes. "You're right. I know I've been preoccupied with training to kill the vamp, and you deserve more than half my attention."

She stifled a groan. He thought it was about him? The only thing about her mate that was so typically male was his ego. Not that she could blame him. He had no idea the monumental secret she was hiding.

"It's not that, Ethan. I can't fault you for wanting to get revenge for your friend. Or hell, revenge for yourself after what she did to you."

Tressa tried not to look, but she couldn't help it. Her eyes landed on the nasty scar at the base of his neck. It would always be there. That reminder of what one of her kind had done to him.

Ethan's hand went to the scar and lingered on it for a moment. "Yeah, but still. It's not fair to you. None of this is fair to you. I've taken over your life with my vendetta, and I don't even know what's going to happen after—"

"Stop," Tressa interjected. "Let's worry about later when it gets here."

Not the healthiest response, but Tressa wasn't ready to risk losing Ethan's presence just yet. Her idea of telling him the truth when he was rocking a post run high was gone, but surely her next destination would perk his mood back up.

"Hey," she said, her lips curling up in a smile. "How do you feel about ice cream?"

"You know, I was pleasantly surprised by your choice of running trail, but I can't say I'm optimistic about this decision."

Tressa laughed and put the McLaren in park in front of Ray's Food

Place, a Fall River Mills staple that carried mostly groceries but also had a deli with ice cream. They'd made a quick stop at the compound for showers, and it was starting to feel like a reset on the day. Her second chance to try again and get him in the right mood to hear the truth.

Or, as Cora would say, it was time for take two.

"Oh, Ethan, my sweet Ethan," she said, shaking her head. "You're going to eat those words."

"And they'll probably taste better than any ice cream from this place."

Tressa slapped his shoulder lightly and climbed out of the car. When Ethan didn't immediately follow, she went around to his side and pulled the door open. Holding out a hand, she asked, "Do you trust me?"

Okay, so there might have been a little more weight to the words than there should be, but if he didn't have enough faith in her to try the tiny ice cream place tucked in the back of the grocery store, she was really screwed when it came to the whole vamp thing.

Ethan stared at her for a moment, then placed his hand in hers. "With my life."

A bolt of lightning shot through Tressa at his words. She could only send a prayer to Lilith that he still felt that way in an hour.

"In that case," she said, tugging him from the car. "Let's grab some of the best bubblegum ice cream you've ever had. Believe me, it's life changing."

When she felt Ethan freeze halfway out of the car, she turned around to see him gaping at her, mouth wide open.

Tressa tossed a glance over her shoulder, searching for the cause of his shock, then looked back to him. "Did I say something bad?"

He eyed her curiously, then shook his head as he finally unfolded his large frame from the tiny car. "I guess I've never met someone else who loved bubblegum ice cream before. Most people think it's gross."

Tressa put a hand to her chest in mock surprise. "Seriously? But it's the best flavor."

He nodded slowly. "I agree. In fact, uh..." He nudged his glasses up on his nose with his pinkie in quite possibly the most adorably innocent gesture Tressa had ever seen.

She ran her hands over his rounded shoulders, trying to get him to meet her gaze. "What?" she asked.

He finally looked up and caught her eyes. "I was just going to say I always thought you smelled a little like bubblegum."

If vampire hearts could skip a beat, Tressa's would be frolicking up and down main street. If only Ethan knew that he smelled like creamy vanilla ice cream to her. Together, they were an exquisite combination.

"Thank you," she said, smiling. "I'll take that as a compliment."

"You should," he replied with a lopsided grin. "I don't like most super-sweet things, but bubblegum flavor is kind of my weakness."

Tressa's heart gave up on skipping and did a full on endzone victory dance. It took everything in her not to throw her entire plan out the window and prove to him right there what she was. Nobody who looked at her like that could possibly let something like a tiny pair of fangs come between them.

Shaking her head, she reminded herself that downtown Fall River Mills was probably not the best place for that revelation. The locals already gossiped that her cadre was probably some kind of cult. They respected their privacy because of the money they spent in the town, but if anyone overheard the word vampire, she imagined news vans would be on their doorstep by the evening.

Resisting the urge to say anything, she dragged him back toward the small in-store ice cream parlor that was going to blow Ethan's mind.

Chapter Twenty-Six

Ethan

"I think I just died and went to heaven," Ethan said before taking another long lick off his ice cream cone.

Laughing, Tressa slid into the driver's seat of the McLaren. "I told you it was amazing."

"And you were one hundred percent right," he said, reminding himself to slow down or risk a brain freeze that might taint the otherwise divine experience.

Tressa paused with her cone to her lips and grinned. "So, what do I get for being right?"

Ethan swallowed his bite and dropped into the car. Shifting his attention over to Tressa, he tracked that mischievous gleam in her eyes. "What do you want?" he asked cautiously, trying and failing not to stare at her lips and the tiny bit of ice cream at the corner of her mouth that begged to be licked.

The only thing that held him back was the firm knowledge that combining the sweet creaminess of his favorite desert with the intoxicating taste of Tressa would shatter the last bit of willpower he'd been clinging to for dear life. One taste, and he'd be testing how easy it was to fuck in a McLennan. Or was it a McLaven? Whatever the name of the fancy car was, he doubted the tiny seats were conducive to all the things he wanted to do to Tressa when he finally got his hands on her.

Tressa hummed for a moment as if deep in thought, then said, "How about we take this ice cream somewhere more *private* and discuss it?"

The way she said "private" sent a tingle down Ethan's spine straight to his stirring cock that had no business waking up when he could do nothing about it. Not that it was ever fully asleep anytime Tressa was around.

"Yeah, works for me," he managed to choke out, feeling the last threads of willpower slipping from his grasp. He took another huge lick to avoid saying something stupid. Something along the lines of suggesting they go back to the compound where he could ravage her for the rest of the day.

While his brain and his dick continued to war internally, Tressa put the car in drive and expertly navigated the small-town streets with one hand as she continued to swipe her tongue over her ice cream.

She only drove for a few minutes down the road before turning into the gravel lot of what looked like an abandoned church nestled against a lush forest. She parked the car around back and turned the engine off.

Ethan stepped out and took a second to look around. Between the large trees and the empty parking lot, they had more than enough privacy for anything Tressa might have in mind.

Or anything *he* had in mind. Watching her take slow, suggestive licks of the ice cream cone while driving had led to a number of naughty thoughts running through his brain, and he was quickly losing the ability to hide how she affected him. Ethan shot a furtive glance her way, taking in how her tongue flicked and swirled across the bright pink ice cream. He couldn't help but envision how that talented tongue might be applied to other tasks. And the look Tressa gave him as she slid onto the hood of the sports car and crooked a finger at him was not helping.

Even though she somehow managed to make it look effortless, Ethan struggled to scramble onto the hood without dropping his dessert, and he winced when his knee connected with the metal hard enough to leave a small dent.

"Smooth, Dr. Rose," she commented, not even trying to hide her snicker.

"Sorry," he replied, twisting his body so his legs were parallel to Tressa's, her bronze skin lit up by the late afternoon sun. "I don't spend much time on the hood of a car."

"No?" she asked, running her tongue up a line of ice cream that was dripping onto her fingers. "You didn't have a spot in the woods where you took girls to go necking when you were a teenager?"

He laughed so hard he almost dropped his cone. "Necking? No, can't say as I ever did that since it's not the 1950's. When I was in high school, we mostly just made out in the back of a movie theater."

Tressa stuck her bottom lip out in a fake pout. "And here I thought you enjoyed being out in nature."

"Oh, I do," he replied, ignoring the drop of ice cream that landed on the car in favor of getting lost in Tressa's dazzling brown eyes. "Which is why I'm having a hard time being a gentleman right now. You bought me my favorite ice cream and took me to a secluded place screened in by towering trees. If I didn't know better, I'd think you were trying to seduce me."

Tressa shifted onto her side to face him and took an obscenely long lick. "Who says I'm not?"

A melted drop slid off and landed on the curve of her breasts, and he couldn't help but stare as the bit of pink ice cream slid down into her cleavage.

If he wasn't hard before, he definitely was now. And the thin track pants he'd thrown on after the shower were officially doing nothing to hide that fact. He regretted not pumping one out while he was scrubbing up under the hot water, but he'd been in a hurry to get back to her and whatever surprise she had planned. That strong urge alone should have told him he needed to empty his balls if he was going to be near her, but after taking care of himself in bed almost every night for the past week, his dick no longer had any interest in his own hand. It wanted her hand. It wanted *her*. And he was quickly forgetting why he'd been so opposed to that idea.

He scooted closer to Tressa until their legs were pressed up against each other. "You're dripping," he murmured, and the widening of her eyes told him the innuendo wasn't lost on her.

"Maybe I am," she said as a second drop landed on the swell of her breasts. "What are you going to do about it?"

Lick it up, his brain shouted, and his head subconsciously drifted closer. He ran a finger across the glistening pink trail on her chest, testing the waters. Was she really okay with this?

He swallowed roughly when he glanced back up, seeing the invitation in her expression.

"I..." He trailed off, his normally reliable brain abandoning him. Then another drip fell from the cone, and he was lost. Any reservations he had melted alongside the ice cream.

He all but dove into her tits and lapped up every last trace of sweetness. "Fuck," he moaned as he sat up straight. The ice cream was good, but all he tasted was her. All he smelled was her. All he saw was her.

Tressa.

She arched her back and tilted her cone slightly, causing another large drop to fall onto her breasts. "Oops," she cooed. "I'm all sticky again."

Ethan met her heated gaze, devoured the last of his dessert in two large bites, then slammed his mouth onto Tressa's, unable to resist any longer.

Her tongue was cold from the ice cream, so he set to work warming it up, caressing it with his own. When a slight whimper escaped from her throat, he pulled back to check in with her.

There was no hesitation on her face, though, only arousal, and the way her hand massaged the inside of his thigh told him she wanted this as badly as he did.

Except she wasn't finished with her dessert. Giving her a seductive grin, he took the cone from her and brushed it down her neck. Then he traced the same path with his tongue, enjoying how the cold of the cream mixed with the heat of her skin.

Sliding his free hand up into her hair, he pulled her in for another deep, exploring kiss, and her small hands started fumbling with the drawstring of his pants. Just the graze of her fingers against his hard cock felt like lightning, and his hips jerked with need.

But despite the fact they were "necking" in the woods behind a church like a couple of teenagers, he had no desire to also blow his load early like one.

He rested his large hand on top of her smaller ones, stilling them before they got his pants untied. "If you keep touching me like that, I'm not going to be able to hold back," he told her, his voice rough despite the soothing chill of the ice cream.

"So don't," she breathed out.

He groaned at the sultry purr in her voice. "Tressa, it's the middle of the day. Anyone could stumble by."

A wicked grin spread across her face. "Trust me, Ethan. Nobody is coming back here. And I couldn't care less if they did."

He stared at her, his eyes slowly grazing up and down her body, taking in her pebbled nipples and the way she squeezed together her tawny thighs that were barely covered by her baby blue mini skirt.

"I don't want to push you into anything," she added gently. "But maybe it's time for you to live a little. Your life can't always be about other people. You spent all your time working on a medication to help others. Now you spend all your time working toward revenge for Jake. Just once, ask yourself this... What do *you* want?"

You, he thought. But the words didn't come out. He felt like he was hovering on a precipice, and once he closed that last bit of distance between them, he could never come back. But maybe that wasn't such a bad thing. She wasn't wrong about his life. He couldn't remember the last time he'd done something for purely selfish reasons.

He could do this. Despite his earlier reservations, it wouldn't actually kill him to take a break and enjoy life for once. There was nothing happening with his mission at the moment, so surely a brief detour with Tressa wouldn't derail everything?

He handed her back the ice cream and leaned in.

"I want..." he began, sprinkling kisses down the side of her neck.

"Go on," Tressa said, angling her head to give him better access.

"I want to..." He slid off the hood of the McLaren and pushed her thighs apart so she was splayed out in front of him.

"Tell me," Tressa sighed, her breath hitching as he began to kiss his way up her legs.

"I want to taste..." His mouth moved higher, and his hands slid under the hem of her skirt.

"What do you want to taste, Ethan?" she cried as he gripped her ass and pulled her to the edge of the car.

He bent down and nipped the soft skin on her neck before brushing his lips against her ear. "I want to taste this sweet ice cream," he whispered, his fingers wrapping around the cone clenched in her hand, "...dripping out of your even sweeter pussy." He gave her a look full of naughty promises as he took the ice cream from her and made his way back down to nestle his body between her legs. With one hand, he shoved her skirt up around her waist, then yanked her panties to her knees.

"Fuck, you're already so wet," he said. Seeing her level of responsiveness to his touch, he nearly tossed the remaining ice cream so he could dive right into a far superior dessert.

But he wasn't done playing with her. She'd teased him for so long, if he was going to break from his mission to finally have a taste of her, he was going to savor it.

Every. Last. Drop.

He dragged the ice cream cone up her inner thigh, then followed the trail with his tongue, lapping up the creamy dessert but pausing just shy of the truly sweet spot.

A loud thump drew his attention up to see Tressa had thrown her head back against the hood, her breasts heaving up and down.

"I don't think so," he growled. "I want those pretty eyes on me. I want you to watch as I make you come undone."

She lifted her head, meeting his gaze, and bit her lip.

Fuck, he wanted to replace those tiny teeth with his own. Wanted to suck on the sensitive skin of her lips and feel her squirm beneath him.

But that would have to wait.

She had been taunting him all day, and now it was his turn to return the favor, with interest.

He grazed the ice cream higher up her thigh, then ran it down the other side, always following close behind with his tongue. But as much as he loved the tiny whimpers she was making, he couldn't hold himself back anymore.

He dipped his finger into the last remains of the ice cream, then circled her clit with his finger.

A tiny squeal escaped her lips, but it devolved into a positively indecent moan when his tongue landed on the same spot. "Oh fuck, Ethan, that's..."

So his little Sunflower had never done temperature play before. Interesting. He'd always been fascinated about the science behind various kinks, such as the mechanism behind cooling and heating the sensitive nerves. Now he had the perfect specimen to experiment on.

He added a little more ice cream to his finger, swirled it over her a second time, then ran his tongue straight up the center of her.

"You taste so fucking good, Tressa."

She let out a strained laugh. "That's just the ice cream."

Ethan pulled away and smirked at her from between her thighs. "You think this"—he held up the remains of her cone—"could compare to you at all?" He tossed the ice cream toward the forest for the animals to enjoy. "Tressa, it doesn't even come close to you. Doesn't hold a candle to the divine taste that is you."

Her cheeks flushed red, and he wondered if no one had ever complimented her before.

Leaning back down, he flicked his tongue over her clit a few more times, then started lapping at her pussy. "I could feast on you all day and not stop until the sun went down."

He pushed a finger inside her, adding a second one when her wetness allowed him easy access. Pumping them in and out, he matched his licks to the pace of his fingers for a second before looking back up at her. "And once darkness fell, that's when the real fun would start."

Tressa's head thumped onto the hood again, and he didn't even tell her to focus on him. He wasn't doing his job unless she became lost to the sensation.

Her hips started bucking against his face, her cries growing louder. "Fuck yes, Ethan! Right there!"

He increased his pace, thrumming his tongue faster as his fingers slid beautifully through her wet heat. "That's it, baby. Let go for me. Scream so loud you scare the wildlife."

He latched his mouth around her clit and gave one strong suck.

"Ethan!" Tressa shouted as her back arched fully off the car, and her fingers tangled in his hair, locking him in place with her solid grip.

Not that he had any desire to move away from her and miss the show. Especially when he knew he was the one responsible for the blissed-out look on her face as her body continued to twitch in the aftermath of her orgasm. Grinning, he licked up every last drop of her release, and it was just as he imagined—far more delicious than any ice cream.

Chapter Twenty-Seven

Tressa

"Sheer perfection," Ethan said, running his tongue along his lips.

Perfect? Tressa thought. Perfect didn't even begin to describe it. She was fluent in eight languages, and she was pretty sure none of them had a word that came even close to what she had experienced.

She should be feeling shame that she'd given in after telling herself she wasn't going to, but damn. Her morals weakened like a vampire in the sun the second he kissed her. It was all just supposed to be a little fun. Teasing him with the ice cream on her tits. She'd wanted to watch him get all red and flustered again before showing her more of that iron willpower he had.

So much for the plan.

Wrapping his hands around her waist, he pulled her off the hood and set her down on unsteady legs. Slowly, he tugged her panties back up and settled them in place around her hips.

"That was incredible, Ethan," she said breathily, gripping his shirt and dragging him close to press a quick kiss to his lips. "But now I think it's your turn."

She still maintained that it wasn't too bad so long as they didn't go *all* the way, and Lilith be damned, she was not going to experience the best orgasm she'd had in three hundred years without offering him the same in return.

Ethan rested his forehead against hers. "You asked me what I wanted, yeah? Trust me when I say I just had it. I'm good."

She pulled back and ran her hand up and down the impressive bulge straining the front of his pants. "Are you sure? Feels to me like you're not finished yet." She increased her pace when she saw his eyes darken.

For all of three seconds.

Ethan took her hand gently and pulled it off his cock.

Wait, did he not want her? What kind of guy ate pussy like a damn champion then called it a day? She could see the evidence in his pants that he clearly needed a release, and she was more than happy to give it to him. Hell, she *wanted* to give it to him. She was desperate to taste her mate.

So why...?

"Do you not want me?" she asked, hating how meek and vulnerable she sounded. She was a fucking vampire. She'd survived the kinds of things that would break most people. She could handle anything life threw her way and do it with a smile on her face and a song in her heart.

Except this. All it took was her mate stepping back from her to crush her spirit.

"Stop," Ethan said.

One word. It was only one word, but the steel and command in his voice brought her spiral to a screeching halt.

"Don't ever think for a fucking second that I don't want you, Tressa. That couldn't be further from the truth."

Okay, he was saying the right things, but...

She dropped her face and scuffed her white sneaker against the ground, drawing a line through the gravel. "So then why...?"

"Hey," he said, two fingers gently but firmly lifting her chin up so she was forced to look at him. "After," he told her, pressing a fleeting kiss to her lips. "When I finally get to have you, I don't want a single thought in my head distracting me from worshipping you. Once I find the vampire and destroy her, that's when I'll get to enjoy the rest of my dessert."

A shiver ran through her at the way he said "dessert." She'd definitely been a fan of the ice cream play—the sting of the cold immediately soothed by the heat from his mouth.

"I could get on board with that," she said, running her hand down his arm and twining her fingers through his. "But that doesn't change the fact that your engine is all revved up with no room to race."

Ethan chuckled and brought her hand up to his mouth. Holding eye contact with her, he dropped his lips to her overheated skin. "Well, if I haven't made it clear yet, I'm not like other guys. I don't care about going fast. I just want to enjoy the ride. And Tressa? I more than enjoyed what just happened between us."

The heat in his eyes was messing with her, but she would just have to trust him. Trust that he was being truthful, and he really did care more about pleasing her than getting himself off.

Tressa opened her mouth to tell him how incredible he was, but the sound of footsteps crunching through the gravel parking lot made them leap apart.

"Well," a smooth female voice said. "I almost hate to interrupt such a perfect moment, but then again, I've already seen far more than I needed to."

Chapter Twenty-Eight

Ethan

They both whipped their heads around, and Ethan froze in place.

His eyes locked on the woman in smartly tailored gray slacks and a pristine navy blouse who was frowning at him and Tressa. If he didn't know better, he would have thought she left from a service at the church and happened to stumble across them.

But he did know better, and he would never forget that face for as long as he lived.

"You," he spat, his fists tightening at his sides. Fiery rage surged in his chest as the hatred he had nursed for the past week roared to life inside him. His hands and fingers tingled with the urge to lash out—to punch, claw, strangle, something. Thankfully though, his rational brain kept his feet locked in place, a small voice at the back of his head reminding him that he had no weapons and was still vulnerable.

It wasn't supposed to go like this. He was supposed to hunt her down. Ambush her. Go in guns blazing and take her out before she could react. This, her being the one to find him, was... not the plan.

Still, he wasn't going down without a fight.

The dark-haired vamp stepped forward. "Allow me to properly

introduce myself. My name is Renata Inês Magdalena Da Silva. You know, I've been looking for you, Ethan Aidan Ambrose. You're the one that got away. I'm still very keen to find out just how you managed that."

Ethan bit back the urge to say 'you and me both' since he had no desire to let her know he was just as clueless. What he needed to do was keep her talking and buy themselves some time. He trusted that Tressa would have a plan. She was a hunter, after all. For all he knew, the trunk could be full of weapons.

"Wouldn't you like to know," Ethan snapped, cringing internally when it came out more like a schoolyard taunt than the firm 'fuck you' he intended.

Renata—because apparently the murderous creature had a name—folded her arms and arched an eyebrow. "Interesting that you don't know either."

Shit, am I that transparent?

"Regardless," Renata continued, "while I do appreciate Tressa's oh so enthusiastic scream alerting me to your presence, I must say that given our history, I did not expect to find you in the arms of another vampire quite so soon. I thought for sure it would take you longer to come around."

Ethan scoffed, his fear overridden by the absurdity of her statement. "Like I'd ever touch one of you undead bitches."

The vampire cocked her head, her dark eyes sliding over to Tressa. "Oh dear," she said, and Ethan thought for a second that she legitimately sounded apologetic. "I didn't realize you were keeping that little fact a secret. My mistake."

Ethan barked out a harsh laugh and turned to look at Tressa, curious to see how she was responding to such a bizarre conversation. He assumed she would be just as amused as he was.

He was wrong.

That wasn't what he saw on her face at all. Instead of amusement or disbelief he saw... fear?

She closed the distance between them and took his hand in hers. "Ethan, I tried to tell you..."

"No," he interrupted, shaking his head.

It wasn't possible. This was another bad dream. Another nightmare. He'd fallen asleep somehow, and he just needed to wake up.

Come on, wake up, he shouted inside his head, scanning the surroundings for something to latch onto. Something out of place that could confirm it was just a dream. It had to be.

Only nothing had changed. The breeze still rustled the trees. The church, with its windows shuttered and paint peeling, still loomed behind them. The remnants of Tressa's ice cream lay a few yards off, a shiny pop of fluorescent pink amongst gray gravel. He could still smell the bubblegum scent, though he wasn't sure if it was the melted dessert or the smell of Tressa herself.

Tressa. Who was looking at him with such pity in her eyes as her thumb stroked the back of his hand.

It wasn't cold. There was no chill to her skin, not like a dead thing should have. Her body was warm and soft. Like a human. She had to be human. There was no fucking way she was a...

"No," he said again, his brain unable to lock onto any other word. He couldn't believe it. He *wouldn't* believe it. He just needed to wake the hell up.

WAKE UP!

But he didn't. Because he was already awake, his nightmare made reality.

Tressa gripped him tighter and opened her mouth to speak, but he ripped his hand from her before she could say anything. He backed away so fast he tripped over his own feet and landed on his ass, staring up at the woman he'd thought was so incredible just seconds ago. The woman he almost abandoned his mission for. The woman he could have seen himself falling in love with.

Only she wasn't a woman.

She was a vampire.

A monster.

Chapter Twenty-Nine

Tressa

Something inside Tressa broke when she saw the expression on Ethan's face. The way he looked up at her as if she was truly one of the irredeemable monsters he believed her kind to be. As if she was no better than the rogue who had butchered his best friend.

Ethan shook his head. "No. It's not possible."

Tressa took another step toward him, and he scrambled away from her, cutting his hands on the sharp stones of the gravel lot.

Tressa's fangs pushed at her gums when she caught the coppery scent, but a sharp intake of air drew both their attention to the rogue who was now eyeing Ethan like he was a four-course meal.

Ethan brought his palms up, and Tressa watched the blood from his cuts ooze down his hands to land on the gravel.

Drip.

Drip.

Drip.

His head jerked up to look at her, but Tressa kept her face calm, stoic, and she forced her fangs to stay hidden. It took all her willpower because Ethan smelled so very, *very*, good, but she couldn't let him see her lose control.

I'm not like Renata, Tressa thought. *I can restrain myself. Please Ethan, see that we are different.*

His expression dropped from pure terror to something more like extreme wariness the longer he stared at her, and Tressa remained perfectly still, waiting.

Renata, on the other hand, prowled toward them, her eyes fixated on the drops of blood. "I've been all over this Lilith forsaken state looking for you, Ethan. And I have not eaten in days. It seems only fair that you fix the problem you caused."

Ethan dragged his gaze from Tressa to Renata. "Go to hell," he barked at the vampire, and Tressa could practically see the gears turning in his head, the shift on his face from concern to calculating.

Oh fuck. Did he really think he stood any kind of chance against her? He was going to get himself killed, and it was all Tressa's fault. She'd let Saiden and Derrick work out with him. Let him think he could actually take on Renata and survive.

He couldn't. Even with years of training, he would never come close to taking down a vampire. Ethan needed to run. He needed to let Tressa distract Renata so he could escape and go hide in the woods.

But he wasn't going to do that because of her. She was about to watch her mate die because she fucked up. Because she had lied to him.

He climbed to his feet and turned his back on Tressa before she could say a word, dismissing her to focus on the vampire. The vampire who was equally focused on Ethan.

Tressa had exactly one shot to save him. One tiny possibility that might allow them to survive.

Sliding her hand into the pocket of her skirt, she found the tiny piece of square metal that every member of the cadre carried when they left the compound. Two quick taps on the button, and her GPS location was sent to Baylin.

She just didn't know if it would bring help in time.

Renata smiled at them, a mildly amused curving of the mouth, and Tressa watched Ethan freeze up as two fangs slowly slid out from behind the vampire's upper canines. They were the same two fangs responsible for the scar on his neck, and Tressa would die before letting them sink into her mate again.

She stepped in front of him and stared Renata down. "You're not going to touch him."

The vampire dragged her eyes away from Ethan, and to Tressa's surprise, she sighed. "I did tell you this wasn't over. Although, I thought it would take longer to find you. I'm quite amazed you didn't disappear. I assumed you would vanish to another country where I might not locate you for years. Isn't that what you normally do? Run away from your problems?"

Tressa grit her teeth. "You don't know anything about me."

"Come now," Renata said, her brows dipping into a disappointed frown. "We already played this game in the hospital. I know *everything* about you. Tell me, is that human truly worth giving up this new life you wanted so badly? After everything you've endured, you would throw it all away for him? You must know that he'll never accept you, Loloma."

Renata's last word turned Tressa's veins to ice. No human or vampire walking the planet should know that name. Not the cadre. Not even the Ruling Coalition. She'd gone to great lengths to ensure she never heard it spoken again.

And for nearly three hundred years, she'd been able to hide from her past.

Until now.

"Don't call me that."

Renata cocked her head. "That is your given name is it not? Loloma? Meaning kindness and compassion. I find it amusing that you started calling yourself Tressa after you died. Derived from ancient Greek, it means 'to reap' or 'harvest,' if I'm not mistaken. I have to wonder, though, if you changed it because you felt like you were no longer worthy of your birth name? Nearly three hundred years, Loloma. Such a long time to keep running from your past. So many lives you've soothed with your Gift, all in an attempt to earn your name back. Would you sacrifice all that to die alongside this human? Would you sacrifice all the future lives you might save?"

Tressa's hands curled into fists, released, and curled again, her nails carving small crescents into the flesh. She concentrated on that ounce of pain as the tiny wounds opened and closed, slicing and healing. Anything to hide from the truth in Renata's words.

"Why are you doing this?" she asked in a steady voice, maintaining a tight grip on her calm as she stalled for time. "Why have you done any of this? Destroying Ethan's lab. Attacking us in the hospital. Killing humans. Why?"

Moving so fast Tressa could barely track her, Renata blurred around them and perched on the hood of the McLaren, crossing her legs and smoothing her blouse as if she was settling into a business meeting.

"Because I do what I must," she said simply. "Things are changing, Loloma, and you would do well to open your eyes. These humans you so badly want to save would never extend you the same courtesy. Truthfully, I have no interest at all in harming you or your family, unless you get in my way. In fact, I will do you a favor because I admire your courage in the face of obvious defeat. Leave now. Drive away, Loloma. Leave the human with me, and I will let you live."

Tressa shook her head and shifted over slightly to keep herself firmly between Renata and the slack-jawed Ethan who still sat sprawled out in the parking lot. "You say you know all about me, but if you did, then you would know that will never happen."

Renata pursed her lips, then took a small, almost imperceptible sniff. A sad smile stretched across her face.

"Ah, yes. That's right. You think he's important because he's your m—"

"Mine," Tressa snapped, cutting off the rogue before she could make a bad situation worse. Tressa didn't need the mate bond dumped on top of everything else Ethan was dealing with. If by some miracle they survived, that would be a discussion for another day. "Ethan is mine, and you're not hurting him."

"You think I want to do this?" Renata asked, tilting her head at Ethan. "I'm sure your friend... What was his name? Ah, yes. Baylin. The Hacker. I'm sure he has already informed you that I have no record of violence with the Ruling Coalition. I'm not some common rogue. Not in the truest definition. I have turned no human against their will, nor do I hunt them for food. I'm simply doing what I must for the greater cause, Loloma."

"I told you not to call me that, bitch," she gritted out.

Tressa never saw the attack coming. One second, she was shooting daggers at Renata, and the next second, fiery pain flared across her right cheek. She looked up in time to see Renata lean back against the McLaren and brush a bit of dust off her shirt.

"Now, now, Loloma," she said, clucking her tongue. "Leave the crude name calling to the humans. You and I are better than that."

"If you're so evolved, you wouldn't be murdering in cold blood," Tressa grumbled, absently rubbing at her face as her increased healing quickly numbed the pain.

Renata waved a hand. "Think what you will. It matters little to me.

The reality is that I'm doing what is necessary for the preservation of our kind. Surely you can't argue with that?"

"I can if it means you're killing innocent humans."

"Innocent?" The laugh Renata let out chilled Tressa to the bone. "Oh, my sweet Loloma. You more than most know what they're capable of. There's no such thing as an innocent human. They're corrupted from birth. Just like the first one was. Always determined to ruin things for our kind. And that one"—she pointed a finger at Ethan—"has proven to be quite problematic."

"Why?" Tressa demanded. "He hasn't done anything wrong."

Renata arched a single eyebrow. "Oh dear. You don't know, do you? Today is simply full of surprises."

Tressa frowned, then glanced back at Ethan who was cautiously climbing to his feet. "Know what?"

"What your precious human has been cooking up in his little lab."

Tressa stiffened before slowly rotating to face Ethan, briefly forgetting the bigger threat was now at her back. "Ethan?" she asked.

His face was hard as he wiped his bloody palms on his track pants. "Not that I owe you anything, but I've already told you all about my work."

"Oh, I doubt that," Renata cooed as she flashed to Ethan's side and laid a hand on his shoulder.

Tressa jolted forward but halted when Renata's fingers dug into Ethan's skin and he cried out in pain.

She relaxed her grip and slid her hand up his neck, playing with the long ends of his hair. "I don't think Loloma would be quite so protective of you if she knew. But I'll save you the tough relationship conversation." Her hand tightened on his hair, and she yanked him closer to her chest, her eyes locking on Tressa. "Either you let me kill him without fuss, and trust me when I say that is the smart decision, or I kill you both. I would rather you not select that option, but it is your choice. Either way, I cannot suffer him to live with the knowledge in his head."

"I'd like to suggest a third option if you don't mind," a deep male voice shouted from above them, and they all glanced up to see Saiden and Derrick crouched on the eaves of the church.

In a flash, they both leapt from the roof to land beside Tressa. Ethan's eyes flared even wider as they darted between her two cousins, and any joy she felt at their arrival was smothered by the level of betrayal that bloomed across his face.

"Ah, The Enforcer," Renata cooed. "We meet again. I wondered which little mouse it was that I heard scurrying over the roof. And you brought The Playboy this time." Her gaze slid over to Derrick. "Come to join the party?"

Derrick scoffed and cracked his knuckles. "Bitch, we are the party. And you're ruining the vibe."

She sighed. "You're not going to make this easy, are you? You won't just let me remove this one tiny, insignificant human and be on my way?"

"Never," Saiden snarled.

"In that case..." She tossed Ethan to the ground and blurred forward. In a single fluid motion, her right hand slammed into Derrick's balls with enough force to lift his feet several inches off the ground, while at the same time her left leg flew out and swept Saiden's feet out from underneath him.

Derrick gave a strangled groan and crashed to his knees, clutching his sack, but Saiden popped back up in an instant and drew two gleaming daggers from his belt. "Going for the balls? Low blow."

Renata shrugged. "I use whatever is available. That's your problem. All of you. So sentimental. You let emotion guide you. You let it stop you from making the tough choices. I have no such qualms." She flew forward and raked her claws at Saiden's face, but he blurred to the side at the last second.

Back and forth they fought, her attacking and Saiden dodging just fast enough to avoid her lethal strikes, taking little more than glancing blows and minor scratches.

Renata flipped away from Saiden and landed on the roof of the McLaren. "Ah yes, I forgot about your pesky ability."

"So give it up," Saiden shot back, wiping a thin smear of red off his cheek. "You know you can't beat me."

"I could, actually, if I was using the full extent of my power," she replied casually, absently cleaning a bit of Saiden's blood from beneath one manicured fingernail. "But as I said, I have no strong desire to eliminate Loloma's family. Besides, I don't need to beat you. I just need to exploit your weakness." Renata leapt off the car, her body shimmering in midair, and Cora landed in front of Saiden.

"Hi, baby," she said, blowing him a kiss.

Saiden took a step back, clearly shocked by his mate's sudden appearance.

Renata seized his moment of hesitation and latched her claws around his neck, digging her talons into his flesh deep enough to send rivulets of blood down the front of his white shirt.

"See, emotions are your weakness."

"They're not *my* weakness, you thunder cunt," Derrick growled as he sent a dagger flying straight for faux Cora's exposed back.

Renata dropped Saiden and dove to the side, allowing the blade to sink into Saiden's gut.

"Derrick!" Saiden grunted, yanking the weapon out.

Derrick grimaced and mouthed, "Oops," as he drew another dagger.

They both whipped around to resume their attack on Renata only to find her...

Gone.

They all scanned the surrounding area, and Tressa opened her senses, searching for any sound as to where Renata disappeared to, but there was nothing.

"We need to get out of here before she returns," Saiden said, pressing his hand to the bleeding stomach wound. "I need to feed and let this heal."

"I'm good on food," Derrick said, "but my balls could use a break before we take her on again. That was not a love tap." He rubbed his crotch gingerly, and Tressa rolled her eyes. Her cousin would be fine in a minute, he just liked to whine.

"My Aston Martin is down the road since someone 'borrowed' my McLaren," Saiden told Tressa with a glare that didn't hold much sincere anger. "We'll head back over there, and I won't leave until I see you drive past. Don't take too long, though. We have no idea if she left or is just waiting."

"Got it," she told him, then took a step closer to examine the gashes on his neck. They were ugly, but not so bad that time and a couple blood bags wouldn't fix him up.

Derrick clapped her on the shoulder and gestured to Ethan. "You know how you're going to handle that?"

Tressa sighed. Every scenario she'd planned for telling Ethan went out the window when Renata had shown up. "Not really," she admitted.

He grinned. "Well, if you need to know what he's thinking, I could always—"

Tressa slammed a hand on Derrick's mouth. "I'm in enough trouble as is, so don't even think about using your Gift on him."

Derrick shrugged and peeled her hand away from his face. "Suit yourself. I offered."

He and Saiden started to walk away, and Tressa called out, "Hey guys?"

They glanced over their shoulders at her.

"Thanks," she told them. She spared a quick look at Ethan, then turned back to them. "I... We appreciate it."

Saiden studied Ethan who was resting against the car and rubbing his scalp where Renata had grabbed his hair. "That's what family is for. Now get him out of here before I regret saving your ass. Don't think I didn't notice the dents in my car." His voice was teasing when he mentioned the McLaren, but the order to get moving was still firm, so she nodded.

Her cousins blurred away, and she cautiously approached Ethan. The whole fight couldn't have taken more than a few minutes, but every one of those minutes was visible in the hard lines of his face.

She would have preferred fear or shock or anything else. The urge to reach for her ability tugged at her, reminding her that she could smooth the worst of it over with a little calming from her Gift, but she couldn't bring herself to use it. Not on her mate. Whatever happened, she wouldn't lie to him again.

"Ethan?" she said, taking another cautious step toward him and holding out her hand.

He stared at it blankly, then pushed away from the car. His eyes fixed on hers, analyzing. Contemplating.

Judging.

"Please say something," she whispered.

There was no love in his voice, no softness at all, when he said, "What do you want me to say, Tressa?"

She dropped her hand, accepting she might have lost the right to touch him ever again. "Anything. Please just talk to me. I'll answer all the questions you have. I'll explain everything. Just give me that chance. I swear I'm not a monster. I would never hurt you."

He cocked his head to the side, and for a brief moment, she thought he might be willing to hear her out. But that flash of possibility disappeared with a blink, his slate gray eyes filling with cold, calculating anger.

"She mentioned my research," he said after a long, bitter silence. "That's why you saved me in the hospital, isn't it? You weren't there to make sure I was safe or help me get revenge. Fuck, I should have known with all that good vampire bullshit you spewed. You say you're not a monster, but you're just like her. Manipulating me for whatever endgame you have. Lying to me. Hell, my research got Jake killed, and you let me believe it was a random vampire attack. You never cared about me at all, did you?"

"No," Tressa cried. She tried to take his hand, and her heart cracked when he yanked it away. "Ethan, that's not it. I *do* care about you. You have no idea how much I care about you."

He scoffed, then glanced toward the forest where Renata had disappeared. "I can't beat her, can I?"

Tressa heard the sorrow in his voice, felt the aura of a broken soul radiating off her mate. "No," she replied gently. "You can't. Definitely not as a human."

"A human," he said, his tense shoulder muscles the only view he was offering her. "You're implying there's another option."

"There is, Ethan," she pressed, sensing a possible opening. A chance to turn it all around. He just needed time to see the truth, and she could give him that time. "I can change you," she told him. "Make you like me. The good vampire rhetoric wasn't bullshit. I swear, most of us aren't killers. In fact, we specifically work to keep mortals safe."

He let out a sad laugh. "You were actually telling the truth about something? You really are a hunter?"

Tressa bit her lip. "Um, sort of? I mostly handle the aftermath rather than the actual fighting. But yes, our cadre's sole function is to protect humanity."

He nodded slowly and turned around, still refusing to look at her, his attention fixed just over her shoulder. There was no emotion in his face. No indicator of how he felt about her. Nothing but cold hard resolve.

"I want you to turn me," he said quietly, and her heart leapt into her throat despite his icy tone. "I want you to make me like you. I'll even tell Baylin everything about my research so he can figure out why that vampire wants me dead."

The sun emerged from behind a cloud, raining beams of bright light onto her mate's face, and it fueled the hope growing in Tressa's chest. If he was willing to work with them, then maybe... Maybe there was still the chance that they could be together. He would see how much she cared, and things might just work out.

But another cloud moved to block the sun again as Ethan's eyes snapped over to lock on hers. "Then I never want to see you again."

And all her hope shriveled up and died.

Chapter Thirty

Ethan

A vampire. The woman he'd been falling hard and fast for was a fucking *vampire*.

And soon, he would be one too. The rational part of his brain kept shouting at him to stop. To wait. To think it through. He was a man of science. He needed to create a hypothesis, run scenarios, and investigate every variable. A decision like this should take months if not years to properly analyze every angle. He would be giving up his entire life to become like them, and that was not a decision to be made lightly.

But then again, what kind of life did he even have anymore? He had no friends or family to mourn him if he vanished. No home to return to. Not even a job waiting for him.

As much as he felt the sting of betrayal from Tressa's lies, the more he took the time to think, the more he could admit the truth of what he'd seen over the past week. She and the others *weren't* actually monsters. They hadn't once hurt him. In fact, they'd laughed and joked together for days. Saiden helped him develop a strength training program that had him nearly back to normal after a week when the doctors told him it would take months or years. Not to mention Derrick had the kind of playful teasing that kept Ethan motivated long after his body wanted to quit. And he'd even spent time in the sun with them, so clearly they weren't entirely creatures of the night. Only an hour ago, he would have called them friends if anyone asked.

Then there was Tressa... For all her lies, he was at least willing to admit she'd never harmed him. Well, not his body anyway. His heart was a whole different story.

So as much as his brain said, "Hold the phone and think this through," the rest of him felt certain that time wouldn't change his decision. There were no downsides to becoming a vampire and only upsides—strength, speed, immortality.

Ok, maybe that last one wasn't accurate. His discussions with Tressa about how vampires functioned told him they could die just as easily as humans if the wound was severe enough. Vampire blood might keep every organ functioning in tip top shape with no decay, but if someone chopped off your head or shoved a chunk of wood in your heart, no amount of fast healing could fix that.

None of it mattered, though. He'd made his decision, and he was sticking with it. Even if he did still have a list of questions longer than his PhD dissertation.

He would have to wait on those, however, because he had zero desire to speak to the woman in the car next to him. Saiden or Derrick could help him. They could teach him everything he needed to know to function out in the world.

As long as they kept Tressa out of it because she was dead to him. She'd lied, manipulated his emotions, and made him feel things for her he hadn't even known he was capable of. In retrospect, he felt like a damn idiot. He should have seen who she was a mile away. Her strength. Her goddess-like beauty. And her eyes. From day one, he had seen something lingering in their depths, hidden behind her too-bright smile and quick wit. He had seen glimpses of the centuries of sorrow she tried to bury deep down.

Fuck, how old was she even?

No, he didn't care. Wouldn't ask.

Dead to me, he reminded himself. That's all she'd ever been. Dead. And just because he planned to sign up for that life—or unlife?—as well, didn't mean he would ever forgive her.

They pulled into the circular driveway, and Tressa put the car in park outside the front door.

Ethan stepped out and waited for her to do the same as he took in the compound with fresh eyes. The lack of large windows along with the notable presence of old-growth trees casting shadows everywhere suddenly made much more sense.

"So, how does this work?" he asked, folding his arms and leaning back against the car. They would have to go in sooner or later, but he wasn't quite ready to return to the mansion full of vampires. He knew about Saiden and Derrick, but what about everyone else? Was there even a single living soul in the building? Or had every person he encountered secretly been looking at him like a Door Dash meal delivered straight to them, hot and ready.

"How does what work?" Tressa asked cautiously as she took a spot at his side, mirroring his lean against the car.

He could see the hope in her eyes. Could see she wanted him to be asking about their future. About their relationship.

The relationship built on a crumbling foundation of lies.

"Becoming a vampire," he snapped, disregarding the tiny bit of guilt that flared when she flinched at the venom in his voice. "How do you turn me or whatever."

Tressa dropped her eyes and picked at her cuticles, making him want to scream at her to stop. He wanted her to stop acting so fucking innocent and hurt and... adorable. He wanted her outsides to match her insides—evil and duplicitous. He wanted her to admit that she never gave a single flying fuck about him.

He wanted... to believe his own thoughts without that hint of reservation that crept in when she looked up at him, those wide brown eyes so very full of heartbreak. He was the one who should be heartbroken. Not her. She didn't deserve to make him feel guilty when he was the one who had been lied to.

"It's... well..." she stammered for a second before finally pulling herself together. "It's not really that complicated. Every vampire has an essence inside of them. You might think of it as something like magic, I guess. It's what keeps us alive forever and grants us our Gift."

"Gift?" he asked stiffly, refusing to let her shy and demure act weaken his resolve.

"Yes," she replied quietly. "Every vampire is blessed with a unique ability. Something specific to them. We call it Lilith's Gift since Lilith bestowed the original Gift upon her daughter, Sura. The first vampire."

He nodded, briefly remembering their earlier conversation about the origins of vamps. He still didn't know that he believed all that angel/demon, heaven/hell nonsense, but if it meant he was going to get a superpower, then she could call it whatever she wanted. "Go on," he prodded.

"So, basically you have to lose a lot of blood first. Sort of an empty vessel kind of situation. Oftentimes a vampire will feed on the human they intend to turn, making it a beautiful moment of sharing lifeforces."

Panic raced down Ethan's spine, and he jerked his head around to glare at Tressa. "Don't you dare—"

"I won't," she said quickly, lifting a hand toward his face then dropping it back down to her side when he shifted away from her. "I know what you've been through, Ethan. I would never do that to you."

When he huffed his acknowledgement, she continued. "Once you're significantly weakened and on the brink of death, I'll share my essence with you. After that..."

She went back to picking at her cuticles, and it was only then he realized how perfect her fingernails were despite the constant damage she inflicted.

Fast healing, he reminded himself. Another clue he'd been oblivious to simply because she had a pretty face and a laugh that lit up his idiotic heart like fireworks on New Year's Eve.

"What?" he demanded, sensing there was more to it than a little magical mojo exchange.

Tucking her hands in her skirt pockets, she sighed. "After that, you die."

He massaged his temples, wondering if vampires still got headaches. "Why do I have the feeling it's not that simple?"

She shrugged. "If you think about it, dying is about as simple as it gets. One moment you're alive, and the next you're dead. Then the essence brings you back as a vampire."

"So how exactly do I die?"

She shrugged again, and the simple action grated on his nerves. He absolutely didn't want to deal with the perky princess, but this reserved creature who kept glancing at him with sad eyes when she thought he wasn't looking was somehow worse.

"How do you want to die?" she asked. "Not many people get to choose how they go. Usually, it's either a last second decision when a human has suffered a fatal wound and faces their forever death, or it's a mutually agreed upon feed and turn between a vampire and their—"

He cocked an eyebrow when she cut herself off. "Still keeping secrets, Loloma?"

She spun her head around so fast he thought he heard something pop. "Don't," she barked, her eyes blazing with a mixture of anger and... shame? It was the first time she'd used a harsh tone with him, and he almost felt bad about saying the name that clearly bothered her. "Don't ever call me that. That girl died a long time ago."

"Fine," he spat back. "Whatever. It's not like I give a shit anymore. Keep all the secrets you want. It's what you do best, isn't it?"

"I'm not trying to keep things from you, Ethan," she protested, the anger in her voice fading back to that soft, kicked puppy tone. "There are just certain things about being a vampire that are a longer discussion. If you would take a second and sit down with me, we can go over this in detail. Maybe we could—"

"Stop," he said, holding up a hand. "I'm not interested. Let's just get this over with. Kill me however you want. Just make it quick and painless."

His analytical brain screamed at him once more to listen to her. To take the time to discuss every aspect before he made what might arguably be the biggest mistake of his life.

Except that was exactly why he was in a hurry. He didn't want to think about it. Didn't want to *overthink* it. His whole life was based on rationality, and look where that got him? Broken and alone.

He was done being rational. It might take him dying, but he was finally ready to live.

Chapter Thirty-One

Tressa

Since meeting Ethan, all Tressa wanted was to turn him into a vampire. It was the driving force behind everything she said and every move she made.

She just hadn't realized how traumatic it would be to actually watch him die.

She should have let one of the others take his life. Somebody else should have sat with him as his blood slowly drained out of his body and into the bags that would save it for later. Somebody else should have endured his painful silence and cold shoulder. Somebody else should have been surrounded by his intoxicating smell as his eyes sluggishly opened and closed, becoming glassy and unfocused.

So yeah, maybe it was a little masochistic for her to refuse help, since any one of the cadre could have at least stayed with him until he was almost gone, but she hadn't been able to bring herself to ask. He was her mate, whether he wanted it or not, and it was her duty to see him through the turn. No matter how much it hurt.

Plus, it had to be her essence that initially changed him. If there was one rule you didn't break, it was the 'vampires are only allowed to turn one human' rule. And never against their will.

At least she didn't have to worry about any fallout from the higher ups. She'd seen what happened to Saiden when he ended up on the Ruling Coalition's radar for changing Cora without her consent. Avoiding that was possibly the only silver lining to the entire fucked up situation.

But it didn't matter how willing Ethan was. It still killed her soul to inject the poison into his veins.

The minutes after that had been the longest of her life, watching as the cloud of violet smoke emerged from her body and entered Ethan's. It should have been a beautiful moment—the connection that was being solidified, like she was sharing a piece of her soul with him. Instead, he had barely allowed her to place a hand on his, the smallest amount of skin contact possible, turning their life-altering moment into something cold and clinical.

She would never forget the look in his eyes—the sheer amount of betrayal and hatred lingering in those stony gray depths. He died still looking at her like that.

And Tressa hadn't even been able to hold him through it.

Tressa dropped into the chair beside Baylin, beyond worn out from the last eight hours of maintaining contact with Ethan while her essence leaked out of her and into him. It wasn't until he was mostly transformed that she could take a break and let Saiden take over turning duty. As long as the majority of the essence used to transform him came from her, that was all that mattered. Saiden could share a slow leak to keep the transition working while she took a break.

She should have slept, but every time she closed her eyes, she saw Ethan staring at her. Accusing her.

No, sleep wouldn't be in her future for a while.

So even though it was very late at night, or possibly very early in the morning, she had trudged over to Baylin's room for an update.

Her cousin pushed back in his chair and propped his feet up on the long table that held his bank of monitors. "It's like 2 a.m., Tress. You could have knocked. What if I was sleeping? Or had a girl in here?"

Tressa let out a mirthless laugh. "Baylin, when was the last time you had a girl anywhere?"

His right eye twitched. Subtle, but she caught it. Before she could probe him about a love life that apparently did exist, he said, "I take it you're here to check on the status of Renata?"

"Yeah," she replied, placing her feet on the table next to Baylin's. "Ethan's still out, but Saiden offered to take over. It's almost time to hook him up to the IV and return his blood, but I don't exactly need to be there for that."

Baylin nodded, giving her a sympathetic look. "I wish I had good news to offer, but I got nothing. I don't know how Renata does it, but she's managed to avoid every camera possible. I hate to say it, but I have no idea where she is."

Tressa slid farther down in the chair and let her head roll back. Her eyes landed on a spider crawling across the tile ceiling, and she simply watched it for a moment, envious of its simple life. Maybe the rogues had the right idea about eternity. Shake off those pesky notions about humanity and focus on the basics.

Hunt. Kill. Feed.

Forever was a long time to drown in your emotions.

Rubbing at her tired eyes, she dismissed that unsettling thought. No matter what happened with Ethan, she was still her. Still Tressa. And she didn't give up that easily, regardless of what that rogue bitch seemed to think.

"What about Ethan's research?" she asked. "Have you had any luck on figuring out why it's such a danger to us?"

Baylin shook his head, then reached under his desk for a water bottle covered in overlapping stickers of metal band logos.

Tressa stared blankly as he took a long pull from it, unable to remember the last time her cousin drank anything that wasn't chock-full of either hemoglobin or a tragic amount of caffeine. Then her nose registered the scent, and she glared at him.

"I still haven't cracked their firewall," he said after a few more deep gulps, ignoring the pointed look she gave him. "Until Ethan wakes up and decides to share, I got nothing. I've researched the history of the company, the other scientists who died in the fire, and even Ethan himself. I can't find any ties to the vampire community that might explain it."

Tressa groaned and pushed off the table to slide her chair over to the silver cooler next to Baylin's couch. "I guess I can't be shocked that nothing is going well." She pulled out a chilled blood bag and stared at it for a second. "You know, I teased Saiden constantly about his messy courtship of Cora, but at this point, I would trade places in a heartbeat."

She released her tiny fangs but couldn't bring herself to puncture the bag. Gently rocking her upturned palm, she felt the weight of the blood swishing back and forth, back and forth, like a sanguine metronome. With each alternating slosh, she felt more like she didn't deserve to replenish her strength. She deserved to suffer.

Retracting her fangs, she tossed the bag back into the cooler and turned to her cousin. "I don't know if he's ever going to forgive me, Bay."

Her cousin dropped his feet to the ground, then reached over to grab her chair. He dragged her back to him and placed his hands on her thighs, his face deadly serious for possibly only the second time ever. "Tress, you know I love you," he said solemnly. "From now till the end of time, you're my family. But for fuck's sake, would you please stop acting like you didn't see this coming the moment you told him that first lie? You had to know this was all going to come crashing down sooner or later."

Tressa cringed and scooted away from her cousin. But no matter how much distance she put between them, Baylin wasn't wrong. He was rarely wrong. Even if nobody wanted to hear it.

She ran a hand through her hair. "I guess I just saw how things worked out for Saiden, and..." She let out a pathetic laugh. "I guess I thought somehow, because he was my mate, it would be the same for me."

Baylin gave her another sympathetic look, and Tressa wished he would go back to cracking jokes. "Don't write him off just yet, Tress. Forever is a very long time to hate someone."

She shook her head. "You didn't see the look in his eyes. He's going to leave, Bay. He said he wanted to help with this rogue hunt, but he told me he never wants to see me again after that. How can I change his mind if he disappears?"

"I won't let that happen," Baylin assured her, tapping on his monitor. "If he needs a wee bit of time after all this, I'll keep an eye on him. Let him cool off for, I don't know, a few decades or so. Eventually he'll calm down."

"Decades?" Tressa sputtered. "Bay, I can barely handle being on the other side of the compound from him. Saiden said it took over a month before he could bring himself to leave Cora behind to go out on a hunt. You think I'm going to survive if he leaves the city? Or worse, the state?"

Baylin groaned, scrubbed at his face, then took another massive swig from his water bottle. "Feck, I wish Raven was here," he muttered. "She's so much better at this whole consoling thing than I am. Look, Tress, I might not have any pretty words, so I'll just be blunt. You fucked up. You lied to him. I get that it was a shite situation, but you still sent it arseways. It's time to cop on and learn to live with the consequences."

Tressa blinked at him. "And now I wish Raven was here too."

"Oh, feck off, *cailín*."

Baylin took another slug from his bottle, and Tressa stared daggers at him. "Bay, what the hell do you think you're doing with that?"

He turned away from her. "It's a water bottle, Tress."

"Doesn't mean there's water in it. My heart is broken, not my sense of smell. And I know you only get that thick brogue when you're drunk, so spill. What happened before I came in here that has you drinking all of a sudden, and why are you trying to hide it?"

He flipped her off, but there was no anger when he said, "Don't worry about me, sweetheart. You got your own issues to deal with. Now if you're not feeling knackered, you should get back to your boyo. Or go literally anywhere that isn't my room. I swear I'm gonna get a feckin keypad for my door so all you shites can't just be barging in."

She debated pushing him but quickly accepted it would be an exercise in futility. Much like his computers, Baylin kept his secrets locked up tight. Tressa hopped out of the chair, then bent down to kiss him on the cheek. "You love us, and you know it. Now stop drinking and maybe get some sleep yourself. Don't make me worry about you too, Bay."

He waved a hand at her to leave, and she did. But not before snatching the bottle from his hand. He made a grab for it, but she danced out of his range and took a deeper sniff.

She'd been right. Whiskey. Probably Bushmills, knowing her cousin.

Disgusting, but given the circumstances, she chugged what was left in the bottle. Her vamp system would burn through it in about five minutes, but that was five minutes that she could stop worrying about Ethan lying dead in the other room.

She needed him to wake up soon. The post transition was never easy, and she wouldn't abandon him for that. No matter how much he hated her, she would never abandon him.

Chapter Thirty-Two

Ethan

He was alone.

He had been nothing. Gone. And when he was Ethan again, he was alone.

It was eerie, how dark the building was at night.

Was it even night? There were no windows in his basement lab, but somehow it felt late. It felt gloomy and ominous. It felt like the time when wicked things claimed ownership of the world, moving through the shadows to steal the lives of any who dared intrude during these unholy hours.

The shadows owned this moment, so the shadows were all he saw.

Except...

There. A red light blinked on a monitor. The only light in the room. Dim at first, and then brighter, his surroundings flashing between the pure darkness of a void and the eerie red glow that showed the walls dripping with blood.

His heart thumped in time with that flashing light.

Thump. Flash. Shadows.

Thump. Flash. Bloody room.

Thump. Flash. Something moving in those shadows.

Thump. Flash. Blood hitting the floor with a drip, drip, drip.

Why was there so much blood?

It oozed from the computers.

It leaked from the lab equipment.

And it trickled from the corner of his lips.

He tried to spit it out, but more filled his mouth the moment he did. Not overwhelming, not choking, just a steady drip of blood sliding down his chin and spilling onto his white lab coat, the crimson stain spreading across his chest.

This wasn't happening. His lab shouldn't be covered in blood. He rushed over to the mass spectrometer, trying desperately to find the source, but the blood came from inside the machine, leaking out of every aperture and orifice in the equipment.

"No," he muttered. "This is wrong. This is all wrong."

"Or is it so perfectly right?" a female voice hissed, the words floating over his shoulder and sliding into his ears like an unwelcome intrusion.

He whirled around, but there was no one there. Only the steady blink of bloody light and menacing shadows.

He glanced down at his wet hands. So much blood. It was everywhere. On everything. And no matter how hard he tried to wipe his hands clean, the blood wouldn't leave. It stained his skin. His clothes.

His soul.

"Light," he mumbled. "I need to find a light."

"No light for you, little moonflower," the voice replied in a taunting tone.

He spun around again.

Nobody there. Just a shadow.

He ran for the door, desperate to escape the bloody lab and the horrific red light.

He grabbed the handle and tugged. Jerked. Yanked. Slammed his foot on the door and pulled with all his might.

It wouldn't budge. There wasn't even a bolt or latch to unlock it. He was stuck inside.

Find a key, he thought, glancing around.

Nothing. No keys. Only blood and shadow.

Try again. Pull harder. Do whatever it takes.

He reached for the doorknob once more, but it was gone. No knob. No lock.

No door.

"No escape," the voice came again, crawling into his brain.

Ethan screamed as he pounded on the space where the door had been only moments before. Just a smooth expanse of wall, as if no exit had ever existed.

"Let me out," he shouted as he backed away from the missing door and bumped into a shelf of test tubes and petri dishes. "I want to go home."

He grabbed the neck of a nearby beaker and smashed its base on the edge of a worktable. He held so tight to his improvised weapon, he feared it might fully shatter in his grip.

The voice chuckled softly. "But Ethan, you're already—"

He didn't hesitate that time. When the voice started speaking, he whipped around. "I will fucking end you!" he screamed as he plunged the broken glass into the chest of the vampire.

"—home." She grinned at him, blood spilling from her mouth in a thick crimson waterfall.

And then she started to change.

Flash of red. Her nose straightened.

Flash of red. Her eyes lightened.

Flash of red. Her skin darkened.

Flash. Flash. Flash. Change. Change. Change.

Until Tressa stood before him, staring down at the glass jutting out from her chest.

"No," he whispered, rushing forward to catch her. "I didn't mean—"

"It's okay," she whispered, lifting a hand to brush back the hair dangling in front of his face. "Everything... is going to be... okay."

Then she died in his arms.

Chapter Thirty-Three

Tressa

"I want to go home," Ethan shouted, and Tressa jumped up from the chair she'd been sitting in for the past couple hours, holding Ethan's hand and waiting desperately for him to come back to her.

She'd learned her lesson from Cora's transition. They had the lights dimmed, and the entire wing of the compound was empty save for whoever was with him.

"No noise, no light, and for Lilith's sake, remember that he is going to be disoriented at first," Eliana had instructed her.

Tressa grabbed for the ear plugs on the nightstand, nearly knocking over a vase of sunflowers in her hurry to get them into Ethan's ears. If he was talking, that meant he was waking up and would need them to muffle his new hyper acute vampiric hearing.

His eyes were still closed, but he thrashed and screamed.

"Ethan," she whispered, trying not to overwhelm his newly heightened senses. "Ethan, it's Tressa. You're going to be—"

Ethan bolted upright in bed and grabbed the heavy crystal vase from the nightstand. Before Tressa realized what was happening, he smashed it on the table and screamed, "I will fucking end you!"

Then he plunged the jagged shards deep into her heart.

Agony tore through Tressa, and she stumbled away from the bed. When her back hit the wall behind her, she stared down at the glass protruding from her chest, blood flowing down its fine etchings. She could feel her heartbeat growing weaker as it struggled to pump around the foreign object embedded in it. Slowly, she dragged her head up, searching for her mate.

His eyes were still vacant, like he was looking but not truly seeing. He stepped forward. "No," he whispered, rushing toward her. "I didn't mean..."

Her legs gave out, and she slumped against the wall, fingers fumbling on the blood-slicked hunk of glass. All the oxygen seemed to vanish from the room, and she struggled to breathe. Struggled to think.

It was a bad idea. She lived long enough to know it was the worst possible thing you could do. But she didn't care. She finally found purchase on the vase and yanked it from her chest. If she was going to die, she was going to do it in her mate's arms with nothing between them.

She looked up at him, saw his glassy eyes running over her body. Was he even with her? Or was he still trapped in the hell of the transition?

He wrapped his arms around her and pulled her in tight, clutching her to his chest.

"It's okay," she whispered. She knew he would blame himself. Knew there was nothing she could do about that. Her mate was a kind soul at the heart of things. "Everything... is going to be... okay." Her head lolled limply to the side, and she struggled to open her eyes. To see him one last time.

"Tressa?" Ethan said quietly, and she could hear the clarity in his voice, even if it sounded like it was so far away. "Tressa, wake up."

He was really there. He was with her.

Ethan.

Her mate.

It wasn't going to be easy for him, but her cousins would help. He would be okay. Her mate was strong, and he would recover.

All she could do was hope that he didn't suffer too much. She opened her mouth one last time to tell him she loved him, but her heart gave its final pump before she could get a single word out.

And then... darkness.

Chapter Thirty-Four

Ethan

The lab dissolved around Ethan, fading into the recesses of his mind like a movie transition.

He blinked rapidly, his eyes flicking to the ceiling, then to the floor, and then darting around the room. Everything was dark yet vibrant at the same time. The individual fibers in the carpet stood out to him, and the texture on the walls was much more visible than before, like a tiny, crater-filled landscape. A coppery tang still filled his nose, and his eyes snapped from object to object, trying to make sense of where the blood had gone. But as he scanned the space that was both familiar and foreign, he couldn't find so much as a drop.

Slowly, it came back to him. The compound. This room. He knew this room. He wasn't in the lab. The blood wasn't real. And Tressa wasn't...

His eyes finally cleared, landing on the one thing he suddenly wanted to see so very badly—Tressa's face.

"Tressa?" he said, gently shaking the sleeping woman in his arms. "Tressa, wake up."

She didn't move.

A slow soft thud caught his attention, echoing in his ears and growing fainter with every beat. He locked onto it, as if the noise might explain what was happening.

That sound was familiar, and there was another one chasing it. Faster. So fast it *pounded*. But the softer thud only faded, faded, faded...

Until it pulsed no more.

Heartbeat, his brain finally supplied, and the reality in front of him was suddenly much worse than any nightmare.

"Tressa!" he screamed, shaking her to wake her up. But she didn't move. He pulled back and stared at the horrific wound in her chest, at the blood that leaked out slowly. So very slowly.

Pain flared in his mouth, a deep ache in his gums, something sharp breaking through at the delicious scent of the blood. Her blood. Like copper and bubblegum. So wrong and yet he wanted to taste it. Wanted to lap it up like ambrosia.

But Tressa wouldn't wake up, and the fear coiling around his heart was far more pressing than the intoxicating blood now coating his fingers.

"Somebody help me!" he screamed again, but the terrified hammering of his own heart was the only answering call to his frantic plea.

"No, no, no," he said, lowering her to the floor and placing his hand over the gaping hole in her chest. "Come on baby, you're a vampire. You can heal this, right? Right?!" Tears rushed down his face, and every awful thing he'd said to her raced through his head.

"You say you're not a monster, but you're just like her."

"It's not like I give a shit anymore."

"I never want to see you again."

He pressed harder on the wound in her chest as he peppered kisses along her slack face and lifeless lips.

There should be a tingle. There was always a tingle when they touched. But now there was nothing.

"No, please God, no." He'd never believed in a higher power, but he knew Tressa had mentioned the whole Adam and Eve thing, so he would pray to whoever he needed to if they saved her. "Tressa, baby, I need you to say something. Tease me about the rose on my ass. Call me a silly name. Please, I need you. I'm so sorry. I didn't mean it. I can't do this without you."

"I never want to see you again."

Cold. She was so cold. She'd never been cold before. He'd always read in stories that vampires were supposed to be icy and pale, but that wasn't his goddess. Not his perfect Sunflower. She was warmth and light, even when his darkness was so strong.

She couldn't be gone.

"I never want to see you again."

"No," he stated firmly. "I'm not losing you, Tressa. I've lost everyone in my life, but not you."

He laid her down and began pumping her chest, doing his best to administer CPR. He felt as much as heard a sharp cracking noise, and a wail erupted from his lungs.

He kept going, though, because some logical voice in the back of his brain calmly reminded him that you weren't doing it right if you didn't break a rib.

So he pumped.

And pumped.

And screamed for help.

Nothing happened. The blood squelched through his fingers with each compression, but she didn't move. Didn't wake up.

"I never want to see you again."

"Damn it, Tressa! You are not leaving me alone," he growled, increasing his efforts.

"Wake."

Thrust.

"The fuck."

Thrust.

"UP!"

Throwing his head back, he howled his anguish to the heavens, then slammed his hands down on her chest.

Specks of violet light erupted from his fingers, swirling in a glowing mist before sinking into Tressa's body.

Transfixed by the tiny sparkles that flowed out of him in a thin gentle stream, Ethan resisted the urge to yank his hands away. He didn't know what was happening, but maybe, just maybe...

They hadn't had this conversation. Hadn't gone over the details of all the different things that vampires could do. Later. He'd said he wanted to discuss everything later. He'd fucked up.

In so many ways.

"I never want to see you again."

"Come on, baby," he whispered, keeping his glowing hands pressed to her chest. "Come back to me."

Her fingers that lay limp against his leg twitched slightly, but that was nothing compared to what he heard.

A thump. A single resonant thump.

And then another.

Hope soared in Ethan.

"That's it, Tressa," he said, pushing even harder against her chest, as if he could force that violet light into her faster. "I need you to wake up, Sunflower."

Her eyelids fluttered. "Ethan..." she mumbled, her sweet voice weak and so very quiet. He didn't know how he heard it, but he did. And it was all he ever wanted to hear for the rest of his life.

"I never want to see you again."

Fuck that shit, he snarled inside his own mind. She was going to wake up, and he was going to show her just how glad he was to see her again.

"That's it, baby," he pleaded. "Open your eyes. Please, Tressa. Open your eyes for me."

Her lids twitched again, then slowly—so achingly slow it felt like time stopped for a moment—her eyes opened.

"Ethan?" she asked, confusion lacing her words as she scanned his face.

"Welcome back," he whispered.

The purple glow receded into his hands, and Tressa glanced down, astonishment lighting her face as she watched it dissipate.

"You scared me," he said. "I thought... I thought you were..."

"I was," she said weakly, her head lolling backward until Ethan snaked his hand around to support it.

He pulled her in close. "Shhh. You're okay. You're with me. Everything is going to be okay."

Tressa blinked a few more times, then pressed on his chest hard enough for him to relax his grip so she could push up to a seated position.

Ethan didn't completely release his hold on her, though. He needed to feel the warmth that was slowly seeping back into her skin. Needed to be surrounded by that bubblegum scent. It blended with something else, something vanilla that he thought might be coming from himself, and together, it was the sweetest aroma he had ever encountered. Like the grocery store ice cream they'd shared only exponentially better.

His eyes drifted over Tressa's face and down her body to the massive red stain that coated her pink satin tank top. He knew in that moment that no nightmare could ever be more terrifying than the memory of watching her die in his arms.

He'd been so awful to her. Acted like such a fucking asshole. Of course she wouldn't admit to being a vampire after he'd just gone through an attack. He never would have trusted her to help him if she had confessed from the beginning. She'd been in an impossible situation, and when he found out the truth, he had only thought about himself. His anger. His betrayal. The logic he relied so heavily on never seemed to show up when it came to her. It always took a backseat to the anger he felt at the utter unfairness of the world.

But it wasn't as strong anymore. The rage inside him. The need for revenge. He still wanted to end that vamp and make her pay for Jake's murder, but the anger was... less. He could see clearly again. Rationally. Tressa had been trying to protect him. Help him when he'd given her no reason to. And he turned on her like a rabid dog.

"What's going through your head, Ethan?" Tressa asked, her voice sounding stronger. More present.

"I'm so sorry," he whispered. "For everything. I don't know why I was filled with so much hatred."

"It's okay," she said, brushing a sweaty bit of hair off his face.

"No, it's not," he protested. "I stabbed you, Tressa. I almost... You almost..." A tear slipped down his cheek, and Tressa took his face in her hands, her thumb tenderly swiping away the bit of moisture.

"Ethan, look at me," she said calmly. "Am I dead?"

He opened his mouth to say "No," but then he remembered the whole vampire thing. "Um... technically yes, I think? I'm a little fuzzy on that."

Tressa burst out laughing, and it relaxed something inside Ethan. Like a Pavlovian response to her joy, the thorny vines of fear, regret, and self loathing that had been wound tightly through every muscle in his body loosened their grip and fell away. Ethan wanted nothing more than to spend an eternity drawing that glorious sound from her over and over again.

"Okay, you got me there," she said when her laughter subsided. "But I'm breathing. And my heart is beating. And I'm looking at you like you're the most incredible thing in the world. I wish you could see it, Ethan." She ran her hands up through his hair, down his neck, and across his shoulders, her eyes taking in every inch of him. "You're magnificent."

He blushed. "Yeah, a magnificent fuck up. The first thing I did as a vampire was try to murder you. It's a good thing we have these nifty healing powers. I had no idea I could bring you back from the brink of death."

"About that," Tressa said, scooting back to prop herself up against the wall. "That's not normal, Ethan."

He blinked. "Come again?"

She ran her hand over the gash in her tank top, her fingers grazing over the smooth bronze skin. "I can't do what you did. None of us can. The closest you get is Cora who has accelerated healing even by vampire standards, but she still can't use it on another person." Tressa paused, a smile breaking out over her face. "It must be your Gift."

"Oh. Interesting."

He hadn't given any thought to what superpower he wanted when she mentioned the whole Lilith's Gift thing, but... healing was pretty cool, right? He chuckled softly to himself. Of course it was. He'd be weeping over Tressa's corpse if it wasn't for his Gift.

"Thank you" he whispered to the ceiling, even though that single phrase would never come close to how grateful he felt that Tressa was alive.

Or unalive. He really needed to have that conversation.

"You're thanking the wrong entity," Tressa said with an amused twinkle in her eyes. "But we'll go over that. I'll go over everything with you. No more secrets. Ever. That is, if you'll let me help you."

"Of course, I'll let you," he said, pulling her back into his arms. "I told you, I'm so sorry for what I said. I reacted harshly. But never again. I'm here with you, Tressa. Until you get bored of me."

She wrapped her arms around his neck. "I don't think I'll ever get bored of you, Ethan. You definitely keep me on my toes."

He kissed her then, his tongue tentatively prodding at her lips for entry, which she promptly granted him. "Fuck," he moaned when he finally pulled back. "How do you taste even better now?"

She grinned. "That's all part of being a vampire. We'll get to that."

"I look forward to it," he said solemnly, before a wicked smirk curled up the corner of his lip. "But in the meantime, I think I'd like to just take a second to enjoy."

He dragged her back in for another kiss. A longer one. A deeper one. His tongue swept into her mouth, tasting just a hint of copper at the corner of her lips, but mostly his senses were suffused with bubblegum and vanilla. He was pretty sure he had just ruined his favorite desert forever, because nothing, not even that amazing stuff Tressa introduced him to, would ever taste a fraction as good as her now that his vampire senses could pick up every nuance of her scent.

Right on cue, as if the near death of his woman never happened, his cock responded to the feel of her in his arms, growing hard in seconds. She always affected him strongly, but he didn't know if he'd ever gone from flaccid to firm quite so fast before. Was that a vampire perk? Super cock?

He jerked away from Tressa and ran a hand through his hair, willing his nether regions to take a chill pill.

"What's wrong?" Tressa asked, leaning back in to nuzzle her nose along his neck.

He allowed himself to enjoy her touch for a minute, then took her by the shoulders and pressed her back gently. He couldn't think straight when her skin was touching his. "I'm sorry, but you taste too good, and I'm not..."

She quirked an eyebrow. "Not what?"

He groaned and not-so-subtly adjusted himself. "I'm not sure I can stop myself from fucking you like a wild animal. Your scent is everywhere, Tressa, and my whole body craves you like a drug."

She settled her thighs on either side of his hips and grinned. "So where's the bad?" she asked.

"You just came back from the dead!" he protested, his hands landing on her hips because he couldn't bring himself to push her away again. "I can't be rutting into you like a damn animal."

"Ethan," Tressa purred as she sank deeper into his lap and wrapped her legs around his waist. "Your Gift is all new territory for me, but it must be pretty damn powerful because I feel fine. In fact... I think I would like a little rutting. Might be just what the doctor ordered."

He arched an eyebrow. "You think so?"

She grinned. "Oh yeah. I would very much like you to fuck me right here, right now. Come on, Dr. Rose, let's take your new vamp body for a test drive."

"Hell yes," he panted, not even registering the silly nickname because everything in his head went blank after 'fuck me.'

He jumped to his feet and hauled her up to his chest, kissing her passionately. She was a slice of paradise in his arms, and she was all his. Not even the sticky red substance coating her skin was a turn off. If he was being honest, it was kind of the opposite...

He ran his hand through the blood on her chest, drawing a red streak across one luscious breast. He held the finger up, then looked over to Tress.

"Is this... Should I..."

"Vampire blood isn't as delicious as human, and it won't do much for you in terms of keeping you running," she explained, "but think of it like decaf coffee. Your body doesn't get any benefit, but the smell might make you crave it anyway." When he continued to eye the red smear on his pointer finger, she added, "You're welcome to try it. If you want."

Ethan lapped up the trace of blood. It wasn't exactly ambrosia, but he could see the appeal. He let the taste linger a bit, and the allure grew stronger.

As he worked his tongue around his mouth to further evaluate this very new experience, it grazed over the sharp fangs that had emerged from underneath his gums.

Fangs. He had fangs now.

And so did Tressa, who was looking at him like she wanted to eat him alive.

He ran a hand over his neck, lingering on the puckered flesh. While he no longer needed his glasses since his eyesight was sharper than humanly possible, the reminder of his attack was still carved into his body, sparking that flash of unease in the pit of his stomach. So much for vamp powers healing *everything*.

"I'm not quite sure yet," he told her. "About the biting."

Tressa pressed a kiss to his scar, lightly dragging her tongue over the damaged skin. "I will never bite you, Ethan. Not unless you ask. I promise."

He stared into her eyes and saw only honesty in them. Honesty and something else. Something deep and reassuring. Something he wanted to explore.

Later. When his cock wasn't about to explode in his pants.

"I trust you," he said to Tressa as he tossed her on the bed, appreciating the way her tits bounced when she landed. He took a step toward her, then flinched when he found himself leaning over her face.

"Oh shit," he said, glancing back to where he'd been across the room.

"You're faster now," Tressa explained. "And stronger."

He bent down and kissed her. "This is incredible," he breathed out. "Fuck, the things I'm going to do you."

Tressa laughed, but before Ethan could say another word, he found himself flipped on his back with Tressa straddling him. "You're forgetting one thing, Doc. As fast and strong as you are"—she brushed her lips over his ear, her voice turning low and sultry—"I'll always be faster and stronger."

Ethan laughed, but it quickly turned into a moan when she wiggled on his dick.

"Fuck, Tressa. In that case, ride me like a vampire."

Giving him a wicked smile, she grabbed Ethan's shirt and ripped it open. "I thought you'd never ask."

When she reached for his pants, Ethan stopped her. "These are actually ones I borrowed from Saiden."

She rolled her eyes. "Like he'll miss one out of the thousand pairs of basic black joggers he owns, but fine." She crawled backward to the foot of the bed, dragging his pants and boxers with her.

His cock sprang free, the hard length slapping against his stomach as he stared down at the goddess looking up at him. She was even more beautiful with his vampiric sight, her inner light shining through and practically making her skin glow. He could see all the unique colors swirling in her eyes. They weren't simply brown. They were a thousand different hues of amber and gold blending into a rich shade of chestnut with white and tan specks scattered around the outer edges.

They were incredible.

She was incredible.

And she was *his*.

"Strip," he ordered her. "I don't want to see anything but you right now."

She grinned and slowly pushed her skirt off her hips before tugging her stained, ripped tank top over her head.

His whole body tightened at the sight of her back arching, those deliciously full breasts straining for release. She locked eyes with him as her fingers teased down the shoulder straps and across the lace edges of her flower print bra. He couldn't decide where to look, his eyes darting back and forth between her sinfully smoldering gaze and the promised treasure hidden in a field of daisies.

In a swift, decisive motion, Tressa unhooked the front clasp and pulled the cups apart, her exquisite breasts finally bouncing free. Ethan's entire body twitched, and his cock bucked into the air as if dancing in approval.

A ragged, near feral moan bubbled up from his chest. "Damn, Tressa, you're going to kill me."

"Then it's a good thing you're already dead," she said, before giggling and adding, "sort of."

She slipped her panties off and stood in front of him, gloriously, perfectly naked.

And wet.

Fuck, he could *smell* her arousal. He could actually scent the sweet liquid between her legs, and when he palmed his cock and rubbed it a few times, the aroma only grew stronger.

"Get over here," he growled, and she smiled before slowly crawling back up his body, grazing her nails firmly along the inside of his thighs as she did.

He groaned at the sensation, at the way his skin lit up, like lightning striking everywhere she touched. Was it a vampire thing? Or a Tressa thing?

A tiny voice in the back of his head whispered that it was her and only her, but all thoughts vanished the moment she took his dick into her warm mouth.

His hips jerked at the unexpected sensation, and he practically choked her on his cock when it hit the back of her throat.

"Shit, I'm sorry, baby," he said, forcing himself to lie still. A herculean feat given the way her tongue swirled up and down the length of him.

She pulled her lips away and smiled. "I'm a vampire, Ethan. I can take it. I can take anything you want to give me."

"Oh, God," he moaned.

"Again, wrong person," she teased. "But we'll talk about that later."

She took him back into her mouth, and he about came from the softness of her tongue and lips caressing his cock. He reached down and tugged on her arms, drawing her away from his leaking dick.

"That feels too good," he explained when she gave him a concerned look. "And fuck if I'm going to blow my first load as a vampire in that perfect mouth. I need to be inside you, Tressa. I need to feel you clenching around me."

She ran her tongue along her lips and positioned herself over his cock, lining him up with her entrance.

"My pleasure," she purred, then sank to the hilt on his dick.

Chapter Thirty-Five

Tressa

It was worth it. Everything they'd been through. Every moment of despair she felt at thinking she was going to lose her mate. Every bit of pain she'd endured when he stabbed her. Even the horrific experience of dying a second time.

All. Fucking. Worth it.

He filled her so perfectly, as if they were made to fit together like puzzle pieces. And maybe they were. Maybe that's what a mate was. The other half of her soul. Her perfect match. The only man she could ever love enough that she would want to spend eternity with him.

She rolled her hips and nearly went cross-eyed. Oh yeah. She could get used to riding this cock for the next thousand years. She wanted to ride it forever.

"Forever is a very long time."

Baylin's words echoed briefly in her head, but instead of sadness, she only felt reassurance at them. Forever. She had forever with Ethan.

It should have slowed her down. Should have made her want to savor every minute of fucking Ethan for the first time. But it had the opposite effect. She wanted to ride him straight into forever at a furious gallop until he erupted inside her. She wanted him to feel what it was like to fuck a vampire. She wanted to show him just what an eternity together could mean.

She picked up her pace, bouncing up and down on his cock, taking him deep inside. His hand landed on her hips, trying to control her pace, but she wasn't having any of that.

He was the newbie. And she was going to teach him everything she could.

Grabbing his hands, she pinned them to his sides and rolled her hips in a circular motion, his cock hitting that perfect angle inside her that set every nerve aflame. They had just begun, but already she could feel a scream building up, clawing for release.

"Fuck, Tressa," Ethan moaned as his hips matched her pace, meeting her thrust for thrust.

"You have no idea," she said, smirking. "I've been alive for a long time. The things I'm going to teach you." She raked her nails down his chest, shivering with pleasure that she didn't have to hold back. The light grooves barely broke the skin, healing between one heartbeat and the next. And the way Ethan moaned at the sensation... Her mate apparently had a little pain kink. Something she was more than ready to explore.

Her fangs started to emerge, demanding that she sink them into her mate and taste him, but she forced them back under her gums.

Maybe one day Ethan would be ready for that, but not for a long time. Not until years after the last nightmare ended would she bring that up again.

She only ever wanted him to feel pleasure.

Bracing her hands behind her, she arched her body and let her head fall back, relishing the deeper position. One Ethan clearly enjoyed as well since the groan he let out stoked the flames building inside her to a fever pitch.

Faster and faster she rode him, her pussy wet and dripping to the point he slipped in and out with ease.

As the pressure grew higher, she flung herself back up to lay forward on his chest. She brought Ethan's mouth to hers, nipping lightly at his bottom lip before kissing him, and the feeling of his hand sliding down to rub against her clit broke her.

The scream that exploded from her when the orgasm hit was so loud she could only imagine she was pushing the room's soundproofing past its limit. Not that she cared. She wasn't in the compound anymore. She was in some alternate universe where she was fucking her mate into oblivion.

Just as her release began to fade and she fell back to reality, Ethan bucked his hips up into her with a sharp snap and erupted. The roar he let out was just as loud, if not louder, as he painted her insides with a glorious heat.

Soundproof? Yes.

Vampire orgasm proof? Probably not.

She collapsed against his chest, not even caring how sweaty they were. All she could smell was their mingling scents. Bubblegum and vanilla. Together, they created the aroma that had teased her for the past three hundred years, hinting at the perfection waiting for her if she just held on. Not that any ice cream would ever be as sinfully delicious as her mate.

And she planned to feast on him for the rest of her undead life.

"Please tell me this is not going to be a thing," Baylin grumbled shortly after Tressa landed back in the chair beside him.

She and Ethan had gone another three rounds after the first one. 'Scientific research,' he'd said. Told her he needed to test how many times he could orgasm now that he was a vampire. The refractory period was still a thing, but she would never forget the look of joy on his face when he realized it was barely a minute or two now.

He was still adjusting to his body, though, so he eventually passed out from sheer exhaustion after a short but awkward lesson on how to consume blood from a bag. She'd let him sleep, not wanting to spoil the real surprise waiting for him. He would soon find out that once he was strong enough, they could fuck for days without stopping. Well, as long as they had plenty of blood and water, anyway.

She blushed at the idea of taking Ethan away from the compound for a few weeks. Just the two of them, alone, maybe on a private island. She'd never asked, but Marquin probably owned one somewhere. He had dozens of mansions scattered across the globe and more than one castle. Why not an island?

"What are you talking about?" she asked Baylin, pleased to see it was a Rockstar in his hand, and his words no longer sounded like he was in an episode of Peaky Blinders.

The glare on his face, however, was a disappointing change from his normal jovial attitude. "You coming in here reeking of sex."

"Hey! I showered," she protested.

"Not enough."

In all fairness, she had joined Ethan in his shower and not gone to her own, meaning she hadn't used the extra-strength antiseptic soap that was needed when you lived in a house of vampires that could smell *everything*.

"Sorry," she said, blushing. "I'll go shower again."

Baylin waved a hand. "Don't bother. My nose has already suffered. Damage done."

"Then I guess that makes us even since that noise you call music is destroying my hearing."

Baylin rolled his eyes but reached over to his speakers to turn the heavy metal down slightly. It was still a low-level assault—most things were when you had supernatural hearing—but he told her once that was why he liked it. The screaming music drowned everything else out so he could focus.

"Happy now?" he asked. "Wouldn't want to upset your fragile vampire senses. What with you being such a delicate flower and all."

"Funny," she drolled.

"Not lately," he muttered before running a hand through his thick auburn hair. "So what's up?" he asked. "The minute you stepped out of his room, the whole cadre became more than aware that you and Ethan patched things up. I doubt you came to gloat, though."

"I would never," she said, feigning shock.

He rolled his eyes and took another chug of his drink. "What brings you in, then?"

She propped her bare feet up on the table holding his monitors. "Can't I stop by and see my favorite cousin?"

He promptly knocked her feet off the table. "You can, but Saiden's on a date with Cora."

"Ha. Ha. Ha." She gave him an unamused look. "But seriously, Bay. I'm a little worried about you. Now that Ethan and I are good to go, I wanted to check in. He's resting for a bit, so I have some time to chat if you want."

Baylin downed the last of his drink, crumpled the can, then banked it off the back wall to land in the trash bin with ease. "So how is the plant boy?"

Tressa grinned. "Oh, he's amazing."

Baylin reached under his desk and grabbed another energy drink. "That's not what I meant, and you know it," he replied, cracking it open.

Tressa shrugged. "I mean, payback's a bitch. I never want to hear about your sex life either."

"Touché. But seriously, how's he doing post transition?"

Tressa watched Baylin throw back half of the drink in one massive slug and frowned. Her cousin's caffeine addiction was no secret, but even for him, it seemed excessive. She made a mental note to ask the cadre about it, but thoughts of Ethan quickly chased away the concern for her cousin's adrenal glands.

"It's incredible, Bay," she gushed. "I mean, we had a rough start with the whole stabbing me thing, but—"

"What?" Baylin demanded, slamming the can on the table and sloshing amber liquid over a keyboard. "He stabbed you?"

She waved a hand. "It's nothing. Water under the bridge. He healed me. Seriously, not even a scratch, Bay. His power is... It's amazing. I'm just worried he's going to want to take up hunting with Saiden now since he has such a useful ability."

"I doubt it," Baylin replied, wiping up the spilled drink. "Saiden told me Ethan never seemed much into the combat part of training. That it was more a thing he was pushing himself to do, as opposed to genuinely enjoying it. I'd say you're more likely to lose your mate to a laboratory than a battlefield."

Her cheeks ached from the massive smile she didn't even try to contain. "My mate. Damn, I'm never going to get tired of that. Saiden was right. It really is the most incredible feeling. I can't believe I found my mate."

"I'm your *what*?!"

They both whipped around to see Ethan standing just inside the doorway of Baylin's room, his jaw stretching toward the floor.

"Ummm..." Tressa's heart started pounding, and it only got louder when Baylin hit the switch to kill his metal music entirely.

Shit. Shit. Shit.

This was not how she wanted to have this conversation. "Ethan, look. About that..."

She hopped out of the chair and took a step toward him, but he held up a hand. She waited as his face cycled through a dozen emotions, praying to Lilith that he would at least give her the chance to explain. Their story just started; it couldn't be over already. She wouldn't *let* it be over already.

"When did you know?" he asked, his voice cautious, wary, and simmering with an undercurrent of pain.

"When did I know...?"

"That I'm your mate," he bit out. "How long have you known and hid it from me?"

Tressa swallowed roughly, and her eyes dropped to the pristine marble flooring. She was almost embarrassed that she briefly debated lying again. But she couldn't. Not to Ethan. Not ever again.

Her eyes lifted to his. "Since the moment I first met you," she said, her voice barely audible in the painfully silent room. His eyes widened, and her heart nearly shattered at the betrayal on his face. "But, Ethan, you need to know—"

"Don't," he snapped, the anger she'd thought gone from his soul flaring to life in his eyes once again. "I first thought you only wanted me because of my research secrets, and I believed you when you said it wasn't that. But now I see it's much worse. You're only interested in me because you believe in some mythical fairytale about fated mates." He scoffed, the dismissal a dagger in her heart. "Do you even like me,

Tressa?"

She opened her mouth to argue that she didn't just like him, but she had fallen head over heels in love with him. He didn't give her a chance to utter a single word, though.

"No," he said, huffing out a weak laugh. "Actually, don't answer that." He shook his head sadly. "I thought... I thought we were done with the lies. But now I'm wondering if that's just who you are. You're the centuries-old vamp, and I'm the newly turned human who couldn't possibly understand your world. Which means I don't get to know anything until you decide it's the right time. You literally promised me a few hours ago that you would be completely open and honest, and the whole time you were what? Hiding yet another monumental secret?"

"It's not like that," she said, cautiously inching forward like she might spook him if she moved too fast. "I can explain everything."

He backed away from her, bumping into the door frame. "No. I just..."

He stared at her for a second, and the anger in his eyes started to fade to something much worse. She would have gladly endured a million botany lectures if it wiped that new expression off his face—disappointment.

Or worse, heartbreak.

He sighed. "I think... I think maybe this is all happening too fast. I got caught up in the dying, and the killing, and the sex. This isn't me, Tressa. I don't do things like this. I've been so consumed by anger for the past thirteen years, and now that I'm seeing things clearly again, maybe I need some time." His voice dropped into a low, sad whisper, and he added, "Maybe I made a mistake."

"Ethan, wait," she protested, taking a hesitant step forward, then another when he didn't immediately flinch. "I told you we would sit down and go over everything. I was going to tell you about the mate bond when we had that conversation. I swear I was—"

"Save it," he said, but his tone wasn't cold. Wasn't vengeful.

It was broken.

"I need some space, Tressa. I'll see you around."

Ethan blurred out of the room, and Tressa started to chase after him, but a strong hand clamped around her wrist.

"I wouldn't do that," Baylin said. "He asked for time, and you need to give it to him. He cares about you, Tressa. Everything will be okay, but maybe allow him some space to process what he's been through."

She curled her hands into fists, suppressing the urge to reach for the doorknob so she could hunt her mate down and beg him to talk with her. "Fine. I guess I can let him go hang out in the gym for a bit."

Baylin's computer emitted a harsh beep, and they both glanced over.

"Well, shit," he said after hitting a few keys and pulling up a security feed.

"What?" she demanded, stalking over to his side.

"When you gave him a tour, did you show him the garage?"

She frowned, trying to make sense of what she was seeing on the camera. "Yeah, I showed him everywhere except the blood storage. Why?"

"Because I'm pretty sure he just stole Saiden's McLaren."

Chapter Thirty-Six

Ethan

He was a vampire.

He murdered, resurrected, and abandoned the only woman he'd ever cared about.

And he just stole a $200,000 car.

Maybe it was the absurdity of the past twenty-four hours, but that last one seemed the most concerning at the moment. He couldn't exactly explain his situation to the cops if he got pulled over.

But he'd needed to get out of that compound, and the McLaren keys had been labeled on the hook inside the garage. He hadn't even hesitated; he took them and left.

It wasn't like they were lacking for vehicles, and he would find a way to get it back to Tressa.

Eventually.

What he needed was a place where he could just sit and think. Preferably in a quiet location since his heightened senses were still wreaking havoc on his attention span. In retrospect, it might have been idiotic to take the car for more reasons than just grand theft auto. How was he supposed to focus on driving safely when he could hear the birds flapping their wings above him? When he could see every squirrel hiding in the evergreen branches? When he could smell, well, everything? How did vampires get anything done when life was constantly bombarding their senses?

And how could he think clearly when a fierce burning in his soul was screaming at him to turn the damned fancy car around and drive straight back to Tressa?

Every mile that took him farther away from her only increased the agonizing feeling, but he forced himself to push through it. He was stronger than whatever vampire mate mojo kept trying to overwhelm him.

Still, it took everything in him to keep his eyes on the road and his thoughts on the task ahead.

Find a safe place.

It should have been such a simple concept, and yet, where on earth would be safe for him? In his brain-addled state, he didn't think encountering Renata would end well. Was there anywhere he could hide that she couldn't find him?

Home, he thought. That's what he needed. He needed the comforting safety of the familiar. The one place that never failed to soothe his soul when he was struggling with life. He would go home.

And not the crappy apartment that didn't even belong to him anymore. No, that wasn't home. That had never been anything more than a place to sleep and store his shit.

Only one place would ever truly be considered home in his heart, even if the person who made it special wasn't there anymore.

Easing back on the gas pedal since he hadn't realized he'd crept up to almost 90mph at some point, he pulled up the map on his phone and typed in the address.

He was headed back to Seacliff.

"Hey, Mom," he said eight hours later when he reached the Seacliff cemetery, just a short walk from the Oregon Coast.

He settled down behind her tombstone, stretching his legs out in front of him as he leaned back against it.

"Sorry, I haven't been to see you in a while. I want to say I have a good excuse, but I really don't. I honestly could have taken a few days off work at any point." He picked at the dirt under his nails that he wouldn't have even been able to see yesterday. "The truth is I didn't know what to say. All you ever wanted for me was to be happy, and... I think I let you down, Mom. I thought helping people would make me happy. I thought curing the disease that took your life would make me happy. I thought..."

He sighed and sank down farther, letting his head thump back against the cold stone.

"I thought a lot of things that turned out to be wrong. It's been thirteen years since you died, and I'm still so angry. So mad at the world." He paused. "I think you would be disappointed in me. In who I've become."

He ran his tongue over the tiny bumps in his gums where his new fangs would emerge from their hiding place. After their wild sex-a-thon, Tressa had shown him how to feed from a blood bag, so he wasn't exactly hungry at the moment. Still, they seemed to respond to his gentle prodding, the tiny curved daggers sliding free of their sheaths.

After analyzing them for a moment, he willed the fangs to retreat. When they did, he let his mind drift back to memories of his mother. Times when he'd snuck out of his bed, crept through the shadows of the garden, and peered into the shed where he would watch her chant late into the night. He didn't believe in magic then. He thought she was just practicing her religion. Now he was starting to wonder if it had been more.

If vampires were real, there was no telling what all existed in the world.

"Or maybe you wouldn't be disappointed. Maybe you would think it was cool. You were always the most accepting and open-minded person I ever met. You'd probably be the first one to buy a 'my son is a vampire' bumper sticker."

He chuckled at the idea, but it didn't lift his spirits for more than a second.

"I think I made the right choice in becoming a vampire. I just think I probably made it for the wrong reason. I've been so obsessed with getting revenge for Jake that I didn't think it through. Hell, I haven't thought anything through lately."

Images of Tressa filled his head. Her smile. Her laugh. Her strength.

And the broken way she'd looked at him when he left.

"I wish you could have met Tressa. I think you would have really liked her. She's funny. So damned funny. Not to mention more than a little sassy. And her heart is incredible. There's so much pain and darkness in her eyes, but she's kept it all out of her heart. I wish I knew how she did it. How she has spent hundreds of years witnessing such horrific things, yet she still manages to see the beauty in life."

He banged his head harder against the stone but barely felt it.

"I think I fucked up, Mom. I've been focused on all the wrong things. And now... Now I don't know what to do."

He stared up at the night sky, taking in the nuances to the celestial tapestry that he'd never been able to see before. The Oregon Coast always had a spectacular view of the stars, but now mere words felt completely inadequate to describe the beauty, the sheer magnitude of the universe staring back at him. It made him feel so small and his problems so very unimportant in the grand scheme of things.

Unable to bear the weight of the universe's judgment, he closed his eyes and let the once faint sounds of nature wash over him. The ocean was almost a mile away, yet the waves seemed to crash against the other side of the road. When the evening winds flowed through the tree branches, the leaves chittered and buzzed like a hoard of locusts. Dozens of unseen nocturnal animals snuffled and scuffled as they emerged from their burrows to hunt or forage. Somewhere along the beach, a bonfire crackled merrily, and he picked up the hiss of a beer being opened as clearly as if the drinker sat next to him. And a gentle blush filled his cheeks when he realized he could hear the euphoric sighs of a couple making love in a cottage just down the road.

The stars made him feel disconnected, but the world at his feet reminded him the opposite was true.

It was a gift, this life that Tressa had given him. The ability to see the hidden wonders of nature. Beauty wasn't only reserved for his flowers. It was everywhere. In everything.

He'd been so wrong to think vampires were innately evil. To have all this at their fingertips and feel only hatred and rage? He couldn't fathom it. He understood what Tressa meant about most vampires being different from the rogues. Those ones that couldn't see the beauty... they were the anomaly.

Maybe it was that comforting realization, or maybe it was knowing he was as close to his mom as he could get, but for the first time, there was not a trace of anger in Ethan's heart. No rage. No pressing need to fix an unfair world or take revenge on a monster. There was only... peace.

Closing his eyes once more, he drifted off to sleep.

Chapter Thirty-Seven

Tressa

"He stopped moving," Baylin announced, and Tressa nearly fell on her face as she lurched out of the chair she'd been half draped over.

For hours, she'd done nothing but stare at the ceiling and hold back the river of tears that would drown her if she cracked that dam even an inch. The anguish of her mate leaving had all but dropped her like a rock, and there wasn't a single thing she could do to distract herself from the pain. That look on Ethan's face before he left was firmly locked inside her mind, forcing her to revisit that moment over and over, refusing to allow her a second of peace.

No, peace was not in the cards for her. Not after how badly she'd fucked up, and not when her mate was dragging her heart alongside the freeway as he raced farther and farther away from her.

"You're sure it's not a pitstop?" she asked, trying not to get her hopes up again. They'd been tracking the McLaren ever since Ethan drove it out of the compound at a speed that would make even Saiden sweat. It had killed her, letting him leave instead of locking down the gates to keep him inside.

But she knew it wouldn't have ended well. She would never make a prisoner of her mate. No matter how much she wanted to. No matter how much the mate bond screamed at her to chase after him. No matter how much her soul ached the farther away he got.

And no matter how pissed Saiden was that yet another person "borrowed" his favorite ride.

"Yeah," Baylin said, pulling up a map on his computer. His hands flew over the keyboard at inhuman speed, and the screen zoomed in on a blinking red dot. "According to GPS, he stopped near a city park in his hometown on the Oregon Coast. He hasn't moved for almost half an hour."

"A park?" she asked, climbing out of her chair to move over to the computer even though she could see perfectly fine from across the room. It wasn't like getting closer to the red dot took her any closer to her mate.

"Looks like," Baylin said, pointing to the map. "Either that or the cemetery across the street, but I don't know why he'd go there."

Tressa scanned the screen, noting the information on the GPS tag—Seacliff Cemetery—and the conversation they had in the garden came back to her. "He went to the cemetery," she said, her voice wilting.

Baylin arched an eyebrow. "Why?"

Melancholy poured off Tressa, her heart breaking for her mate that was so far away. "My guess? He was feeling confused and scared, so he sought out the one person he could always rely on. His mom."

Baylin frowned. "I looked into him, though. Isn't his mom—"

"Dead?" Tressa supplied. "Yeah. I imagine she's buried there."

Baylin eyed her curiously. "So why...?"

"Come on, Baylin. Haven't you ever felt so lost that you just wanted the comfort of your family and would take that in any form you could get?"

"Honestly?" he asked, turning back to the computer, his voice and body tight. "No. The only family I care about lives under this roof."

Tressa rested her hand on his arm, a small gesture to let him know she wouldn't pry.

After a moment, his shoulders relaxed. When he glanced back up at her, he was smiling again, though it didn't quite reach his eyes. "Besides, they always come to me." He winked. "Even when I don't want them to."

Tressa pulled her hand back and smacked him with it. "Stop acting like you don't love it, and maybe we'll stop barging in all the time, Baylicious."

"A vampire can only dream," he grumbled, then sat back in his chair. "So what, you think Ethan went to the cemetery to visit his mom's grave?"

Tressa's finger drifted over to the monitor, brushing against the red dot that was her mate. "I know he did. She meant everything to him. You might not understand, but I know what it's like to miss your mom so much that even a cold stone with their name on it would be a small comfort."

"Oh," Baylin said, and the word lingered in the air between them for a long moment before he cleared his throat. "What are you planning? Are you going to leave him be or..."

Perching on the edge of the table, Tressa picked at her cuticles. "I don't know, Bay. I'm out of my depths here. My heart is screaming at me to take the next fastest car and get to him as quickly as I can."

"Then what's the problem?"

Tressa sighed and tucked her hands under her butt so she could focus. "The problem is that my brain doesn't know if showing up right after he asked for time and space is the best plan of action. It could end up being the final stake in the coffin of our relationship."

Baylin groaned. "Did you just make a really awful vampire joke?"

"Little bit," she replied with a forced grin. "I'm doing everything I can to not fall apart here, Bay. Let me have my bad puns."

He huffed out a short laugh. "Fair enough. But slightly offensive joking aside, I can't tell you what to do, Tress. He's leaving himself wide open to an attack, and we both know he can't take on Renata by himself. But I hear what you're saying about not wanting to push things so hard they snap. Shit, Saiden is lucky that Cora even speaks to him after the crap he pulled."

"You're not wrong there," Tressa agreed dryly. "Why is it that most vampires are shit at telling their mates the truth?"

Baylin shrugged. "Maybe because people these days freak out when romantic things move too fast? Telling a modern-day human that a cosmic power believes you're destined to be together after your first handshake is unlikely to get you anything other than a restraining order."

"Ugh," Tressa griped. "It makes no sense. Their lives are so short, you would think they would jump at the chance to skip the dating game and go straight to happily ever after."

"You can't expedite love, Tressa. It takes time."

Love.

Maybe that was the problem. She'd never told him she loved him. And maybe it was crazy since they'd barely known each other a couple weeks, but she'd been falling since the first moment she looked into his slate gray eyes. Three hundred years meant she had encountered a lot of men, and not a single one even gave her stomach a flutter. Ethan, on the hand, made her feel like she had a belfry full of bats inside her.

She couldn't lose that feeling.

She couldn't lose *him*.

Tressa slid her ass off the table and went over to the silver cooler in the corner of Baylin's room. Snagging a blood bag, she sank her fangs in and sipped it slowly as she mulled over her options.

Really there weren't that many. She either gave him space or she didn't. But really, what she kept hearing was, she either risked her mate's life to potentially save her relationship, or...

She tossed the empty pouch in the trash. "Call Derrick," she told her cousin as she grabbed a few more bags from the cooler.

"Come again?" Baylin asked, narrowing his eyes at her pilfered supplies. "Why do you need Derrick, and why are you guys always stealing my blood bags? Can't you go to the cellar and get your own?"

"Nope," she said. "I have a plane to catch."

Maybe she was about to make the biggest mistake of her life. Maybe she was about to ensure her mate never spoke to her again. Maybe she shouldn't have been such a dumbass by preventing Saiden from going after Ethan when he initially offered...

So many maybes, and she was definitely questioning the insane logic that led to that last one.

She made a lot of bad calls when it came to her mate, but one thing was for certain: if she left him alone, he was a sitting duck for Renata.

And Tressa wasn't about to wait around in the safety of the compound to see if he survived or not.

Pausing in the doorway, she tossed a glance over her shoulder at Baylin. "I don't care if Ethan ends up hating me for the next five centuries. He's my mate, Bay. I won't risk his life. If he needs space to decide how he feels about me, I'll give it to him. I'll give him space for the rest of eternity. But not until after that bitch is dead and I know he's safe."

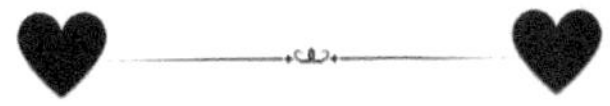

"You know," Derrick said through the plane's headset, "I don't mind that you guys basically use me as your own personal air Uber, but could you look a little less mopey about it?"

"You're one to talk," Tressa pointed out, and Saiden snorted at her side.

"She's not wrong, cousin," Saiden said. "Being away from Cora always sets me on edge, and Tressa may or may not have fucked things up with her mate forever. What's your excuse, huh? Why have you been such a sourpuss lately? I spilled blood on your Armani jacket yesterday, and you didn't even blink."

The sigh that came through the headset was loud even without vampiric hearing. "It was a Tom Ford, actually, and I don't want to talk about it."

"Do you need a little pick me up?" Tressa asked, moving from the back seat to the co-pilot chair.

"Nah," Derrick said. "Appreciate the offer, but I don't need your mood mojo to make me feel better. I sort of deserve to feel like shit right now."

Tressa studied her cousin, taking in his tense face and the laser focus he maintained on the controls. It was strange, considering Derrick could fly a plane in his sleep. In fact, if she believed his story, he'd once spent a week in Milan with a supermodel and had passed out at thirty thousand feet after testing just how much liquor a vampire needed to get truly smashed. He said he'd woken up to a half-naked woman screaming as the plane was nosediveing through the clouds, but it hadn't phased him for a second.

Granted, not all of Derrick's stories were real—or at least she hoped they weren't—but his ease in the cockpit was not an exaggeration.

"If you say so," she muttered. "As long as you're on your game when Renata shows up."

He scoffed. "Oh, I'll be on my game. I might not have Saiden's super special spidey sense, but—"

"Do *not* call it that," Saiden snarled.

"Why?" Derrick asked, glancing back at him with a genuine look of confusion. "You let Cora use that term."

"That's because Cora is my mate."

Derrick thumped his chest. "And I'm family."

"You're a jackass that I can't seem to escape."

"A jackass who has saved your life how many times now?"

"And you never let me forget it."

"Admit it, Saiden. You love me."

"If it gets you to shut up, then sure. Think whatever you want."

Tressa leaned back in the chair, enjoying the exchange between the guys. Despite what Saiden would never admit, she knew he really did love his cousin. And Derrick had lightened up a bit at the bantering, so Tressa had no intention of interfering in their little squabble. She would wheedle his problem out of him after she solved her own.

Checking her watch, she saw they would be landing at the airstrip just outside of Seacliff in the next fifteen minutes. Which meant she was running out of time to figure out what she was going to say.

Please Lilith, don't let him hate me, she thought, keeping her eyes locked on the blinking dot on her phone.

He hadn't moved from the cemetery for the past two hours, and she didn't know what to make of that. A not-so-small part of her was terrified they were too late and Renata had already gotten to him. If they arrived at the cemetery only to find his permanently dead body draped over his mother's headstone, Tressa didn't think she would survive it.

She wouldn't *want* to survive it.

"Hey, Derrick?" she called out.

"Yeah?" he asked, glancing over at her.

"Fly faster."

Chapter Thirty-Eight

Ethan

A soft tickle on his nose pulled Ethan from sleep, and he blinked at the faint spears of sunlight just peeking over the horizon. He glanced at his watch and groaned. Five a.m.

Maybe he was more suited to the life of a night creature than he realized, because five a.m. was not typically a time he wanted to be awake.

Brushing aside the moth that had landed on his cheek, he climbed to his feet and stared down at his mother's grave.

"Well, Mom, any bright ideas on what I should do now?"

Whoever coined the phrase "as quiet as a graveyard" was clearly not a vampire, because his ears were filled with sound—the chirping of early morning birds, the scuffling of squirrels, the passing of cars on the main road.

So much noise, and none of it was what he wanted to hear.

He ran his hand over the top of the headstone, his vampiric eyes picking up every tiny crack in the seemingly smooth rock. Nothing was ever what it appeared to be on the surface.

"I miss her voice, Mom. I miss her laugh. Fuck, it hasn't even been twenty-four hours, and I feel empty. Like a piece of me is missing. I don't think I can live without her. I don't know if it's the whole mate bond thing, or something else, but..."

"That's not it."

He flinched at the somber voice that floated over from behind him. So familiar but also filled with so much hesitancy. So much worry. It was her, and yet it was not.

He slowly turned around to see Tressa standing beside a tree on the edge of the cemetery twenty or thirty yards away. He shouldn't have been able to hear her at that distance, but her voice was clear as day. And so was the fear distorting her beautiful face.

His nose twitched at a familiar copper-tinged scent—almost but not quite hidden by her sweet smell—and his eyes traveled down to her fingers. Blood under the nails. She'd been picking at them again. Because of him.

"What do you mean?" he asked, fighting the urge to rush over to her. To take her in his arms and kiss her until she forgave him for running away like a jackass.

"What you're feeling," she replied, taking a few tentative steps toward him then stopping herself.

It killed him. To see her so shy and reserved. It was like everything that made her Tressa had been siphoned away. He wanted her to make a bad joke. Or tease him. Or call him some silly name like 'Dr. Rose.' Hell, he'd even take 'Science Boy' if it made her smile like she used to.

He wanted his mate back.

"How do you figure?" he asked, shoving his hands in his pockets so he didn't do something stupid like grab her and kiss her senseless. Maybe that had been their problem from the beginning. They kept giving in to their lust when they should have been talking.

"The mate bond," she replied. "It does draw you to a person and urges you to find them when they're gone. It makes you feel this sense of rightness when you're together, like you just know that the person belongs in your life and it hurts to be away from them. But the bond doesn't make you care about their feelings. Doesn't make you want to do anything in your power just to see them smile. It doesn't..." She sighed. "It doesn't create feelings in you that wouldn't otherwise exist. It doesn't make you *love* them."

She stuttered over the word love, and he didn't know what to make of that. Did she love him? Could she love him after everything he put her through? Could he love her? They'd only known each other for... Had it really only been two weeks? But he couldn't deny that he felt something. Something that was more than just a sense of rightness.

He craved her with every breath. And not just her body, but her heart. Her soul. He wanted to be the reason she laughed or smiled. He wanted to be the reason the glow in her eyes never went out. He wanted to be the light that made his Sunflower bloom.

And yes, he also wanted to make her scream with pleasure. If he was being honest, just seeing her had things stirring in multiple places in his body. Some slightly more awkward than others given he was standing next to his mom's grave.

"So, how do you feel?" he asked, hauling his caveman brain back to more important matters. "About me? Mate bond aside, what do you feel for me, Tressa?" He took a few steps toward her, closing the space between them to something less monumental and more manageable. A gap that could be overcome, if she was still willing.

Pausing a few yards away, he waited for her response.

She dropped her eyes and picked at her nail for a second. When she looked back up, some of the fear had been replaced with... hope?

"When I first met you," she began, her words hesitant as if she was choosing them carefully, "I felt excited. You don't understand, Ethan.

For vampires, finding your mate is the one thing you spend your entire undead life waiting for. Being in a relationship with another vampire is almost impossible because you both know your mate is out there somewhere. And being with humans is, well, it's never more than temporary at best. So when I felt the connection between us and knew what it meant... I was filled with all this joy."

She sniffled, and Ethan had to fight the urge to wrap her in his arms and comfort her. The only thing that held him back was knowing that the moment he got his hands on her, all talking would cease, and they needed to get everything out in the open if they had any chance at a future.

"And of course that happiness was followed immediately by this intense fear about how you'd react," she continued. "You'd just been attacked by one of my kind. She almost killed you. She *did* put you in a coma for months. What was I supposed to say? 'Sorry you think vamps are undead monsters, but I promise I'm a good one. Oh, and by the way, the universe also thinks we are destined to spend eternity together. Want to go on a date?' Tell me I'm wrong, but I don't think that would have gone over well."

Ethan laughed softly and moved forward, cautiously eating up a little more of the distance between them. "Fair enough. But you didn't really answer my question, Tress."

She cocked an eyebrow, and he took another step forward.

"You told me how you *felt*. I want to know how you *feel*."

She curled in on herself, and the hope filling his chest deflated a little.

"I don't know how to answer that, Ethan," she replied quietly. "At least, not in a way that will make sense. I waited almost three hundred years for my mate, and when I finally found you... you were the most gorgeous guy I'd ever met. You were smart, much smarter than me, and so very clever. You also had the same rage simmering under your skin that I've struggled with. I instantly knew you were my other half." She looked up at him with wide, vulnerable eyes and whispered, "Ethan, I was half in love with you the first day we met."

He inched closer. "And now? After everything? After I said... those words to you back at the compound?"

She finally took a step toward him, eliminating all but the last bit of distance between them. "Now I feel like I *know* I'm in love with you. You're my perfect match, Ethan. The universe knew we would complement each other beautifully, but you're the one who made me fall so deeply and completely in love with you. I just wish I could do the same for you."

Her eyes dropped to the ground, and he surged forward, lifting her chin with one finger to pull her face up. "And you think you can't?"

Tears pricked at her eyes. "I don't know. It could just be wishful thinking, but I want to. I want you to understand how sorry I am that I lied to you. I never meant any deception. I never meant to hurt you or take your choice away. I never meant—"

"Shut up, Tressa," Ethan interrupted as he cupped the back of her head with his other hand. "None of that means anything to me any-more. Right here, right now is all I care about. I love you, Sunflower, and this is our start. This is the beginning of our story." He gave her a wicked grin. "And I think I know how I want to kick it off."

She smiled, the light returning to her eyes. "Really? And how's that?"

He leaned in close to her, letting his hot breath ghost over the shell of her ear. "I want to take you somewhere and make love to you. I want to memorize every curve and dip of your body until they're so ingrained in my mind that I know you better than I know myself. And once that's done... Once you understand that I love you now and will continue to do so for the rest of time... that's when I want to chain you to a bed and fuck you until we've fully tested out the limits of my new vampire body."

A shiver ran through Tressa, and he wrapped his arms around her, pulling her into his chest.

"I think I could be open to that," she murmured, rising up on her tiptoes to kiss him.

Tiny shocks crackled across his skin when their lips met, and he let out a primal groan. His tongue dove into her mouth as he surrendered to the blissful taste that was Tressa. He hoped vampires didn't need much oxygen because he wanted to drown in her. Wanted to claim her as his.

His love.

His mate.

His forever.

Without breaking contact for a second, he slowly walked her backward until she hit a tree, and then he gripped her ass and lifted her up. She wrapped her legs around his waist, rubbing herself against his crotch, and he moaned at the contact.

For about two seconds.

"Fuuuck," he swore, frustration drawing out the curse as he pulled away and pressed his forehead to hers. "We can't do this."

Tressa's legs went limp and fell to the ground. When she spoke, her voice was coated in misery. "I... I understand, Ethan. You need more time. You need—"

"I need *you*," he growled, then kissed her again to make sure he shut that nonsense down before it even got started. The last thing he wanted was more space from her.

"So what's wrong?" she asked when he pulled away a second time.

"We're vampires," he answered.

She jerked back a bit and gave him a confused look. "Yes. And?"

"And if vampires exist, then who the fuck knows what else exists. On the off chance that ghosts are a thing, I'd rather not get caught feeling you up less than twenty feet from my mother's grave."

Tressa's explosive laugh echoed through the cemetery, bouncing off the headstones. "Okay. That's fair. I haven't heard anything about ghosts, but better safe than sorry." She ran her nose along his neck, nuzzling the spot just behind his ear. "In that case, where do you want to go?"

"Hang on, lovebirds," a male voice interrupted.

They turned to see Saiden and Derrick strolling toward them.

Tressa gently extricated herself from Ethan's arms and hissed at her cousin. "I thought I told you to stay by the rental until I called for you?"

"Oh, you did," Derrick said, amusement twitching at his lips as he scanned their mussed clothes and hair. "But I thought you might want to know Baylin pinpointed Renata's location, and she's here in Seacliff. Arrived shortly after we did. Still interested in taking her out?"

Ethan stiffened at the words. Renata. The rogue. The mission that had been so important to him was now within his grasp.

Except... he didn't harbor the same hatred in his heart. The unending drive to seek revenge for Jake's death no longer haunted him. He loved Jake like a brother, and he would feel the loss for the rest of his days, no matter how many of those he ended up having. But it wasn't Ethan's fault. He had no way of knowing his research would lead to a vampire attack that should have killed both of them.

He would never forget Jake, but that didn't mean he needed to die along with him. Not when he had something to live for standing by his side and biting her lower lip as she looked up at him.

And yet...

That bitch had slapped his mate in the face.

He didn't *need* to kill Renata, but he sure as hell *wanted* to.

"What do you say?" he asked Tressa. "Want to go stake a vampire?"

She pressed a kiss to his cheek. "Nobody actually uses stakes anymore, babe. That's so old school and extremely impractical. Too much opportunity for something to go wrong."

"She's right," Saiden said, stepping forward and opening his jacket to reveal an assortment of weapons tucked into various pockets. "We've upgraded since the dark ages."

Ethan scanned the arsenal, then grinned at Saiden. "In that case, load me up. I might not be as skilled as you guys, but if I'm going to be part of the cadre, I guess it's time for my initiation."

Saiden and Derrick exchanged a brief look, then turned back to Ethan with big smiles on their faces.

"Welcome to the family, cousin," Derrick said, and something in Ethan blossomed at the words. He knew the cocky vamp hadn't meant anything much by them, but still. A family. It had been so long since he'd had one of those. The last time he felt anything like that was...

"Do you mind if we make a stop somewhere first?" he asked as they headed toward the road.

"We don't know how long Renata will stay in one spot," Saiden answered. "Why? What do you need?"

"There's a woman who lives nearby," Ethan said as they left the cemetery and crossed the road to the waiting McLaren. "She was friends with my mom. Kind of like an aunt to me. I couldn't bring myself to see her after..." He shut his eyes for a second, then continued. "My mom always told me I should go to her if I was ever in trouble. Said she was a powerful witch. I never gave it much thought, but with this whole 'vampires are real' thing..." He shrugged. "Who knows?"

Tressa slipped her hand through Ethan's and squeezed. "Of course we can go see her real quick. Like you said, who knows?"

"Fine," Saiden grumbled as they reached the car. "But you get to drive the rental. Nobody lays a finger on Selene ever again."

Tressa paused with her hand just shy of the door handle and slid her eyes over to Saiden. "Selene?"

Saiden ran a hand through his hair and looked away. "Cora's become fond of the McLaren, so she named it Selene," he muttered. "Said it was fitting since the car was hot, sleek, and badass. I don't get the reference, but it made Cora smile, so..."

Ethan slapped Saiden on the back and handed over the keys. "I get it man. No worries. Selene is all yours."

Saiden just grunted and dropped into the driver's seat.

Derrick tossed the rental keys to Tressa, then climbed in next to him. "We'll follow you guys," he called, shutting the door.

Tressa led Ethan down the road to where a black town car was parked. She paused at the driver's side door and looked up at him. "Are you sure you're ready for this?"

Ethan lifted their joined hands, pressed a kiss to her knuckles, then headed for the passenger side. "Are you kidding me?" He shook his head as he climbed into the car. "Sunflower, we're going to pay a visit to a witch before we try to murder an ancient vampire who will likely kill us first. I don't think anybody would be ready for that."

Tressa slid into the driver's seat and leaned across the console to kiss him. "I like when you call me Sunflower."

He ran a hand down her cheek. "Baby, I'll call you whatever you want for the next thousand years. We just have to kill Renata first. Nobody touches my mate and gets to continue breathing."

Tressa laughed, kissed him again, then put the car in drive.

"Oh, that bitch is toast."

Chapter Thirty-Nine

Tressa

"What in Lilith's name is she doing?"

When Derrick said Baylin had pinpointed Renata's location, Tressa assumed they would be going to a house or abandoned building. Something befitting the vicious killer they all believed the rogue to be.

But that wasn't the case at all. After a brief stop at an adorable cottage that Ethan had disappeared into for a few minutes, they sped over to the spot where Baylin had caught her on camera. The last thing they expected to see was a parking lot leading down to a beach.

And more shocking than that was what they found when they stepped onto the soft sand.

Renata was just sitting by the water's edge, the waves rolling in and out to gently lap at her toes with each pass. Her arms were wrapped around her knees, and she didn't so much as flinch when they arrived.

Given her age, there was no way she hadn't heard them approach. In fact, she might have heard them from miles away for all Tressa knew. So why was she just sitting there acting like another tourist enjoying the sunrise?

"It's got to be a trap," Saiden said, his hands ghosting over the daggers in his belt.

"I agree," Derrick said. "And I don't like it. There's the bait, but where's the hook?"

They all scanned the surrounding area, but as far as they could see, there was nothing but empty sand for miles.

Tressa turned to Ethan. "Is this normal? For the beach to be deserted?"

Ethan scratched the back of his neck and glanced toward the vacant parking lot. "I'm not sure. It is pretty early, so it wouldn't be packed, but we're also still in tourist season. For there to not be a single morning jogger or person walking their dog? It's definitely suspect."

"Told you," Saiden said. "Trap."

"Nobody is arguing with you, Sadie Bear," Tressa said, patting him on the shoulder.

He let out an annoyed chuff. "Remind me again why you're here?"

She blinked at him. "Where the fuck else would I be? It's *my* mate she's trying to murder. You think I'm going to go get a damn pedicure and wait for you three to take care of the men's work?" She snorted. "You know me better than that."

Saiden chuckled. "I know. But it's not often I get to be the one teasing you." His eyes darted up and down the beach. "So how do we play this? I didn't bring my rifle, so long range is out. And I don't really want to start tossing grenades on a public beach. Explaining that to the cops would be hell even with Tressa's ability."

Derrick cracked his neck and rolled his head side to side. "If you bust out the semi-automatic, we'll have police swarming us in minutes, and I have more important things to do than sit in a jail cell. I say we go old school. It's four against one. A handful of blades and my fists should get the job done."

Tressa opened her mouth to say she was pretty sure Derrick's hands had far more experience with activities of a less violent nature, but her cousin turned to Ethan before she could get the snarky comment out.

"You any good with a weapon, Ethan?" he asked her mate. "I know we didn't get past hand-to-hand in your training."

Ethan gave him a dubious look. "No offense, but of all the things you know about me, what makes you think I'd be good with a weapon? Besides, I don't think the few days that you spent dropping me on my ass really counts as training considering the situation." He pulled a small green vial from his pocket. "The best I got is this potion the witch gave to me, and it mostly just smelled like weak tea before she corked it. She wasn't even clear on what I'm supposed to do with it. Just told me 'I would know when the time was right.' Whatever that means." He shoved it back in his pocket and gave them all an apologetic look.

"Okay, then," Derrick said, pursing his lips as he glanced at Tressa and Ethan. "So we got two, uh, less than skilled fighters, one total badass, and a Saiden. I still think we can take her."

Saiden glared at Derrick. "You're the badass in this scenario? You, who spends more time flirting than fighting? Riiight." Saiden rolled his eyes. "Regardless of that highly inaccurate assessment, deciding on a plan isn't getting us anywhere. I say we just go in and play it by ear. If she's got something up her sleeve, we'll deal with it as we go. I can guarantee you she knows we're here, so no point in chatting about it now."

"I agree." The voice floated over on the wind, and they all whipped their heads to the rogue who hadn't moved from her spot on the beach. She cocked her head to the side but kept staring out at the ocean. "There's something very surreal about listening to a group of people plotting your demise. And while it was amusing at first, I find that I've grown quite bored of it."

Slowly, Renata climbed to her feet and brushed sand off her pleated gray pants, still refusing to even look at them.

"Wait," Ethan sputtered. "She could hear every word we said even over the waves?"

Tressa arched an eyebrow. "Of course. Vampire, remember?"

Ethan threw up his hands. "I mean, I can't make out much beyond our small circle, what with that loud crashing filling my ears." He glanced from Tressa to Saiden. "What the hell, man? Why the fuck were we standing here coming up with a plan if she could hear the whole thing?"

"I don't know about the rest of you," Saiden said with a grin. "But I was buying us some time."

Tressa glanced at him warily. "Time for what?"

"To prep this."

In a single smooth motion, Saiden jerked the pin from the small metal cylinder that appeared in his hand and lobbed it at Renata. It rocketed toward the vampire, gas spewing from the canister. Time slowed to a standstill as they watched it fly through the air, and...

Renata whirled around at the last second and snapped her hand up. Her palm connected with the cylinder and sent it sailing over her head to splash down harmlessly a dozen yards out to sea.

Even from their far distance, Tressa could see the slight frown that stretched Renata's mouth for a fraction of a second before she fixed a harsh glare on them.

"Seriously?" Derrick said. "Did you really think that would work?"

"Worth a shot," Saiden grumbled. "Fuck, she's fast. I thought that would at least throw her off balance. How ancient did Baylin say she was again?"

"I don't remember, but she's definitely old enough that I'm debating calling this off until we have reinforcements," Tressa said. She knew Ethan wanted the rogue dead, but since rationality seemed to have retaken control of his brain, surely he would see the futility in attacking one whose speed and strength far outweighed any of theirs.

"That was quite rude," Renata said, and between one blink and the next, she went from the edge of the water to standing only a few feet away from them.

"You're trying to kill my mate," Tressa snarled. "And we're the rude ones?"

Renata sighed. "Do you know the damage that canister and those chemicals will do to the local sea life?"

Four jaws dropped consecutively as they all stared at her.

"That's what you're mad about?" Derrick asked, barely able to contain his laughter. "Some fucking fish?"

She clucked her tongue at him. "Don't be disrespectful. Those creatures suffer enough at the hands of humans. They deserve life just as much as any other living"—she paused—"or non-living being."

Once Tressa managed to shake off the surprise of Renata's response, she put her hands on her hips and glared. "Then why the hell are you trying to kill Ethan if you're so pro-life?"

"I told you. His research could mean the end of all vampires. We cannot allow that to happen."

"Who's 'we?'" Ethan interjected. "So far you're the only one I've met with homicidal tendencies."

Renata glanced up to the sky as if searching for answers. "She's not ready to meet you yet. But the day will come. Perhaps sooner rather than later."

"Why are you doing this?" Tressa demanded. "You never gave us an answer last time. Baylin scoured every file in the Coalition archives searching for your motive, but you've never so much as harmed a single human or other vampire. What changed?"

"The world is what changed," Renata replied, tucking a wayward strand of hair behind her ear. "We can no longer hide in the dark as we once did. The humans are becoming... unpredictable. We have a responsibility to maintain balance since they will not."

"And killing my mate?" Tressa growled. "The one person who means everything to me? That's what you call balance?"

Renata gave the slightest dip of her head. "I'm afraid so, Loloma."

"My name is Tressa, bitch," she gritted out. "Do you hear me? And the only thing getting balanced here is your spleen on my hand." She stepped forward and folded her arms in what she hoped was an imposing power stance. "If you want Ethan, you go through me."

"And me," Saiden added.

"And me," Derrick chimed in.

"And even if you get through them," Ethan said, stepping up to Tressa's side. "I'll never go down without a fight. You murdered my best friend. Drank him dry right in front of me. You think I'm going to believe this bullshit that you're acting in the benefit of mankind or something? Fuck that. I saw you. That look in your eyes as he struggled to escape? You killed him, and you fucking enjoyed it. So tell yourself whatever lies you want about 'doing what's best,' because when you meet your maker, they'll know the truth."

For the first time, Renata smiled. "Oh, I don't know about that. Something tells me Lilith isn't quite so interested in the actions of her children anymore."

"Then I guess we'll have to make sure justice finds you anyway," Derrick declared, cracking his knuckles.

"By all means," she replied. "You're welcome to try."

Chapter Forty

Ethan

Blood pounded in Ethan's ears, and the frenzied beat of his heart seemed to vibrate through his bones. After weeks of nightmares, endless hours of training in the gym, and constant memories of shattered glass and Jake's blood dripping from ivory fangs... he was finally going to get his revenge.

Except he had no fucking clue what to do.

He thought he was over it—the violent, all-encompassing need to make her pay—but from the moment he saw Renata sitting by the surf, one voice screamed in his head, "Kill!" while another threw out plans of attack that were immediately dismissed as downright reckless. Visions of the hospital and church parking lot flashed through his mind, and with his logical brain reactivated, he was fully aware he was no match for the sheer speed and power of this creature. He still wanted nothing more than to tear out her throat with his bare hands, but his survival instincts left him quivering with impotent rage.

He finally had something and someone to live for, and he wasn't going to carelessly throw it away. He had to be smart. If he couldn't beat her with brawn, it had to be brains. But his brain glitched the moment he was finally ready to listen to it.

The thundering of the ocean waves and his own pulse were deafening, and he nearly missed the moment when the three vampires at his side launched their attack. Blurs of pastel, black, and brown flew forward, and all hell broke loose.

At first, Ethan couldn't make heads or tails of what was happening. He could only see a whirlwind of limbs and the occasional arc of ruby red blood flying through the air to splatter on the sands around them. The harsh staccato of fists meeting flesh popped off faster than a string of firecrackers as the cadre didn't let up their assault for even a second.

And not a damn bit of it made any difference.

Renata maintained her smile throughout, and there wasn't a scratch on her.

She moved through combat with an ethereal grace, bending, twisting, and weaving among the other vampires like a willow tree thrashing in a maelstrom. Though she was clearly fighting purely defensively—focused on dodges and blocks—she manipulated the other three with the ease of a puppet master, using them against one another. Each slash or punch was not so much deflected as it was redirected toward someone else. Tressa, Derrick, and Saiden were continuously knocked into one another, their limbs fouling each other's strikes and their knives drawing friendly blood.

With a twist of the hips and a sharp upswing of her arm, Renata spun an attacking Derrick in front of her, and he accidentally buried his knife in Tressa's bicep when she came flying in with her own dagger. Before he could dislodge his blade, Renata planted a hand on Derrick's shoulder and vaulted over him. The momentum sent him crashing into Tressa, knocking them both to the sand.

Slipping behind Renata silently, Saiden closed in on her, but his dagger flashed through empty air as she dove forward in a summersault that sprayed a wave of sand into his face. Renata popped up from her roll only to blur back over to Derrick and Tressa as they rose from their tangle. She viciously tore out the blade lodged in Tressa's arm and sent it tumbling end over end for Saiden's heart.

Though still blind to his surroundings, Saiden threw himself to the side, and the blade merely sliced through his shirt, scoring a line across his ribs.

Off to the side, Ethan finally overcame the initial shock of watching their combat. Just because he wasn't going to be reckless didn't mean he was going to sit on the sidelines the whole time. Not when he had a love worth fighting for.

He surged forward, hoping to tackle Renata to the ground while her back was turned and give the cadre a chance to collect themselves. If they could all pile on at once, her speed wouldn't matter for shit when pinned under four bodies.

He only needed to close a few yards, a dozen steps at most, and with his new speed it should be over in...

A flash of sky and water whizzed past his face as he soared through the air to crash into the surf, a hot lance of pain spreading across his ribs.

Spitting out sand and seawater, Ethan pushed up to his hands and knees to see Renata smirking over her shoulder at him, her arm still extended from the backhand that had sent him face first into the ocean.

"Dammit," he cursed. He could run faster than some cars could drive, yet Renata still made him feel like he was all but human again.

He let out a frustrated roar, but it quickly died in his throat when he saw Tressa spring to her feet and charge Renata. The rogue whirled to meet her, skin rippling and shimmering. In the most surreal experience ever, Ethan watched Renata transform into... himself?

Worse. She turned into a version of him he barely recognized—cringing in fear, hands held up, abject horror pasted across his face.

Tressa stumbled when she pulled up short, her eyes wide with shock, and worry spread across her face. Ethan could only imagine what was running through her head, faced with a vision of her mate so obviously terrified of her.

Before he could shout at Tressa to kick his own ass, Renata shifted back into herself and blurred forward. "Your will is weak, Loloma," she snarled, then launched a push kick into Tressa's chest.

There was an unmistakable crack of bone, and Tressa was launched a dozen yards away, sand swirling up in the vacuum created by her sudden departure.

Something broke within Ethan as he watched his mate tumble down the beach. Something deep and primal howled its fury, and his analytical brain that was still stuck in processing mode gave way to neanderthal anger once more.

Ethan tore from the surf and flashed forward, heedless of danger, his vision awash in red. Snatching up a driftwood log as he ran, Ethan gripped the heavy wood in both hands as he bellowed his defiance and ripped loose a home run swing with every ounce of strength he could muster. When the log whiffed through the air as Renata simply bobbed beneath the blow, the inertia of the swing pulled Ethan off balance, and he toppled to the ground.

Instead of landing in the sand, though, an iron grip seized him by the belt at the small of his back. Pain exploded in his head as he was violently flung through the air to crash into Saiden who'd been stealthily approaching from behind Renata.

They hit the ground hard, and Saiden cried out in agony when his shoulder twisted at an odd angle, the jagged end of a fractured clavicle tearing through the fabric of his shirt. Blood spurted out, spreading swiftly across his chest.

"She's too fast," he said, reaching up to press his hand to the gushing wound. "Even with my Gift, I can barely keep up."

Ethan yanked his own shirt off, balled it up, and handed it to the wounded vamp.

Saiden let out a pained grunt as he popped the bone back inside and held the wad of fabric to the wound. His eyes darted from the downed Tressa over to Derrick, who was locked in his own dance with Renata. A dance he clearly wasn't leading.

He shifted to look at Ethan. "I don't think we can beat her."

Chapter Forty-One

Tressa

Tressa burned.

Fire ripped through her side where exploring fingers found a massive bruise blooming around the rough edges of a broken rib just peeking through her skin.

First, seeing a facsimile of her mate cringing in fear had been a red-hot brand to her soul, then seeing the real Ethan flung like a rag doll, his head and limbs snapping just as loosely, set bile churning in her throat and rage roiling in her mind.

She struggled through a few shallow inhales until she could finally breathe despite the excruciating pain threatening to double her over. The bleeding under her skin repaired itself within a moment or two, but the muscle and bones beneath would take several minutes or more, an eternity in a fight like this.

Not that she had any plans to surrender. Broken ribs were an absolute bitch to deal with, but at least she could still function, even if each panting breath felt like shards of glass grinding into her side, and each step forward felt like a tiny gremlin was slamming a pickaxe among said glass.

Tressa sealed away her physical agony, locking it deep in the vault of her mind that housed all the pains of a different variety. Her mate needed her, and she would not fail him.

Your will is weak, Loloma.

Renata was right, partially anyway. Loloma had been weak. She survived long enough to escape from Fiji, escape the sickness that had taken her mother, all so she could hunt down and end the pathetic existence of her father.

Not that she ever called him father. He was just the white man who'd shown up two and a half decades earlier, forced himself on her mother, then took off with the rest of the English sailors back to his 'civilized' life. When her mother finally revealed his name on her deathbed, Tressa made a promise that he would not be allowed to live for what he'd done.

She'd endured untold suffering to cross the ocean and hunt him down in that dingy brothel, only to discover she couldn't do it. Couldn't take a life in cold blood. She'd left him untouched and ran away. She'd been too weak, and she'd failed her mother.

But then Loloma died in a dark alley, and Tressa was born.

And the first thing she had done after waking up as a vampire was return to the brothel to murder her father, feasting on his blood until there was not a drop left in his body.

When she had seen what she'd done, had seen the women cowering in the corners and weeping softly as they waited for her to drain them as well, she'd vowed that she would never take a life again. Would never become the monster that lurked under her skin, craving retribution for all the evils of the world by any means necessary.

Until now.

I'm going to rip that bitch's head off and toss it to those fish she cares so much about, Tressa thought as she rose to her feet. She would not run away. She would not bury her darkness under a smile and a joke any longer. She would use it.

Seeing Ethan moving again as he climbed off Saiden lifted a weight from her shoulders, and fresh vitality surged through her.

She rushed forward to help Derrick right as he got knocked to the ground by Renata. "Glad you could join me," he grumbled, sliding a short knife from his boot and springing to his feet. "Thought you were going to take a nap or something."

"Nope," Tressa said with a determined grim, taking the offered blade. "I'm fully awake."

Tressa danced to the side, trying to keep her profile slim and protect her injured ribs, while Derrick shifted to flank Renata on the left. She stepped in with a quick yet clumsy upward slash before spinning the knife in her hand to reverse into a hard plunging stab at Renata's heart. Flowing alongside Tressa's attack, Derrick slid in low, slicing at the rogue's hamstring.

Neither connected.

Renata flipped her leg up to avoid Derrick's attack and brought it down hard in an axe kick, her heel driving into the nape of his neck. Pinwheeling her arms as she bent at the waist, Renata snaked her hand over Tressa's wrist and redirected her downward blow straight into the meat of Derrick's shoulder.

Snarling like a pissed off badger, Tressa ripped her blade free and spun around with a cursing Derrick close on her heels. Rage drove each of her unskilled strikes, but three sharp slashes from her knife encountered only empty air as Tressa pursued her prey.

She briefly regretted not training in combat with Saiden more often, but some part of her hadn't wanted the knowledge. Hadn't wanted the temptation to kill again. And while protecting her mate wasn't the same thing, she was starting to think her newfound justification might not actually mean shit against the much older rogue.

Still, she refused to accept defeat, and her fourth swing met with glorious resistance as it sliced a long furrow along Renata's upper arm. The smile of satisfaction that lit up Tressa's face vanished just as suddenly as it had appeared, though. A fist flashed out and sank into her stomach, the vicious uppercut forcing every ounce of breathable air from her lungs as she was lifted off her feet.

Before gravity could bring Tressa back down to earth naturally, Renata snatched one ankle and whipped her arm in an overhead arc to slam Tressa's body deep into the sand. She caught Derrick blurring toward her, but the world flashed black for a moment, and she couldn't see what happened to her cousin. She could only feel a symphony of pain and could only register a vague sense of him careening off to the side.

The sounds of the combat, the screams of the seabirds, and the crashing of the waves disappeared, replaced by a steady high-pitched whine boring through her skull. Flashes of shadows flitted across her vision, taunting and teasing her with how useless she was, until finally, tingling sensations started fluttering through her numb limbs as her muscles sluggishly came back online.

The shadows faded away to reveal Derrick leaning over her, a knife gripped in each hand. His shirt was ripped in a dozen places, and dried blood lined his arms in parallel cuts where nails had raked and clawed.

Tressa began to push herself up, rising onto one elbow, when Derrick was suddenly flung away from her, and Renata's foot smashed down on Tressa's knee like a meteor strike.

Pain more intense and powerful than anything Tressa had ever felt before coursed through her, and blood flew from her lips as an anguished scream burst from her lungs. She tried to move, tried to force herself to get up and fight through the agony, but it consumed her. Destroyed her.

"Stay down," Renata growled, her face blocking out the rising sun as she loomed over Tressa. "I don't want to kill you, Loloma, but I won't let my own desires jeopardize my mission. You simply cannot win this fight."

Chapter Forty-Two

Ethan

"I don't think we can beat her."

"We have to win this," Ethan snapped back at Saiden, ripping his attention away from his mate as she raced toward Renata with vengeance in her eyes. As much he wanted to simply watch her, he knew he needed to get Saiden back into the fight for them to stand a chance.

"Look, Ethan," Saiden said, his eyes dropping to the wound that still gushed blood. "I don't want to give up either, but I didn't survive three centuries of fighting by being careless. Sometimes you have to recognize when you're outmatched and a tactical retreat is the best option. Just run, Ethan. She only wants you. We'll hold her off long enough for you to get away, then regroup to develop another plan. But you have to go *now*."

Ethan only half heard the urgent plea, his eyes drawn to the crimson spreading across Saiden's shirt. His vampire vision picked out the glistening edges of the stain wicking through the fabric, crawling fiber by fiber, reminding him of a similar image from only a day ago when his Sunflower had nearly died. Ethan's eyes flared wide, and he grabbed

Saiden's shoulder.

"What the fuck?" Saiden cried out as Ethan the makeshift bandage away and thin streams of sparkly purple haze began seeping out of his fingers. Just as he had with Tressa, he pressed his hand to the wound, willing the violet cloud to soak into Saiden's shoulder and heal him.

A grimace spread across Saiden's face, and he let out a string of curses, but Ethan maintained the contact, even as the sickening crunch of bones rearranging themselves reached his ears. What was likely only a few seconds felt like a lifetime as he tried to focus on the purple mist and not the sound of Tressa's pained gasps behind him.

Saiden's litany of muttered expletives died off as the last traces of the wound smoothed over, and Ethan slumped into the sand, a sense of pride filling him.

"Lilith take me, that was the weirdest fucking sensation," Saiden said, rolling his shoulder a few times. "I've seen Cora heal in less than a minute from a severe wound, but that... That was nearly instantaneous."

A scream of agony ripped through the awe-filled moment, and both men swiveled their heads back toward the fight to see Tressa crumpled on the ground, her knee bent at a disturbing angle. Renata stood over her, growling for Tressa to stay down, while Derrick struggled to climb to his feet behind them.

Without a further word, Ethan grabbed a fist full of Saiden's shirt and hauled him to his feet. Twin puffs of sand flew into the air as the vampires blurred toward their targets.

Once more, Renata's form rippled and twisted to reveal Cora flinching at Saiden's approach. The image didn't slow his charge forward, but he did bobble the grab for his knife laying in the sand as he sped past it. Bellowing in frustration, Saiden dismissed the weapon and launched into a series of sharp strikes with his elbows, fists, and knees, while Derrick gathered himself and moved to attack from the rear.

Ethan slid to a stop in the sand next to Tressa and clamped one hand over her leg and the other over the bone jutting from her lower ribs. His eyes raked up and down her body, searching for more injuries, but he saw nothing beyond an assortment of fading bruises. Bursts of glittering amethyst swirled about his hands, and her rib crunched into place at the same time her knee gave a wet pop as it reset itself, shredded tendons and muscle stitching back together in an instant.

Her hands locked onto Ethan's face, her nails digging in just a hair shy of painful, and she pulled him into the softest lips and sweetest mouth he would never get used to. The kiss was fast, heated, and over far too soon, but it was everything Ethan needed to feel rejuvenated.

Releasing her grip as their lips separated, she whispered, "You're incredible." Then she leapt to her feet and returned to the fray.

It took an almost embarrassingly long moment for Ethan to clear his mind and spin around to reorient on the chaos behind him.

The other three vamps surrounded Renata who had returned to her own form, but she still looked nothing less than mildly amused.

"I can do this all day," Saiden snarled, yanking another dagger from a sheath at the small of his back.

"I don't care what you do, Enforcer," Renata hissed as she threw out a hand to stop Derrick's incoming charge, clamping her fingers around his throat. "You think any of this has accomplished anything? You think you're actually winning?" She laughed, then tossed Derrick forward, sending him crashing into Saiden and Tressa with a force that had them all tumbling to the sand again. "I've entertained this for a while as a courtesy. Nothing more."

"A courtesy?" Saiden huffed as he spat sand out of his mouth.

"For her," Renata said, nodding toward Tressa. "So she could believe in the end that she truly did her best to save her mate. When the final death comes swiftly to a loved one, it eats at you over the years. The feeling that you could have done more. *Should* have done more. You often think to yourself how things could have gone different-ly. Perhaps if you fought harder, acted faster, or been smarter, then maybe, *maybe,* you could have saved them. I respect Tressa enough to grant her the comfort of knowing she did her best to prevent his demise. But make no mistake, all of this"—she gestured to the four of them crumpled in the sand—"this was merely a kindness. And I'm afraid that kindness has now run out."

She leaned down, plucked a small piece of driftwood from the sand, and cracked it in half, leaving a sharp jagged point. "I'm sorry, Loloma. I imagine your mother would be very disappointed in me, but I have no choice. The only thing I can offer you is your life and that of your friends. This is the final time I will extend to you this opportunity. Leave the botanist behind, and I will not hunt you. For your mother's sake."

Ethan rushed over to Tressa's side as his mate stared blankly up at Renata for a second before giving the rogue a nasty sneer. "I don't know what trick you're trying to pull, but it's not going to work. What the hell could you possibly know about my mom?"

Renata gave her a small smile. "Everything, Loloma. I did spend a century with her after all. Until you came along."

Chapter Forty-Three

Tressa

Tressa's sneer dropped away as realization hit her. "You're not talking about my human mother," she said, shaking her head. "You mean the vampire who turned me. That's how you knew my birth name. She was the only one I ever told."

Renata dipped her head in acknowledgment. "A secret she shared with her own maker. You should know just how proud she was of you. Every time you left her to go wandering, she would come to me and talk for hours about how incredible you were."

"Wait," Derrick interrupted, waving a hand. "Are you trying to say you're Tressa's... what? Vampire grandma or some shit? Because that's a little too soap opera for even my tastes."

"You watch daytime television?" Saiden asked, scrubbing his face. "Now you're just embarrassing yourself."

"Hey, don't knock it til you've tried it," Derrick shot back.

"I don't need to try it," Saiden argued. "I've also never shoved a cucumber up my ass, but I know I won't enjoy it."

Derrick smirked. "How unfortunate for Cora."

"You leave my mate out of this."

"I would, but it sounds like she's in desperate need of a good—"

"Finish that sentence and I'll gut you on this beach."

"SILENCE!"

They all went quiet, and Tressa turned to face Renata who was giving them a look of disappointed annoyance, like they were children fighting on a playground. Which, to be fair, wasn't far off.

"Loloma," Renata said, stepping forward and holding out a hand. When Tressa only scowled in response, Renata let it fall back to her side. "As I was saying, your mother made me promise to look after you if anything were to happen to her. And while I had no desire to spend all my time with the fledgling vamp who took her away from me so often, I have occasionally checked in on you from a distance over the past two centuries. You've never been far from my mind ever since that mob in Spain took her undead life before I could stop them. So you see, each time I've told you that I didn't want to hurt you, I truly meant it. But I will if I have to. This is bigger than either of us. Bigger even than the promise I made to your mother. Ethan cannot live. The risk is too great."

Fury blazed through Tressa that Renata dared to play on her emotions. That she thought any sob story would convince her to sacrifice her mate and the love she'd waited an eternity for.

"Corinne wasn't my mother," Tressa snapped. "She was just a lonely vampire who found a broken young woman in an alley and offered to make her powerful. She might have guided me, might have been proud of who I became, but she never truly loved me. She was a teacher, not a mother. The only real mother I had was the woman who raised me in Fiji. Her name was Kasanita, and she's the one whose face kept me going when I nearly starved on that ship crossing the ocean. The one whose voice whispered in the back of my mind to stay strong as those sailors..." A tear formed in the corner of her eye, but she fiercely wiped it away. This bitch didn't deserve her tears.

"Tressa," Ethan said softly.

She held up a hand for him to be quiet as she climbed to her feet. "I don't care if we share some fucked up vampire lineage. You're not my family, and you never will be. These guys behind me? They're my family. They *actually* love me. If you think I'm going to walk away and leave you to murder my mate, guess again. You'll just have to kill me first."

Renata scanned Tressa's face for a long moment, then sighed. "If that is your wish." She blurred forward and locked her hand around Tressa's neck.

"Wait," Ethan shouted as he scrambled to his feet. He stepped up beside Tressa, and her heart shattered when she saw the resignation in his eyes.

"Don't," she choked out through the iron grip slowly crushing her windpipe. She could see exactly what her perfect mate had running through his head. "Please, Ethan. Don't do this."

"I have to," he said, brushing a bit of sand off her cheek. "I'm sorry, Sunflower, but I won't let you die for me."

Renata relaxed her grip just a fraction, and slowly turned her head to look at the love of Tressa's undead life. "Yes, Ethan? You have something to say?"

He nodded.

"Let them go. You can have me."

Chapter Forty-Four

Ethan

"You can have me."

The words rang in his ears, surprising even himself with how sure he sounded. How confident. He loved Tressa. There was no doubt about it. And he refused to let her die for him. Refused to let her *family* die for him.

He could finally save someone he cared about.

"Nobody else needs to get hurt," he told Renata. "There's been enough pain. It needs to stop."

She eyed him warily, as if she didn't expect him to actually co-operate. "That is true," she said before tossing Tressa to the ground beside the others and holding out her hand. "It is a shame that your intelligence is to be your downfall, but what you have created cannot exist. And your death is the only way to guarantee it will never be duplicated."

When he didn't immediately take her hand, she grabbed his arm and jerked him closer to her. He couldn't help but cringe at the proximity as her scent filled his nostrils. It was cloying, and he felt like he might choke on her rotten, perfumy smell. It had been faint when she first sank her fangs into him months ago, but this time it was overwhelming, and he fought the urge to gag. He wanted his last scent to be that of Tressa's. Wanted his last sight to be her beautiful chestnut brown eyes. Instead, it seemed like he would leave the world being forced to endure flashbacks of Jake's death.

It bothered him, the fact that he still had no idea why his heart medication could be such a risk to vampires. He'd hoped Baylin could figure it out once he shared the information with him, but they hadn't had time for that. There hadn't been time for a lot of things he wanted to do before dying.

He chuckled sadly to himself, wondering if he won the award for shortest stint as a vampire ever. If he had to give up eternity, though, he was glad it was for Tressa. Nobody deserved to live more than his Sunflower.

But Renata was naïve if she thought killing him would actually solve anything for long.

"It won't end, you know," he told her, resisting the urge to spit in her face as he stared into the hollow voids that were her eyes. "Someday, another scientist will come up with the same theory I did. You can destroy me. You can destroy my research. You can destroy every computer and every lab that had anything to do with it. But you can't destroy human curiosity. Eventually, someone will discover the same thing I did."

"Perhaps," she said as she dragged the rough piece of driftwood over the scar on his neck, tearing it open just enough to send a small stream of blood dribbling down his chest. "And that is why I will remain ever vigilant. That is the purpose that has been given to me. After five hundred years, *she* has offered me a reason to continue this unending existence. So long as humans keep stumbling across things they don't understand, I will be here. Watching in the shadows. Cleaning up the mess."

She sniffed his neck, then licked up a tiny bit of his blood. "You really do taste delicious, even now that you've been turned. I can barely smell anything but vanilla and bubblegum when you and Tressa are around. And that brain of yours? So much potential. I can see why she fell for you. I truly am sorry about this, Ethan."

When she slid the driftwood down his chest to rest above his heart, he squeezed his eyes shut, bracing himself for the end.

"Wait!" Tressa screamed, and he cracked one eye open to see her at his side, her hand gripping Renata's wrist. "Can I just say goodbye? Please?" she begged, the sorrow in her tone causing more damage to his heart than any stake ever could.

Renata glanced back and forth between them before the tension in her face went slack. "Fine," she conceded, some of the edge in her voice fading. "You may say your farewell."

"Can you let him go?" his mate pleaded softly, her gaze fixed on Renata. "Just so I can kiss him one last time. It would mean everything to me."

Renata's eyes narrowed for a fraction of a second, and then she sighed. "You do know there is nothing that can be done to save him, right? If you are attempting a... What do the humans call it? A Hail Mary?" She shuddered. "It will do you no good. And I might be less inclined to make his demise quick and painless."

Tressa shook her head, placing her other hand over the one tightly wrapped around the stake. "I promise. It's not that. Just one last kiss."

Remembering his mate's Gift, Ethan watched as Renata succumbed, and a small, sad smile curled up the corner of her mouth. "How could I deny you such a simple request?"

She released her hold on Ethan and stepped back, gesturing for Tressa to go ahead.

"Oh, and one more thing, Loloma," Renata said, halting them as they reached for each other. "While I enjoy having the rough edges of my anger soothed as much as the next person, if you try to use your ability on me again, I'll tear your pretty head from your shoulders. Family or no."

Tressa gulped, nodded, then turned back to Ethan. She wrapped her arms around his waist and locked her eyes on his. "I know why you're doing this, Ethan," she said in a quiet voice even though every vampire on the beach could clearly hear their exchange. "And I think your mom would be proud of you. I think your mom's *friends* would be proud of you too."

The pointed look she gave him carried more than just the weight of goodbye, and he searched her face, struggling to understand what message she was trying to convey. He turned the words over in his head, parsing them for any clue.

Friends.

That was the word she had put emphasis on. But what could that possibly have to do with...

It hit him like a fastball to the face, and he could only hope Renata didn't catch the slight widening of his eyes before he schooled his expression.

His mom's friends.

The witches.

The potion.

"You'll know when the time is right." That was what the kind, older woman in the 50's swing dress had said.

He smiled at Tressa. "I agree," he said, running his hand down the side of her arm to rest on her hip, inches away from his own pocket that held the small vial. "I think she would be proud."

He pulled his mate to his chest with one arm and kissed her with all the passion he felt just in case he failed. While he let his head fill with all the beautiful moments they'd spent together, his hand slipped away from her hip and moved to his own, sliding into the loose pocket of the black track pants he was glad he'd chosen over tight jeans.

His fingers curled around the bottle, and Tressa let out a tiny moan, deepening the kiss. He slowly pulled the potion from his pocket, his thumb brushing against the cork stopper as he tested to see how easily he could pop it off.

Time stood still as he debated.

Drink or toss.

Both were viable options, but he couldn't decide. The witch hadn't been clear. In fact, she'd been purposefully vague about what the hell he was supposed to do with the liquid. Was it poison or protection?

Drink or toss.

He'd told her exactly what he was going up against—an ancient vampire—and she hadn't even blinked. Simply disappeared into her kitchen for a moment, then returned with the vial, telling him it was the exact thing he needed.

Drink or toss.

His mind flashed back to when Saiden had hurled the gas canister. How easily Renata had caught it. There was no way he could throw the bottle fast enough to catch her off guard.

Drink or toss.

He could see only one realistic choice, and he had to try.

Drink.

As he slowly pulled back from their kiss, he lifted the potion to his mouth, dragging it up between their bodies so Renata wouldn't see. He leaned in close to Tressa, pressing his forehead to hers.

Please let this work.

His thumb pressed against the cork lid, loosening it.

"I love you," he whispered to Tressa.

"I love you too, Ethan. Whatever happens, I—"

Before Tressa could finish her sentence, she was flung away from him with a pained yelp, and a hand clamped down on the one holding the potion, pausing it less than an inch from his lips. He looked into Renata's dark eyes, and a sinking feeling coiled in the pit of his stomach.

"I'm disappointed," she said sadly. "I told you not to try anything, and yet you didn't listen."

Ethan swallowed roughly. He could see the vial. It was so close, yet the grip holding him might as well have been carved from marble for all he could move his hand.

He'd failed.

Renata glanced down at the bottle and then back up to Ethan. She dug the tip of the stake into his chin, forcing him to look at her. "I am curious, though. What exactly did you think you were going to do?"

"Nothing," he snapped. If he was going to die, he would at least show her that he wasn't afraid. It was all he had left.

Renata arched an eyebrow. "I don't believe this is nothing." When he didn't respond, her face twisted in anger. "Tell me what this is Ethan, or I might not choose to spare Tressa when this is done. I've been more than patient with you all, and I've gotten nothing but lies and disrespect in return."

He glanced over at his mate who was still lying on the beach where Renata had thrown her, barely able to lift her head to look at him. The fear he thought he'd suppressed came rising back up. He didn't care what happened to him, but he had to know Tressa would be okay.

His shoulders sagged. "I think it's a protection potion," he admitted. "My mom was some sort of witch. One of her friends gave it to me."

Renata stared at him, her eyes searching his, and then she tossed her head back and laughed. "A protection potion? Delightful." She pried the small vial out of his hands and sniffed it. "I don't smell anything. Are you sure she didn't give you water? A bit of false courage?"

"Doesn't matter now," he gritted out. "Does it?"

"No," Renata said, pressing the stake into Ethan's chest. "It doesn't."

The wood burrowed through skin and muscle, inching toward his heart. He ground his teeth together through the agonizing pain. He wouldn't beg for his life. Jake had begged, and it hadn't saved him.

Maybe Ethan should have died in that lab. Maybe it would have been better if he'd never met Tressa. Never had that brief moment of happiness. That teaser of what could have been.

Maybe dying would be easier if he didn't know what he was leaving behind.

"I'm sorry to drag this out," Renata said, and it actually sounded like she meant it. "But I did tell you what would happen if you tried anything."

She pressed a little harder, and Ethan heard his sternum crack. Blood filled his lungs, and he coughed, sending small red splatters across Renata's face. When she pulled him in close, every aspect of her looked exactly the same as it had that night, right down to the flecks of blood on her skin.

"Do it," he bit out. "I'd rather die than spend another second looking at your hideous face."

The smirk she gave him belied any sense of the civility she claimed to have. "In that case," she replied, the vacant depths of her dark eyes prepared to swallow his soul, "your wish is finally granted."

She lifted the potion in front of his face and crushed the vial.

"Goodbye, Ethan."

Chapter Forty-Five

Tressa

Tressa braced herself for the final push. The final thrust that would lodge the stake into Ethan's heart and tear him away from her forever.

But it never came.

"What...?" Renata choked out, gaping at her hand that was sizzling and slowly turning black. "What is this?" She released her hold on the stake and stumbled back from Ethan.

Tressa blinked at her, then glanced at her mate who was staring at Renata, seemingly just as shocked as she was.

She let out a cry of pure gratitude when the realization struck her. Ethan's mom and her friends really had been honest-to-Lilith witches.

And she was really fucking glad Ethan hadn't drank that potion.

Renata fell away from the group, flailing wildly as if she could dislodge whatever dark magic was ravaging her body. Her skin cracked, smoked, and began to burn. Ragged screams filled the air as she clawed at her seared flesh, only managing to knock off loose hunks of black char that crumbled to dust before they even hit the sand.

Saiden and Derrick rushed over to help Tressa to her feet, and all four of them watched, stunned, as the blackness crawled up Renata's arm, across her neck, and down the other side, rapidly devouring her entire body.

Nobody moved for what felt like an eternity. Then Tressa's brain kicked back on, and she turned to Ethan.

Who still had a stake lodged in his chest.

She raced forward and pulled him into her arms just as he collapsed. She carefully lowered him to the sand, her fingers wrapping around the sharp piece of wood, ready to yank it out of him.

"This isn't over," a raspy voice wheezed, and Tressa whipped her head up in time to see Renata fall to the ground, her disintegrating legs unable to hold her upright. "She will come for you. She will restore balance." Renata's eyes locked on Tressa's, the only part of her body left that wasn't flaking away in the breeze. "The world is changing, Loloma. Enjoy your happiness... while... you..."

Her final words were lost as her body slumped forward and crumbled into a smoldering pile of ash.

For a fraction of a second, there was no sound save for the perpetual thundering of the waves. And then the world exploded back into action as Saiden and Derrick blurred over to her side, and Tressa turned her attention back to her mate who was still bleeding in her arms. She closed her eyes for a second, and when they flew open, relief filled her.

"You're going to be okay," she told him. "Your heart is beating fast, but it's steady. She didn't pierce it."

Saiden crouched down next to Ethan while Derrick plopped his ass in the sand and slapped Ethan on the thigh. "Guess you're stuck with us."

Ethan's head lolled back. "Well, that's... good to hear."

Tressa gawked at him. "It's 'good to hear?' You defeated the rogue who murdered your best friend without getting yourself killed in the process, and that's the best you've got?"

Ethan dragged his head up and gave her a wry grin. "Sunflower, I'm a vampire with a wooden stake embedded in my chest. Do you really expect me to be eloquent right now?"

Tressa burst out laughing and pressed a kiss to his forehead. "Fair enough. Okay, I'm going to pull this out, and you're going to use your fancy new Gift to heal yourself, okay?"

When he nodded, she yanked the stake out and flung it into the ocean. She pressed her hand to the wound on his chest as his blood oozed between her fingers and dripped onto the pale sand. "Okay, Doc. Your turn," she told him.

Ethan closed his eyes, and Tressa waited for the violet light to appear.

But nothing happened.

"Why aren't you healing?" she demanded. "Ethan, use your Gift. Heal yourself."

His eyes flew open. "I... I can't," he said, staring at her wide-eyed. He reached over and plucked out a piece of driftwood that had become embedded in her calf during the fight. A thin stream of blood spilled out, and his hand instantly became wreathed in a purple glow. He grazed his fingers over the small gash, and it sealed shut. But when he brought his hand to his chest, the light faded away.

"I guess my power doesn't work on myself," he told them.

In a flash, Derrick had his shirt off and pressed to Ethan's wound. "It's okay, new cousin. You still have vampiric healing. We just need to get you a couple bags of blood, a bottle of Hennessey, and a comfy bed to lie in for a few days, and you'll be back on your feet in no time."

Ethan groaned, and Tressa gently pushed Derrick aside so she could be the one to help patch up her mate. Most of the tension had eased out of her when she'd heard his heartbeat holding steady, but the amount of blood soaking through the shirt still had her worried. Until she could run her hands over smooth, unblemished skin, she wasn't leaving his side.

Holding pressure with one hand, she used the other to wipe away the blood on his chin that had spilled from his mouth. She gazed into his eyes and sighed. "Oh, Ethan. What kind of doctor can't fix himself?"

"The undead kind, apparently," he said with a chuckle, and the last bit of tension in Tressa faded away. If he was able to find the humor in the situation, he was going to be okay.

They were all going to be okay.

"She will come for you. She will restore balance."

For now.

Chapter Forty-Six

Ethan

Three Months Later

"You work too hard."

Ethan popped his head up, and a wide smile spread across his face at the appearance of his beautiful mate. He dismissed the microscope he'd been bent over in favor of watching her stroll toward him. "You say that every time you come in here."

"Because it hasn't ceased being true," she said, plopping her cute butt down on the stool next to him.

"Well, what do you expect me to do? The scientist in me is still trying to accept the insane fact that using apple blossom extract for my heart medication meant I accidentally created a poison for vampires that was undetectable by smell."

It hadn't taken long for Baylin to figure things out once Ethan had the time to sit down with him and go over everything. After that, they'd run some tests on the broken bits of glass Saiden carefully recovered from the beach. Turns out it was nothing more than water with a few drops of apple juice. Ethan had initially been disappointed that it wasn't an actual magic potion, but that quickly took a backseat to all-encompassing horror at how such a small amount turned Renata to ash in less than a minute. It had led to Ethan being terrified of his own shadow for days, afraid there was somehow an apple lingering around every corner waiting to jump out and steal his new life with Tressa.

Of course, that anxiety faded after the fifth time Tressa reminded him that he was a vampire and could smell apples a mile away. The liquid inside the bottle may have been nothing more than juice, but since none of them had caught the scent after the witch gave it to him, the running theory was that the bottle must have been enchanted. Apparently, there was something to the whole concept of real witches after all.

And perhaps that was how he managed to survive his lab burning down. Neither the cops nor Baylin had been able to figure out how he was found lying just outside the burning building when Renata had left him for dead inside. More fuel for the theory that there were greater magical forces at work in the universe.

He just tried not to think too much about how the witch in Seacliff had gambled with his life, considering how close he'd come to drinking the 'potion.' If there was a mystical guardian angel watching over him, he was definitely keeping them busy.

Tressa's laugh brought him out of his thoughts and back to the climate-controlled greenhouse laboratory Marquin had constructed for him within the first week of their return. When Tressa said he was rich, she wasn't joking.

"Well, it wasn't like I had time to give you a full lecture about the history of vamps," Tressa teased. "Next time I'll be sure to start with our weaknesses and make sure I cover *all* of them."

Ethan grinned and grabbed his glasses from the table. There was nothing vision-altering in the frames given his vampiric sight, but when Tressa told him she thought they were sexy, he'd had a special pair made just for her. "It's just so fascinating. I mean, I grew up hearing the story about the apple and the garden of Eden just like everyone else, but still... To find out there was supposedly a spark of heavenly magic in the apple Adam brought with him when he was kicked out of paradise, and therefore all apples on earth are lethal to vamps is... It's a little difficult to wrap my brain around." He paused, then let out a sigh. "And still a little disappointing, considering how beneficial that medication could have been. The Camellia should yield effective results one day, but we won't have enough blooms to do real testing for years. The apple blossoms really were the perfect plant in the meantime, given their abundance in nature and high concentration of antioxidants."

Tressa peered around him at the equipment on the table. "So does that mean your new experiment isn't going well?"

Ethan perked up at that. If there was one thing he loved, it was talking about his work with his mate. She would never be as invested in plants as he was, would never see the Middlemist Red Camellia as anything but a pretty flower, but she always let him ramble on for as long as he wanted, and that meant everything to him.

"Actually, it's showing a lot of promise," he told her. "Once I accepted magic had to be real, I started to wonder if maybe it was related to vampirism in some way. If you think about it, how else do you explain our existence, let alone the individual Gifts we possess?" At Tressa's inquisitive look, he continued. "So I started to wonder if this 'magic,' or whatever it is, did something to alter my blood. I think..." He trailed off to let the dramatic effect build. "I think I might be able to find a way to use the healing magic in my blood to neutralize the apple poison. If that works..."

Tressa gasped. "Ethan, are you saying you could create an antidote?"

He held up his crossed fingers. "Maybe, just don't get your hopes up quite yet. It's still just a working hypothesis."

Tressa propped her chin in her hand and gazed at him, that light in her eyes sparkling brighter than ever. "Trust my mate to find a way to mix magic and science."

Ethan shrugged. "I think Arthur C. Clarke said it best: 'Magic is just science we don't understand yet.' If I keep working at this, there's a chance I can uncover the deeper layers of how it works, and then..." He leaned over to Tressa and kissed her. "Who knows what things I can do with this. And it's all because of you, Sunflower. You gave me an eternity to spend developing new ways to help both people and vampires."

His glasses slipped down on his nose, and Tressa nudged them back into place. "Only you would get excited to live forever so you could keep doing work, Dr. Rose."

Ethan winked at her, then turned back to his research. He didn't even mind the cute nickname anymore. Yeah, he had a rose on his ass for the rest of eternity. But it also meant he would never forget Jake, so he could put up with a little teasing.

"Now I just need Saiden to agree to capture a rogue and keep them alive so I have someone to test my theories on," he said, adjusting the eyepiece on the microscope.

Tressa dropped her head to the table and groaned. "Well, there's definitely no shortage of those lately, and I'm afraid it's only going to get worse given everything that's happened. Saiden is headed down to LA for Cora's premiere tomorrow, but maybe when he gets back you can talk to him about finding a way to do experiments. Just don't go all mad scientist on me, okay?"

Pushing his microscope away, Ethan slid his hand under Tressa's cheek and lifted her face back up to meet his. He kissed her softly, lingering with his lips pressed lightly against hers. "No promises. You wouldn't love me if I was boring."

"You know I love you for so many reasons," she murmured, running her hands up the back of his neck into the long hair he hadn't gotten around to cutting.

Though, considering how deeply he melted whenever she gripped it firmly and tugged, he might just forget a little while longer.

"And I you," he whispered. He pulled back and gave her a heated look. "If you're not busy, the sun has gone down, and you keep saying I could use a break. Care to join me in the garden?"

Tressa's lips curled up into a knowing smile. "I might still have grass in my hair from the last time, but what the hell. I don't think we've done it by the Hyacinths yet."

Ethan's face lit up. "Look at you spouting off flower names."

"Of course I was going to learn," she said, sliding his glasses off and tossing them on the table. "My mate is a botanist after all."

"And you will always be the most beautiful flower in my life."

He jumped from the chair and drew her in for another kiss. When they broke away, she gave him a mischievous grin, then blurred away. He could chase after her, but he'd never catch her. Not until she wanted him to. And it wasn't like they were in a hurry.

He still had days where it was hard to remember that it was all real. That he had a fully stocked lab at the compound, unrestricted access to samples of the Camellia that would soon have its extracts isolated, and even a few part-time human lab techs to help with the easier work. None of them were Jake, of course. They could never even come close to his friend's intelligence and wit. But he'd learned to accept that and embrace the positives—he now had the chance to twist magic into science and genuinely find a way to do good in the world.

To help people was all he ever wanted for his life.

To be happy was all his mother ever wanted for him.

And Tressa had given him both.

His Sunflower.

His light in the dark.

About the author

T. M. Kirk writes paranormal rom-coms and romantasy books filled with snarky banter, spice, and side characters that love to steal the show. Originally from Alaska, she is a rolling stone, eternally searching for that perfect place to call home. Currently residing in California with her partner and two fur babies, her days are spent riding her motorcycle, traveling to new places, and creating fantasy and paranormal worlds as a much needed escape from reality.